MW01674966

Incidents in My Life

SALZWASSER
VERLAG

D. D. Home

Incidents in My Life

Reprint of the original, first published in 1864.

1st Edition 2022 | ISBN: 978-3-75259-220-7

Verlag (Publisher): Salzwasser Verlag GmbH, Zeilweg 44, 60439 Frankfurt, Deutschland
Vertretungsberechtigt (Authorized to represent): E. Roepke, Zeilweg 44, 60439 Frankfurt, Deutschland
Druck (Print): Books on Demand GmbH, In de Tarpen 42, 22848 Norderstedt, Deutschland

INCIDENTS IN MY LIFE.

BY

D. D. HOME.

WITH AN INTRODUCTION BY JUDGE EDMONDS.

FIFTH EDITION.

NEW YORK

1864.

CONTENTS.

CHAPTER VII.

CHAPTER VIII.

CHAPTER IX.

CHAPTER X.

CHAPTER XI.

CHAPTER XII.

INTRODUCTION

TO THE AMERICAN EDITION.

It is now about fifteen years since there occurred at Rochester, in the State of New York, some incidents of so unusual a character as to excite a very lively attention.

These incidents were, the locomotion of ponderable objects without any perceptible mortal agency, and the creation of sounds without any discoverable human origin; and through their instrumentality, such an intelligence displayed as enabled conversation to be carried on with the unseen power that was acting thus strangely in their midst.

Through the conversation thus opened, it was professed that these things were done by the spirits of those who had once lived on the earth, and that the object was to open a communication between the living and the dead.

Such a claim was received by an almost universal disbelief—by vehement condemnation of the impiety, or unsparing ridicule of the credulity which could receive or avow it.

Still the thing went on, and impelled by curiosity or the love of the marvelous, people began to investigate—and as investigation progressed, the belief in the spiritual origin of the phenomena spread, until in a short time, people of all classes and positions in society, and of all conditions of intelligence and education, inquired—and most of those who inquired, believed.

Confined originally to one locality, it soon spread to other parts of that State and to adjoining States. Limited, at first, to three young girls as the "mediums" through whom these things were done, the power was soon manifested through others, of different sexes and ages.

The ordinary newspaper press of the day was alive with the details and discussion of the incidents and their origin Periodical papers were established, devoted to the topic and numerous volumes were published with the same pur pose. The whole matter was subjected, both as to the facts and their sources, to the severest scrutiny which ingenuity and acuteness could devise. Solutions of the mystery, professing to be satisfactory, put forth even under the auspices of such men as Sir David Brewster, and Professors Faraday and Agassiz, were of frequent occurrence, and the press and the pulpit seemed to unite in one voice of denunciation of the monstrous fraud and delusion.

Still the thing moved steadily on, until before the expiration of the first decade after its advent, the instruments through whom the things were done were counted by thousands in this country, and the believers by millions, and kindred manifestations were breaking out throughout the world, and appearing on different continents, among people of diverse nationalities and language, simultaneously, without any missionary effort on our part, and apparently without preconcert with us or between themselves.

Thus at length—through this instrumentality and by the testimony of these hosts of witnesses—was established in this country the marvelous fact of *inanimate matter moving without mortal contact, and displaying intelligence, and that intelligence so great as to "speak in many tongues," and to read the inmost unuttered thoughts of man.*

Among the early instruments used to bring about such a result in this country, was D. D. Home, whose experience is given in the ensuing pages. He was of a mild and gentle disposition, sincere and simple-minded, yet of a passive rather than an affirmative character, with a strong devotional tendency.

He was never known much in this country as a medium.—

His powers were not more remarkable than those of many others who were in daily use at the time, and during a good part of the time that elapsed between the development of his powers and his departure for Europe, his mediumship was confined to a very small circle, consisting of gentlemen of education and of means, who were, through him, thorough ly investigating the subject.

Such an investigation, by men of science, of learning, of intelligence, and of standing, was earnestly sought and repeatedly urged by the educated ones of those who, on witnessing the phenomena, found in it, a profound mystery. It was often said to that class of men, whom we were wont to regard as our teachers and leaders in knowledge, "Here is something that we cannot fathom. Come you to our aid! Here are incidents for which we can find no origin in the laws of nature known to us, which we are told are not supernatural, but in conformity with nature. Come ye and discover this unknown and extraordinary power which thus tends to lead us into the domain of the magical and the miraculous! Here is an intelligence displayed by inanimate matter which professes to be that of the dead. Come ye to our rescue, and unfold to us, if it is possible, some other theory than the spiritual, as explanatory of these uncommon events.—For if that cannot be done, and this thing is what it professes to be—a communion with the spirits of the departed—the importance of this new phase of human life cannot be exaggerated"

To such appeals the response was often favorable, and such investigations were had in different parts of the country; which resulted not so much in the discovery of the nature of this new power, as in establishing to all who would expend a thought on the subject, the reality of its existence, and in some degree, what it was capable of achieving.

As soon as this end was attained in this country, demonstrations of that character almost wholly ceased among us, and spirit communion assumed a new and most interesting phaec.

Meanwhile Europe lagged behind the celerity of our movement, and as we were beginning to read in this New

Testament from God to man, we could occasionally hear that her people were just entering on their A, B, C.

So that when Home arrived in England, in the possession of a power then quite common in this country, but almost unknown there, he at once attracted great attention—and it will be seen in the following pages, how wide-spread and earnest was that attention among the higher classes, as well on the Continent as in England. The same lively interest in these, the primary steps of the Communion, was displayed there that had been seen here, some ten years before. That interest still continues there. I will mention as an instance of this, that some time ago I received a letter from Home, requesting leave to send me the advanced sheets of his forthcoming work, in order to their publication here; and when I received those sheets, they came to me, not from him, but from a friend, because he had been sent for by the Emperor of the French and had departed for Paris.

The office which his book will perform in Europe will be somewhat different from what it will perform with us. There, it will be mainly to establish the fact of spiritual intercourse. With us, we have an abundance of testimony on that point, not only in the oft recorded experience of the past, but in the great number of private Circles, now scattered all over our land, where every one may see and judge for himself.

To some in this country too that will be the office of his book, but to very many it will be different, and the book will find its chief interest in the plain, simple detail of fact, and the great accumulation of testimony in support of that detail, and in the fact that it is a clear delineation of the first step of many which have been taken within the last fifteen years.

That first step has been pretty thoroughly investigated in America, until a great revolution has been wrought in the public mind as to its actuality.

The next thing—and we are prepared for that now in this country—is to obtain for the subsequent steps the same thorough and searching scrutiny.

And it is the object of this introduction to bespeak for those subsequent steps the closest investigation that science, education and acuteness can give. It is impossible for any one mind or any small number of minds to do that wisely and well. It requires very many minds and numerous observations and a gathering together of the results of very many inquiries, before a satisfactory conclusion can be arrived at, and every possible objection be foreclosed. Just as in astronomy, the discoveries of the last hundred years have exceeded those of any prior equal period, because of the largely increased number of observers and improved means of observation. It may be the same in spiritual intercourse. Many things now obscure may be rendered clear; many things deemed impossible may be shown to be possible; and many things which to the uninstructed mind may be terrifying, may be rendered at once attractive and salutary. All that is wanted is patient, persistent investigation.

This appeal of mine would however be incomplete, if I should omit to define more particularly what are the topics for which I supplicate a scrutiny, and so I proceed to mention them.

First. If it be true that the spirits of the dead can commune with us, then it must be, that they can reveal to us what is the state of existence into which they were ushered on dying, and what is the mode of life they are leading there. This they profess to do, and this seems to me to be the primary and main object of this whole movement. I have myself received a great deal of information on this subject. Some I have already given to the world, but there is a great deal more that I have not. I am ready to give it as soon as I find the world ready to receive it—not amid the furor of superabundant wealth, with all the selfishness, luxury and extravagance which follow in its train, nor amid the evil passions which civil war engenders—but bye and bye, when the afflictions which God is bringing upon us shall have performed their destined office of softening our hearts, and opening them to the entrance of the gentle voice which is now coming to us in ever-increasing tones from beyond the grave.

As the life on earth is never exactly alike in any two persons, so life in the spirit world is never alike to any two immortals. Behold then! How many spirits must commune with us, and how many mortals must engage in that communion before enough can be obtained for us to be able to say and to feel that we know what is the life beyond the grave. As in astronomy it took the observations of many, many persons for several thousand years, to enable us to arrive at the truth in regard to our planetary system, so this far more momentous truth must come to us in the same way, as the result of many observations by many persons. What can one man, or even a score do in this respect? The question is easily answered. How few have ever read or believed what I have published in regard to the spirit world! Yet let the inquirer be convinced of what this book of Home's teaches, namely, that there is such a thing as direct communication with departed spirits, and he can himself make his own inquiries, and receive direct answers to himself, and thus from personal observation may come to believe that which he finds it so hard to receive through me. Others and others again doing the same thing, the result would be such an accumulation of testimony that there would be as little doubt upon this subject as there is now of the actual existence of spiritual intercourse.

And when that time shall come, when a rational knowledge of what the great change—the mortal putting on immortality—actually is, shall be substituted for the dreadful fear of death which now so often frightens man from his propriety, and enslaves his mind with a worse than Egyptian bondage, what imagination can picture the vast increase that will flow to the happiness, the wisdom, and the purity of man!

Second. Another topic, on which much evidence has already been received, but much more is necessary to a full understanding, is involved in the question in what manner, and to what extent are we, in the mortal life, surrounded and affected by the spirits of the departed?

There is abundant evidence to show that we are ever surrounded by them, and much to induce us to believe that every mood of mind has its kindred spirit; whence it would seem to follow that we are ever liable to be influenced for good or evil by our unseen companions. But many important questions arising out of these facts are yet unsolved. For instance: To what extent and under what circumstances can the attendant spirits influence us? And what is our protection against the evil of this influence?—Can we ourselves control it by controling our mood of mind? And if we need help, can we obtain it, and how? Here perhaps will be found the solution of the oft disputed proposition of the efficacy of prayer. Here, perchance, we may learn that as God always works through his instruments, so the mood of mind which prompts us to pray, may drive evil far from us, and draw closely around us the ministering spirits who may be charged with the function of answering our petitions, and who might not otherwise be able to approach and do for us that which they see, as well as we do, is needful for us.

And here too, perchance, may be found the solution of many mental conditions which ignorant doctors are apt to treat as incurable insanity. I have seen a good many cases, and myself cured several, where the physicians had been appealed to in vain.

It is not long since that I was invited by one of our Medical Societies to attend the reading of a paper on Insanity by a German Doctor. In some remarks I made on that paper, I took occasion to call the attention of the faculty to this subject, and detailed to them several of the cases in which I had cured, and I did so in the hope that they would investigate for themselves, and see whether there was not something in that. Unhappily, in their publication of my remarks, they omitted this part, and with it an inquiry, which I cannot but think highly pertinent—"Whether the medical profession might not find in these and cognate cases something worthy of their most careful investigation?"

And now in this connexion I may repeat the question already asked—If the inquirer believe in the communion announced in these pages of Home, and he can, by availing himself of that communion, learn the cause and the cure of any number of cases of Insanity, be they many or few, why not investigate? Does mere investigation hurt? It never hurts any thing but error, and sometimes perchance the first propounder of the truth—but the truth itself it never hurts.

Third. Another deeply interesting topic, on which some revelation has been had and more may be, is/What is the soul? And how is it connected with the body? What form or covering does it assume, when corruption puts on incorruption? And what are its relative powers before or after death?"

In this topic are embraced the phenomena of sleep and dreams—of clairvoyance (long a subject of dispute, but now received as a fact, though involved in profound mystery)—of the spirit photographs—of a spiritual telegraph, and the philosophy and explanation of spirit communion.

On all these subjects many facts and principles have already been learned, and many more may be. Enough has been learned to show us that we need not remain in ignorance any longer.

For instance: One winter, four or five years ago, I tried some very interesting experiments. Two *seances* were held at the same time, (allowing ten minutes for the difference of longitude) in New York and Boston. Careful records of what occurred at both places were preserved—and upon comparing them, it was found that the two parties, though two hundred and fifty miles asunder, conversed with each other as if present face to face. The *modus operandi* was shown to me, and many explanations given. The experiments were continued for several weeks, but it was found that they were attended with danger, and they were abandoned. The cause of that danger was discovered, and it was found that in due time it could be obviated.

Since these experiments, I have made no continued efforts in that direction, but I have experienced many incidents calculated to show the practicability of such a communion among us even in this earth life.

Another instance will be found to be in the spirit photographs, which profess to be likenesses of the departed as they now live in the spirit life. Several years ago I received from the far West—Illinois I think—some crude specimens of this phenomenon, and was informed of what was intended and what it was hoped would be attained. Now a more matured form of it has appeared in Boston, and many pictures have been taken, which there is every reason to believe are likenesses of the departed as they exist now. Time and repeated observations will show how this is. And if it should become a well established fact, surely every one will see at a glance how powerful is the evidence thus given of an existence beyond the grave.

Connected with this subject is the power of seeing and delineating scenes and objects in the spirit land. I have received much evidence in this regard, and have in my collection some interesting specimens, all of which tend to show feasibility and the need of further investigation to develope the power.

Fourth. I will refer to one other topic and close, and that is the power of foretelling future events.

I have in my library a book published in London in 1707 in which is detailed a prophecy, given through just such a spiritual intercourse as we are now experiencing, that the Bourbon family would be expelled from the throne of France, and the reason was given, viz. its general profligacy and its persecution of the freedom of religious opinion.

The last time I lectured to the Spiritualists in New York, which was in May, 1861, I read two papers, one given about eleven years and the other about five years ago, in which our present civil war was foretold—in one of the papers somewhat blindly, until the events made it clear—but in the other most explicit and distinct.

These all related to public events, where the prophecies were published to the world before the events happened, but I have had a great many instances within my own observation where private events were truly foretold.

Five years ago, I published a tract on this subject, with a view to calling attention to it. I have seen nothing since to change my views, but much, very much to confirm them, and to show me that here is a power capable of being understood and improved by us, and of being made available to us.

These four topics are all that I deem it advisable to refer to now. But they are by no means all that are connected with Spiritual Intercourse that are of deep and abiding interest, on which some knowledge has already been obtained and more may be by proper inquiries.

It is, as I understand it, only through the instrumentality of Spiritual Intercourse that that knowledge can be obtained. No man certainly will use that instrumentality who does not believe in its reality, or who regards it as a fraud or a delusion. And in this, it seems to me, lies the chief value of Home's book, and the lesson which it teaches.

If the Book does no more than merely work conviction in some minds, of the reality of communion with the Departed, it will be of some value, for it will carry consolation to many a heart now suffering under a load of doubt or affliction. But if it goes farther, and leads intelligent and instructed minds into an investigation of the higher truths connected with the subject, it will be a great good indeed. For my part, I do not believe that we have yet "attained the end of knowledge of either the works or the word of God."

J. W. EDMONDS.

NEW YORK, March 29, 1863.

INCIDENTS IN MY LIFE.

CHAPTER I.

EARLY LIFE: I BECOME A MEDIUM.

I WAS born near Edinburgh, in March, 1833. When I was about a year old, I was adopted by an aunt, and I accompanied her and her husband to America when I was about nine years old. I was very delicate as a child, and of a highly nervous temperament; so much so that it was not thought that I could be reared. I cannot remember when I first became subject to the curious phenomena which have now for so long attended me, but my aunt and others have told me that when I was a baby my cradle was frequently rocked, as if some kind guardian spirit was tending me in my slumbers. My aunt has also told me that when I was about four years old, I had a vision of the circumstances attending the passing from earth of a little cousin, I being at Portobello, near Edinburgh, and she at Linlithgow, all which proved to be entirely correct, though I had mentioned persons as being present about her, who it is thought could not have been there, and had noticed the absence of her father on the water, at a time when it was thought that he must be with her at home.

When about thirteen years of age, the first vision which I distinctly remember occurred. I was, from my delicate health, unable to join the sports of other boys of my own age. I had, a few months before the vision which I am about to relate, made the acquaintance of a boy two or three years my senior, and somewhat similar to myself both in character and organization. We were in the habit of reading the Bible together, and upon one occasion, in the month of April, as we had been reading it in the woods, and we were both of us silently contemplating the beauties of the springing vegetation, he turned to me and said, "Oh, I have been reading such a strange story!" and he told me a ghost story connected with the family of Lord ———, and which I have since found to be well authenticated. A portrait of the lady to whom it occurred still exists in the family, and is known as the lady with the black ribbon. The present Lord ———, who is of the same family, has told me that he was born in the chamber where the spirit appeared. My friend Edwin asked me if I thought the story could be true, and I said I did not know, but that I had heard strange things of that kind. We then agreed that whichever one of us should first be called from earth, would, if God permitted it, appear to the other the third day afterwards. We read another chapter of the Bible together, and we prayed that so it might be to us. About a month from this time, I went with my family to reside at Troy in the State of New York, a distance from Norwich, where Edwin lived, of nearly three hundred miles. I had been to spend the evening at the latter end of June with some friends, and nothing had occurred during the evening to excite my imagination, or to agitate my mind; on the contrary, I was in a calm state. The family had retired to rest, and I at once went to my room, which was so completely filled with the moonlight as to render a candle unnecessary. After saying my prayers, I was seated on the bed, and about to draw the sheet over me, when a sudden darkness seemed to pervade the room. This surprised me, inasmuch as I had not seen a cloud in the sky; and on looking up I saw the moon still shining, but it was on the other side of the darkness, which still grew more dense, until through the darkness there seemed to be a gleam of light, which I cannot describe, but it was similar to those which I and many others have since seen when the room has been illuminated by spiritual presence. This light increased, and my attention was drawn to the foot of my bed, where stood my friend Edwin. He appeared as in a cloud of brightness, illuminating his face with a distinctness more than mortal. His features were unchanged except in brightness, and the only difference I saw was that his hair was long, and that it fell in wavy ringlets upon his shoulders. He looked on me with a smile of ineffable sweetness, then slowly raising the right arm, he pointed upward, and making with it three circles in the air, the hand began slowly to disappear, and then the arm, and finally the whole body melted away. The natural light of the room was then again apparent. I was speechless and could not move, though I retained all my reasoning faculties. As soon as the power of movement was restored, I rang the bell, and the family, thinking I was ill, came to my room, when my first words were, "I have seen Edwin —he died three days ago at this very hour." This was found to be perfectly correct by a letter which came a few days afterwards, announcing that after only a few hours' illness, he had died of malignant dysentery.

My mother was a seer throughout her life. She passed from earth in the year 1850, at the age of forty-two. She had what is known in Scotland as the second sight, and in many instances she saw things which were afterwards found to have occurred at a distance, just as she had described them. She also foresaw many events which occurred in the family, and foretold the passing away of relatives, and lastly, she foretold her own four months previously.

I was then seventeen, and was residing at Norwich, Connecticut, and my mother was living at Waterford, near New London, twelve miles distant. One day I suddenly felt a strong impulse that she wished to see me, and I walked all the way in consequence of this impression. When I got home, I felt an impression that she had something particular to communicate to me that evening. When we were alone I turned to her and said, "What have you to say to me, mother?" She looked at me with intense surprise, and then a smile came over her face, and she said, "Well, dear, it was only to tell you that four months from this time I shall leave you." I asked incredulously how she knew, and she said, "Your little sister, Mary, came to me in a vision, holding four lilies in her hand, and allowing them to slip through her fingers one after the other, till the last one had fallen, she said, 'And then you will come to me.' I asked her whether the four lilies signified years, months, weeks, or days, and she told me 'months.'" I had been quite impressed by this narration, when my mother added—"and I shall be quite alone when I die, and there will not be a relative near to close my eyes." This appeared to me to be so improbable, not to say impossible, inasmuch as the family was a large one, and we had many relatives, that I said to her, "Oh, mother, I am so delighted you have told me this, because it shows that it must be a false vision." She shook her head. Mary was a little sister who had been taken from earth under most trying circumstances about four years previously. My mother was out for a walk, leaving the child at home, and on returning, having to cross a running stream, and whilst she was on the bridge over it, she saw what appeared to be some loose clothes floating on the water, and hastening to the side to see what it was, she drew out the body of her child.

The apparently impossible prophecy was literally fulfilled, for by a strange complication of circumstances, my mother was taken ill amongst strangers, and a telegram which they sent on the last day of the fourth month, announcing her serious illness, only reached us about half-past eleven in the morning. Being myself confined to bed by illness at the house of my aunt, and she being unable to leave me, the telegram was sent on to my father. That same evening, about twilight, being alone in my room, I heard a voice at the head of my bed which I did not recognize, saying to me solemnly, "*Dan, twelve o'clock.*" I turned my head, and between the window and my bed I saw what appeared to be the bust of my mother. I saw her lips move, and again I heard the same words, "*Dan, twelve o'clock.*" A third time she repeated this, and disappeared from my sight. I was extremely agitated, and rang the bell hastily to summon my aunt; and when she came I said, "Aunty, mother *died to day at twelve o'clock*, because I have seen her, and she told me." She said, "Nonsense, child, you are ill, and this is the effect of a fevered brain." It was, however, too true, as my father found on going to see her, that she had died at twelve o'clock, and without the presence of a relative to close her eyes.

My mother has also told me that her great uncle, Colin Urquhart, and her uncle, Mr. Mackenzie, were also seers, and gifted with the second sight.

A few months after my mother had passed from earth, one night on going to bed, I heard three loud blows on the head of my bed, as if struck by a hammer. My first impression was that some one must be concealed in my room to frighten me. They were again repeated, and as they were sounding in my ears, the impression first came on me that they were something not of earth. After a few moments' silence they were again heard, and although I spent a sleepless night, I no longer felt or heard any repetition of them. My aunt was a member of the Kirk of Scotland, and I had some two years previously, to her great disapprobation, become a member of the Wesleyan body—but her opposition was so violent that I left them to join the Congregationalists. On going down to breakfast in the morning, she noticed my wan appearance, and taunted me with having been agitated by some of my prayer meetings. I was about to seat myself at the breakfast table, when our ears were assailed by a perfect shower of raps all over the table. I stopped almost terror-stricken to hear again such sounds coming with no visible cause; but I was soon brought back to the realities of life by my aunt's exclamation of horror, "So you've brought the devil to my house, have you?" I ought here to state that there had then been some talk of the so-called Rochester knockings through the Fox family, but apart from casually hearing of them, I had paid no attention to them; I did not know even what they meant. My aunt, on the contrary, had heard of them from some of the neighbors, and considered them as some of the works of the Evil One. In her uncontrollable anger, she seized a chair and threw it at me. Knowing how entirely innocent I was of the cause of her unfortunate anger, my feelings were deeply injured by her violence, and at the same time I was strengthened in a determination to find out what might be the cause of these disturbances of our morning meal. There were in the village three ministers, one a Congregationalist, one a Baptist, and the other a Wesleyan. In the afternoon, my aunt, her anger at me having for the moment caused her to lose sight of her prejudices against these rival persuasions, sent for them to consult with her, and to pray for me, that I might be freed from such visitations. The Baptist minister, Mr. Mussey, came first, and after having questioned me as to how I had brought these things about me, and finding that I could give him no explanation, he desired that we might pray together for a cessation of them. Whilst we were thus engaged in prayer, at every mention of the Holy names of God and Jesus, there came gentle taps on his chair, and in different parts of the room; whilst at every expression of a wish for God's loving mercy to be shown to us and our fellow-creatures, there were loud rappings, as if joining in our heartfelt prayers. I was so struck, and so impressed by this, that there and then, upon my knees, I resolved to place myself entirely at God's disposal, and to follow the leadings of that which I then felt must be only good and true, else why should it have signified its joy at those special portions of the prayer? This was, in fact, the turning point of my life, and I have never had cause to regret for one instant my determination, though I have been called on for many years to suffer deeply in carrying it out. My honor has been called in question, my pride wounded, my early prospects blighted, and I was turned out of house and home at the age of eighteen, though still a child in body from the delicacy of my health, without a friend, and with three younger children dependent on me for support. Of the other two clergymen, the Congregationalist would not enter into the subject, saying that he saw no reason why a pure-minded boy should be persecuted for what he was not responsible to prevent or cause, and the Methodist was so unkind, attributing it to the devil, that I derived no comfort from him.

Notwithstanding the visits of these ministers, and the continued horror of my aunt, which only increased as each manifestation was developed, the rappings continued, and the furniture now began to be moved about without any visible agency. The first time this occurred I was in my room, and was brushing my hair before the looking-glass. In the glass I saw a chair that stood between me and the door, moving slowly towards me. My first feeling was one of intense fear, and I looked round to see if there were no escape; but there was the chair between me and the door, and still it moved towards me as I continued looking at it. When within about a foot of me it stopped, whereupon I jumped past it, rushed down stairs, seized my hat in the hall, and went out to wonder on this wonderful phenomenon.

After this, when sitting quietly in the room with my aunt and uncle, the table, and sometimes the chairs, and other furniture, were moved about by themselves in a singular way, to the great disgust and surprise of my relations. Upon one occasion, as the table was being thus moved about of itself, my aunt brought the family Bible, and placing it on the table, said, "There, that will soon drive the devils away;" but to her astonishment the table only moved in a more lively manner, as if pleased to bear such a burden. Seeing this, she was greatly incensed, and determining to stop it, she angrily placed her whole weight on the table, and was actually lifted up with it bodily from the floor. My only consolation at this time was from another aunt, a widow, who lived near, whose heartfelt sympathy did much to cheer and console me. At her house, when I visited her, the same phenomena occurred; and we there first began to ask questions, to which we received intelligent replies.—The spirit of my mother at her house in this way communicated the following: "Daniel, fear not, my child. God is with you, and who shall be against you? Seek to do good: be truthful and truth-loving, and you will prosper, my child. Yours is a glorious mission—you will convince the infidel, cure the sick, and console the weeping." This was the first communication I ever received, and it came within the first week of these visitations. I remember it well. I have never forgotten it, and can never forget it while reason and life shall last. I have reason to remember it too, because this was the last week I passed in the house of the aunt who had adopted me, for she was unable to bear the continuance of the phenomena, which so distressed her religious convictions, and she felt it a duty that I should leave her house, and which I did.

One of the singular manifestations which occurred during this first week, was in connexion with Mrs. Force, a neighbor. I should mention that by this time the neighbors had heard of what was occurring in my presence, and were beseiging the house in a way that did not tend to sooth the religious susceptibilities of my aunt. Being one evening at the house of Mrs. Force, the raps were heard, and the alphabet was used in the way that has now become familiar to many. The name of her mother was in this way given, announcing her presence, and words were spelt out, reproaching her with having so long forgotten her half-sister, who had been married some thirty years previously to a farmer, who removed to the far west, and had not since been heard of. Her mother went on by means of the alphabet and the raps, to state the name of the town where this daughter by a former husband lived, the number of their children, and each of their names. Mrs. Force wrote to the address thus given, and received a letter in reply confirming every particular; and the family was in this way again brought together, and mutual sympathies were interchanged. On visiting Mrs. Force the following year, I found that she had had one of her newly found nephews to visit her the previous autumn.

I go into these particulars not to revive or to cause painful recollections to any one, but merely to show the history of my mediumship, and the mysterious working of Providence in thus throwing me before the public. Had it not been for this chain of circumstances, these truths might have remained unknown so widely as they now are.

Although the manifestations had only lasted a week, they had become known not only to the town, but through the newspapers they were becoming public all over the New England States; and when I left my aunt's house, I went to a neighboring town, Willimantic, and was received at the house of a friend there. Whilst I was with him, these phenomena were repeated, and those present investigated them in the most determined manner. I find the following account of what occurred stated in a newspaper of March, 1851:

"At request, the table was moved repeatedly, and in any direction that we asked to have it. All the circle, the Medium included, had their hands flat upon the table, and we looked several times under the table while it was in the most rapid motion, and saw that no legs or feet had any agency in the movement. The table was a large and heavy one, without castors, and could not be moved by Mr. Hayden in the same manner by all his exertion with his hands laid open upon the table. At one time, too, the table was moved *without the Medium's hands or feet touching it at al*. At our request, *the table was turned over into our lap.* The table was moved, too, *while Mr. Hayden was trying to hold it still!* Mr. Hayden took hold of the top at first, and failing that way, he grasped the leg, and held it with all his strength. The table did not move so freely as before. It would move a little way from Mr. Hayden, and then the invisible power would suddenly relax its effort, when it would spring back with the exertion of Mr. Hayden."

I was then eighteen years old, and on seeing this article which made me so public, I shrank from so prominent a position with all the earnestness of a sensitive mind; but I now found myself finally embarked without any volition of my own, and, indeed, greatly against my will, upon the tempestuous sea of a public life. From this time I never had a moment to call my own. In sickness or in health, by day or night, my privacy was intruded on by all comers, some from curiosity, and some from higher motives. Men and women of all classes, and all countries; physicians and men of science, ministers of all persuasions, and men of literature and of art, all have eagerly sought for the proofs of this great and absorbing question of the possibility of spiritual causes acting on this world of nature. For myself, I have no apology to offer for the occurrence of these unwonted manifestations in my own case. As will have been seen, they came to me quite unsought, and with all the unpleasant and painful accompaniments which I have described. I have not, and never had the slightest power over them, either to bring them on, or to send them away, or to increase, or to lessen them. What may be the peculiar laws under which they have become developed in my person, I know no more than others. Whilst they occur I am not conscious of the mode by which they are produced, nor of the sort of manifestation that is about to occur. Any peculiar sensations that I may experience during certain of the manifestations, I will describe as far as I can, while mentioning the visions or external phenomena. Beyond being of a highly nervous organization, there is nothing peculiar about me that I am aware of; but I continue to have delicate health, and I firmly believe that had it not been for these phenomena, I could not have lived till now. In this belief many physicians of high standing have given their testimony to bear me out. Frequently during the most severe visitations of illness, my pains have been suddenly soothed in a mysterious way, and many times when it would have been impossible to have moved me in bed, for fear of in creased hæmorrhage from the lungs, my head has been slowly lifted, and my pillow has been turned by unseen hands. This has been repeatedly witnessed by many persons. Especially, I would say, that I do not on this account or on any other, consider myself morally superior to others, nor should any one believe that these phenomena come to me, or to others, on account of moral or immoral qualities. On the contrary, with the great blessings which have been showered on me, and the ineffable proofs which I have received of God's providence and goodness to me, I feel myself only worse than others that I should have made so little progress in the path of good. I have to thank God for many kind friends, not less than for many bitter enemies, since they keep my mind in an equilibrium, and do not suffer me to feel any pride, at what is no doubt but an accident, so to speak, of my organization.

These extraordinary occurrences have, with some exceptions, continued with me ever since the time I stated as their commencement, and they have extended their range, to my astonishment not less than to that of others, in the most striking manner. They have proved to me and to thousands of careful and able investigators, the existence of spiritual forces which are calculated to revolutionize the current ignorance both of philosophy and of theology, as men have made them. The exceptions to which I refer have been of periods during which the power has left me entirely; for instance, from the 10th of February, 1856, to the 10th of February, 1857, during which time I had no external token of spirit power, though I on several occasions had visions, one of which was my seeing the manner in which a brother passed from earth. He was frozen in the Polar Seas whilst out bear-shooting with the captain and officers of his ship. Falling into a fissure of the ice, he was not found till the following morning. I saw all this in a vision at the very time of its occurrence, and informed my family of it five months before the confirmation of the intelligence arrived. On several other occasions, the power has ceased for shorter periods, and generally I have been told beforehand, both of the times of its cessation and return. I could never detect any physical cause for such cessation, nor any difference in my general feel ings of health, although the reason given for the withdrawal has commonly been on the ground of health. Upon several occasions, however, the reason given was that it was withdrawn from me as a reproof for having done that which I knew to be wrong.

CHAPTER II.

BEFORE THE WORLD.

I REMAINED in Willimantic but a short time, and then I went to Lebanon, a few miles off. There I was received in the family of an old resident. After I had been with them a few days, I saw a spirit who called himself Uncle Tilden. I asked a lady, a member of the family, if she recognized the name, but before she had time to make answer, the spirit made signs to me that he did not wish the lady to tell the name, and that he would come on another occasion to me, when he could have more perfect control. In the course of a few days he came whilst I was entranced, and signified that certain papers which his family had been seeking for years, and for which they had given up the search as hopeless, would be found in a house which he described as situate near Cleveland, Ohio. They were the title-deeds of some land which had become valuable for building purposes, and out of which a lady was entitled to her thirds, but which by reason of the loss of the deeds, were withheld from her, and she was in consequence living in very straitened circumstances. He described to them minutely through me the part of the garret, and the form of the box in which they would be found. Her son was written to with these particulars; the search was made, and the deeds were found as described.

The second week of my stay at Lebanon, I had been to pass a day or two with an English family residing about three miles off. One afternoon I suddenly became unconscious or entranced, and on awaking, the lady of the house told me that I had been speaking with some spirit, who directed me to proceed at once to the house of a Mr. B——. I had seen two brothers of this name one evening a week previously, and no interchange of visits had been made or proposed, and I felt that it would be most awkward for me to call on them, saying only that I had been sent by my unseen friends. The distance was also six miles from where I then was, and three miles of the journey I would have to walk. I knew that when I returned to my friends at Lebanon, I could have their conveyance; but still I had not any inclination to pay the visit. As soon as this was fully decided in my mind, I was again made unconscious, and on recovering, I was told that I had received strict injunctions to leave at once, though no reason was assigned why I should go. I then felt, however, that the order ought to be obeyed, and I went to my room for the purpose of dressing for the journey. While there, my reasoning faculties again assumed the ascendancy, and I thought that if I were thus sent, I ought at least to know for what purpose. However, I soon again felt myself impelled by a force far superior to mine, and which to have even attempted to resist would have been folly. On leaving the house, all this left me, and I walked the three miles to Lebanon, wondering what could be the cause of this singular errand. On arriving, I stated to my friends there all that had occurred, and they also thought it would have been quite as well to have ascertained why I had been sent. Finding that they agreed with me in this, I now again fully determined to proceed no farther, but I was quickly made insensible, and on awaking I found that orders had been given by the family to have a horse saddled, and that I was admonished in a gentle but firm manner, for my want of Faith and overweening curiosity, whereas I ought, I was told, to have followed as a child would its teacher, or an indulgent parent.

Before I left the house to complete the journey, the sun had set, and now rain laden clouds were fast overshadowing the sky. The road was lonely, and for the month of April the weather was uncommonly chill. I had agreed in my mind that my guardians had been teaching me a useful lesson, and I resolved that thenceforward I would not seek to know their purposes. In this frame of mind I reached what I knew from description must be the house of Mr. B——, and as I was about to dismount, the first rain drop fell on my un gloved hand, and with the contact came the most vivid impression that Mr. B——'s mother was dangerously ill. I rang the bell, and Mr. B—— having seen me, came himself to open the door. As he did so, I said, "Your mother is ill, and I have been sent to say what will relieve her." His look of intense surprise baffles description, as he said, "How on earth could you have known of her illness, as it is only an hour since she fell ill, and we have sent in another direction for a medical man, but I fear he will not arrive in time to save my poor mother, as she seems sinking so rapidly." On entering the house, I stood waiting to see what impression I might receive. Whilst I was standing, I was thrown suddenly into a trance, and I was told by Mr. B—— that in that state I led the way to his mother's bed room, and that after making a few passes over her with my hands, the acute pains left her, and that in a few minutes' time she was in a quiet sleep. Whilst in the trance, I also mentioned simple remedies of herbs for immediate use, and others for continued use. I was then led by the unseen power into the sitting-room, and there returned to my normal state, greatly surprised when these things were related to me. The doctor arrived in about an hour, to find his patient quite out of danger, and on examining her, he said that from the nature and violence of the attack, it would in all probability have been fatal, had steps not been taken at once to alleviate the symptoms. A letter written a few weeks after to a friend by Mr. B——, says that his "mother has not had such health for eighteen years past, as she now enjoys; she follows implicitly all the instructions given though Daniel, and the effect is magical."

I remained in Lebanon till the month of June, having sèances nearly every day, my mediumship principally consisting of visions, movements of the table and furniture without my touching them, and of the rapping sounds through which intelligent messages were received. Whilst there, in the beginning of June, all these external manifestations ceased entirely, and I left Lebanon about the middle of June on a visit to Mr. G—— at Boonton, New Jersey. I had still visions frequently of the spirit friends of persons who were perfect strangers to me, describing their appearance; and the spirits gave me their names, and dates of their departure from earth, with answers to other questions of a test nature which their relatives asked. These came to me whilst I was in an abnormal or trance state, and in which I was unconscious of natural surroundings, but with a facility of speech far superior, as I was told, to that of my ordinary condition, and through which I transmitted with readiness the replies of the spirits to the questions asked of them. I was so exceedingly sensitive at this time, that the playing of sacred music would frequently throw me into a trance state, in which I am always in companionship with spirit friends, and that in as perfect and palpable a manner, as in my ordinary external state I am with my friends of this world. Through these means hundreds of persons became convinced of the truth of spiritual communion, and found their sceptical tenets no longer available. I then found, as I still find, that all honest, deep-rooted scepticism rather call calls out than prevents the proofs of which it stands so much in need; and atheists, deists, and infidels were thus often brought to a belief in Providence and direct spirit guidance.

About the middle of July 1851, I went to Brooklyn, New York, on a visit to Mr. C——. Whilst here I had the pleasure of first meeting the learned and good George Bush, an eminent theologian and Professor of Hebrew and Oriental languages at New York. Profes sor Bush was quite prepared to acknowedge the possibility of such phenomena from his acquaintance with the writings of Swedenborg, and with the subject of Mesmerism, and the spiritual experiences of Jung Stilling and others. He was also a profoundly learned man, with a more open and child-like mind than often falls to the lot of those with so much worldly knowledge. He had made, morever, the greatest sacrifices, by giving up his worldly prospects in the Church, in avowing his belief in Swedenborg's works. Professor Bush took a deep interest in observing the mental phenomena which occurred through me, though there were no external manifestations. The communications he received were of such a nature as to leave no manner of doubt on his mind, as to the real presence with us of those who had gone before. Amongst other names, he told me that I had given him that of an old school-fellow, whom he had forgotten for many years, and that this school-fellow referred to a dream which the Professor had had on the very night on which the boy had passed from earth, although he was not then aware even of the boy's illness. The spirit of the boy now told through me the whole of the Professor's dream, which was that whilst they were playing together, he suddenly saw his school-fellow taken from him, and heard his voice saying, "I leave you, George, but not for ever." A dream of forty years previously, was thus brought to his remembrance. The Professor was so strongly impressed with this, that he called on me the next day, and wished to have me reside with him for the purpose of studying for the Swedenborgian ministry. I went to the house with the intention of so doing, but within forty-eight hours I saw in my waking state the spirit of my mother, who said to me, "My son, you must not accept this kind offer, as your mission is a more extended one than pulpit preaching." On seeing the good Professor, I told him of this spirit message. He expressed regret, but no surprise, and so I returned to my friend, Mr. C——, and remnined with him till the end of August. I frequently afterwards saw Professor Bush, with whom the most kindly intercourse was interchanged. Here again in New York many were convinced.

I returned to Lebanon, but I was not able to see any strangers on account of my very delicate health, and in the month of September my young friend, the son of Mrs. E——, fell ill, and I saw the spirit of his father, whom I had not known on earth, though I had frequently seen him, and received communications from him both in the trance and waking state, on my former visit to Lebanon. He came to me whilst I was alone in my room, and standing near me, said, "Ezra will be with me within three weeks—go to him." I was then staying with a Mr. F——, about three miles from the boy. I obeyed the spirit message, and went at once, and found Ezra ill. He wished me to stay with him, but the family thought it was a passing illness, and that I might prolong my visit for a few days to Mr. F. I did not tell them what I had seen, and in about four days afterwards they sent for me to come to them, as Ezra was worse. I went, and with his sister I took care of him, till his departure, which occurred on the nineteenth day of his illness. He was about eighteen, and had become conversant with the facts of spirit intercourse through me a few months before, and had himself become a partial medium, receiving occasional communications, principally from his father, by means of the rapping and the alphabet. Soon after my first visiting him in his illness, on his sister leaving the room for a moment, he took the opportunity of telling me with perfect composure, that he knew he should not recover, as he had been told by raps on his pillow, by his father, that this was his last illness. This extraordinary composure remained with him throughout, and I had told the family ten days before of my vision, which prepared them for the coming change. About two days before his leaving us, the doctor asked me to break it to him, when I informed him that Ezra had been long aware of it. He doubted this from seeing him so composed, and I desired him to stand at the door and hear what I would say to Ezra. I then went to his bed, and told him that the doctor had left some news for him. He laughingly said, "I suppose it is to tell me that I am going. Little does he imagine that I have already decided who my bearers are to be." The doctor now came into the room, and taking his hand, said, "My dear boy, if I had not heard this, I could not have believed it. You have everything to make life happy, and yet you are so willing to leave it." A few hours after this, a deacon of the church visited him, who was much opposed to these things, to the extent even of telling untruths and misrepresentations. He argued with the dying boy, trying to take away his happy belief, but fortunately without the slightest success. The boy told him that he willingly placed all his hope in the hands of an allwise God, and that he felt that the change would be most happy for him. The last evening of his stay on earth, several persons came to the house, and I was told by one of them that it was for the purpose of watching to see if he did not recant or turn coward at the last. I told this to Ezra, and he requested that they should be brought into his room, where I left them for a few hours' rest. At half-past one in the morning, Ezra sent for me, and I found them still there, he having been speaking with them great part of the time. In speaking to his mother, he said, "Only think, dear mother, I shan't be lame there." He had been lame since he was six months old. He asked me to look out of the window, and to tell him what kind of morning it was. I told him it was bright moonlight, and he recalled to me a conversation we had some months previously, in which he said he should like to pass away in the moonlight, whilst I had said I should wish to go at sunset. He expressed a wish that no one should wear mourning for him. He asked me to take his hand, and whilst I held it, his face suddenly assumed a beatified expression, and he pronounced my name, as if calling me to witness some happy vision passing before his eyes, and the breathing ceased.

This is one of the many happy death-beds which I have witnessed, and such consolation given at a time like this is sufficient proof of the loving wisdom of our Heavenly Father in allowing such things to take place. Some may be surprised to find an apparent prophecy in this case given both to the boy and to me, but perhaps a larger view of spiritual insight may teach us that such is only apparent to us in this natural sphere, and that to those who have spiritual insight and perceptions, there probably was some bodily change in his organism which made clear to those in the spiritual state the mortal character of his disease. Since his departure, he has been frequently present with me, impressing me to write messages to his mother and sister. Sometimes my hand has been taken possession of apparently by him, and used in writing his own autograph. In a letter received from his sister dated the 9th of February, 1852, she says, " Ezra was with you to a certainty when you were writing, for that is his autograph and chirography; the kindness of the advice almost overwhelms me, when I think how spirits watch over and comfort us."

The following is an account taken from a newspaper of other manifestations at this time.

" After several communications had been spelled out, a request was made that the table might be moved, in order to convince some present who were sceptical. Accordingly very soon slight movements were perceptible, which soon became very rapid. A light was placed upon the floor under the table, and one remained on the table. Our hands were raised so that the ends of our fingers only touched. One end was then moved up so that it was poised on the two opposite legs upon an elevation in the floor, and in this position it remained for awhile, keeping time with music, by rocking; and in the same way questions were answered, three movements being considered an affirmative, and one a negative; and after numerous questions were given and as many satisfactory answers received, three gentle raps were heard at the door by a part of the company, and the question was asked if any one was rapping at the door? and immediately three decided movements of the table were made, and accompanying them were three more decided raps at the door.

"An emphatic call for the alphabet followed, and spelled out, 'Spirits—Door;' the question was asked if there were spirits at the door who wished to come in? Three raps.

"It was suggested that they were to help in moving the table, and an affirmative reply immediately followed. Then commenced larger and more decided movements—the table being slid freely about the floor. and raised alternately one side and then the other several inches; and at one time it was raised nearly to an angle of forty-five degrees, poised on two side legs, and then by oscillating movements the time was correctly kept to several tunes sung by the company.

"Several unsuccessful attempts were made to bring the table to the floor, which were relinquished for the fear of breaking the leaves. By request it was carefully let down on to one side, and in a moment raised again to its proper position. One of the company then seated himself upon the table, and it was moved about and raised up so as to render it necessary for him to hold on, and this, too, with as much ease apparently as before. Again, by request, it was slid while one was pushing against it in an opposite direction to the uttermost of his strength."

I remained in Lebanon up to the end of January, 1852; the physical manifestations having spontaneously returned in October previously, and with increased power, and with the new phase of unseen hands touching me and others with whom I was sitting. We frequently were touched by them, and on some occasions a spirit hand was placed within our hands as palpably as if it were a real living hand, though invisible to us. It would remain quietly in our hands until we tried to close them upon it, and even then it was not withdrawn, but as it were melted away in our grasp.

I went to Springfield, Massachusetts, an entire stranger, but having heard of Mr. Henry Gordon, a medium there, I asked for and was directed to his house. He received me most kindly, and said that he was about to have a séance that evening, requesting me to join them. I did so, but the contending influences prevented the occurrence of manifestations. Those who were there assembled had to leave at an early hour, and Mr. Gordon accompanied them, leaving me with five or six of his friends who had come in in the meantime. Among these were Mr. and Mrs. Elmer, the former being a believer, but Mrs. Elmer having violently opposed it. I was thrown into a trance, made to sit near her, telling her the names of her mother, father, brothers, and sisters; then of her children, all of whom were in the spirit world; and I repeated to her the last words of two of her children. Turning to an older lady in the room, I did the same and so on through all those who were present. Mr. and Mrs. Elmer have since been my friends, and at their house some most remarkable manifestations occurred. I stayed with them for some time, and great interest was excited by the accounts given by the very numerous witnesses who came to see the manifestations. Whilst here the power was very strong, and frequently I had séances six or seven times a day, at each of which as many were present as could be accommodated. Their house was besieged by visitors, and often outside in the street there was a concourse of anxious inquirers People came from a distance, even from the extreme west and south of America, having seen the accounts given of me in the newspapers of the previous year. It was here that one of the Professors of the University of Harvard came and joined some friends in a rigid investigation of the phenomena, and after several sittings they published the following statement of the result of their investigations.

THE MODERN WONDER—A MANIFESTO.

The undersigned, from a sense of justice to the parties referred to, very cordially bear testimony to the occurrence of the following facts, which we severally witnessed at the house of Rufus Elmer, in Springfield, on the evening of the 5th inst:—

1. The table was moved in every possible direction, and with great force, when we could not perceive any cause of motion.

2. It (the table) was forced against each one of us so powerfully as to move us from our positions — together with the chairs we occupied — in all, several feet.

3. Mr. Wells and Mr. Edwards took hold of the table in such a manner as to exert their strength to the best advantage, but found the invisible power, exer-

cised in an opposite direction, to be quite equal to their utmost efforts.

4. In two instances, at least, while the hands of all the members of the circle were placed on the top of the table—and while no visible power was employed to raise the table, or otherwise to move it from its position—*it was seen to rise clear of the floor, and to float in the atmosphere for several seconds, as if sustained by some denser medium than air.*

5. Mr. Wells seated himself on the table, which was rocked for some time with great violence, and at length, it poised itself on the two legs, and remained in this position for some thirty seconds, when no other person was in contact with it.

6. Three persons—Messrs. Wells, Bliss, and Edwards—assumed positions on the table at the same time, and while thus seated, the table was moved in various directions.

7. Occasionally we were made conscious of the occurrence of a powerful shock, which produced a vibratory motion of the floor of the apartment in which we were seated—it seemed like the motion occasioned by distant thunder or the firing of ordnance far away—causing the table, chairs, and other inanimate objects, and all of us to tremble in such a manner that the effects were both seen and felt.

8. In the whole exhibition, which was far more diversified than the foregoing specification would indicate, we were constrained to admit that there was an almost constant manifestation of some intelligence which seemed, at least, to be independent of the circle.

9. In conclusion, we may observe, that Mr. D. D. Home frequently urged us to hold his hands and feet. During these occurrences the room was well lighted, the lamp was frequently placed on and under the table, and every possible opportunity was afforded us for the closest inspection, and we admit this one emphatic declaration: *We know that we were not imposed upon nor deceived.*

WM. BRYANT,
B. K. BLISS,
WM. EDWARDS,
DAVID A. WELLS.

The following account also is given in the "Shekinah" of 1852, of manifestations occurring at this time, which will show the power which they had then acquired.

"On the 28th day of February, 1852, while the undersigned were assembled at the residence of Mr. Rufus Elmer, Springfield, Mass., for the purpose of making critical experiments in the so-called spiritual manifestations, the following, among other remarkable demonstrations of power, occurred in a room thoroughly illuminated. The table, around which we were seated, was moved by an invisible and unknown agency, with such irresistible force that no one in the circle could hold it. Two men—standing on opposite sides and grasping it at the same time, and in such a manner as to have the greatest possible advantage—could not, by the utmost exercise of their powers, restrain its motion. In spite of their exertions, the table was moved from one to three feet. Mr. Elmer inquired if the

Spirits could disengage or relax the hold of Mr. Henry Foulds; when suddenly, and in a manner wholly unaccountable by us, Mr. Foulds was seated on the floor, at a distance of several feet from the table, having been moved so gently, and yet so instantaneously, as scarcely to be conscious of the fact. It was proposed to further test this invisible power, and accordingly five men, whose united weight was *eight hundred and fifty-five pounds*, stood on a table (without castors), and the table, while the men were so situated, was repeatedly moved a distance of from four to eight inches. The undersigned further say that they were not conscious of exerting any power of will at the time, or during any part of the exhibition; on the contrary, they are quite sure that the exercise of the will is a serious impediment to such manifestations.

"At the close of these experiments it was perceived, on lifting one end of the table, that its weight would increase or diminish, in accordance with our request. Apprehending that the supposed difference might be justly attributable to fancy, or to some unconscious variation in the manner of applying the motive power, it was proposed to settle the question by weighing the end of the table. At the first experiment it required a force equal to nineteen pounds to raise the end of the table. This was fairly tested to the entire satisfaction of all present. The spirits were then requested to apply the invisible power. The balance was now applied in precisely the same manner as before, when the weight was found to have been suddenly increased from six to twelve pounds, varying as the mysterious force was increased and diminished, so that it now required a force of from twenty-five to thirty-one pounds to separate the legs of the table from the floor. Mr. Daniel D. Home was the medium on this occasion, and it is worthy of remark that during the performance of the last experiment, he was out of the room, and in the second story ot the house, while the experiment was conducted in the back parlor below.

"The undersigned are ready and willing, if required, to make oath to the entire correctness of the foregoing statement."

The original paper was sigued by John D. Lord, Rufus Elmer, and nine others, living at Springfield, Mass.

The account proceeds: "Lights are produced in dark rooms. Sometimes there appears a gradual illumination, sufficient to disclose very minute objects, and at others, a tremulous phosphorescent light gleams over the walls, and odic emanations proceed from human bodies, or shoot meteor-like through the apartment. These phenomena are of frequent occurrence, and are not accounted for by any material hypothesis, unless, indeed, they could be comprehended under the popular generalization which ascribes the whole to human fraud and delusion. I have seen these lights in all their variety. On one occasion, when a number of friends were assembled at my house, there occurred a gradual illumination of the apartment. It appeared like the twilight half an hour after the dawn. The light continued to increase for about fifteen minutes, and then it gradually diminished.

"On the 30th of March, I chanced to be one of a company convened at the house of Mr. Elmer, in

Springfield, Mass., Mr. Home being present, when the room was darkened, to see if the mysterious illumination would occur. Immediately the gross darkness began to be dissipated, and in a few minutes the forms of all the persons in the room were distinctly visible Without disclosing her purpose to any one, Mrs. Elmer mentally requested that the spirits would restore the darkness, and, almost instantly, the change was perceived by the whole company, and soon every form was lost in the deepening gloom."

This was the first appearance of these spirit lights that I had seen when others were present, though I had several times seen them when by myself, since their appearance on my first vision of Edwin as before described. Although the physical manifestations had increased, and were so continuous, yet the internal power of vision had not left me, as will be seen from the following, which was published and signed by Mr. S. B. Brittan of New York, to whom occurred the fact which he describes.

"Last winter, while spending a few days at the house of Mr. Rufus Elmer, Springfield, I became acquainted with Mr. Home. One evening, Mr. Home, Mr. and Mrs. Elmer, and I were engaged in general conversation, when suddenly, and most unexpectedly to us all, Mr. Home was deeply entranced. A momentary silence ensued, when the medium said 'Hannah Brittan is here!' I was surprised at the announcement, for I had not even thought of the person indicated for many days, or perhaps months, and we parted for alltime when I was but a little child. I remained silent, but mentally inquired how I might be assured of her actual presence. Immediately Mr. Home began to exhibit signs of the deepest anguish. Rising from his seat he walked to and fro in the apartment, wringing his hands, and exhibiting a wild and frantic manner and expression. He groaned in spirit, and audibly, and often smote his forehead and uttered incoherent words of prayer. He addressed me in terms of tenderness, and sighed and uttered bitter lamentations. Ever and anon, he gave utterance to expressions like the following:

"'Oh, how dark! What dismal clouds! What a frightful chasm! Deep—down—far down!—I see the fiery flood! Hold! Stay!—Save them from the pit! I'm in a terrible labyrinth! I see no way out! There's no light! How wild!—gloomy! The clouds roll in upon me! The darkness deepens! My head is whirling! Where am I?—'

"During this exciting scene, which lasted perhaps half an hour, I remained a silent spectator, the medium was unconscious, and the whole was inexplicable to Mr. and Mrs. Elmer. The circumstances occurred some twelve years before the birth of Mr. Home. No person in all that region knew aught of the history of Hannah Brittan, or that such a person ever existed But to me the scene was one of peculiar and painful significance. She was highly gifted by nature, and endowed with the tenderest sensibilities. She became *insane* from believing in the doctrine of endless punishment; and when I last saw her, the terrible reality, so graphically depicted in the scene I have attempted to describe, was present, in all its mournful details, before me!

"Thirty years have scarcely dimmed the recollection of the scene which was thus re-enacted to assure me of the actual presence of the spirit. That spirit has since informed me that her present life is calm, peaceful and beautiful, and that the burning gulf, with all its horrible imagery, existed only in the traditions of men, and in the fitful wanderings of her distracted brain."

At Springfield, also, there were many instances of the sick being healed. I was so sensitive to any one who came near me in a diseased state, that I not only myself felt but accurately described their symptoms, and the seat and causes of the disease. One case which I remember was that of a person who had been ill for many years with no apparent cause. I brought to his mind an accident which had occurred to him some years previously, and which I was impressed to tell him was the cause of his suffering. When he applied to a surgeon and related the circumstance, the surgeon told him that I had been no doubt correct in attributing his illness to that accident. My own suffering in sympathy with other people's illness was often so great, and was indeed was so frequent, that I was often warned by my spirit friends against coming in contact with sick persons.

In May, 1852, I went to New York, and was at once received by investigators of the phenomena, mediums having increased largely in number, both in public and private circles. My days and nights were fully occupied by investigators of all classes and conditions. The following account of what he witnessed is given in the words of Dr. Hallock, a physician of New York

"Two communications, spoken through Mr. Home as a medium, were read by the Secretary. They were given on the 10th inst., at the house of Mr. Partridge. The first was preceded by physical manifestations, intended to identify the spirit about to communicate. The second embraces several topics.

"Mr. Home said, a male and female were present, who wished to commune with Mr. P.

"Directly, sounds and motions were made as of a violent storm—the roaring and whistling of the wind, the rushing of water, and the breaking of waves—sounds as if a vessel was straining at her anchor and laboring in a heavy sea, amid which she was held by her chain cables—her joints creaking, and she rolling from side to side. The picture of a shipwreck was so true, that it made the cold chills run over me. The medium spoke of a boat with machinery in it, and went through the motions of dying 'mid the raging waters and a dark storm. The Spirit making these demonstrations to identify her presence, is one whose life was lost by the wreck of the steamer Atlantic, in November, 1849. She gave the following communication:

"'*But, oh! it was not death!* Bright spirits were hovering around, and bore me to their happy home; but it would be no home to us, if we were not permitted to return and watch over our dear friends we have left behind.

"'To me, the storm has passed and gone, and with it went all the storms of life. From that breaking barque, I passed to one the winds could not beat. It was anchored home in the heavens, and my spirit was nearer God—more easily developed, and was amid influences more pure and holy, just what they ought to be for man's advancement.

"'Kindness never goes unrewarded; and for yours, she wishes to express her deep obligation, not thanks merely, but a deep and abiding sense of it.

"'Be upright and kind, and it will prepare you for brighter spheres.

"'Be patient, as God is. Think of His forbearance, for ages past, with the blindness, the hardness, the perversity of man. If man had possessed His power, he would, in his impatience, long since have annihilated earth and all that inhabit it.

"'Think not of the grave. To us, it is past and forgotten. To you, it is but an entrance into a new and more glorious existence.

"'Oft in the silent night, when the busy toils of life are hushed and the mind is at rest from its cares, we hover around and watch over you, happy, indeed, at being able then to impress our presence upon you.'

"The question is often asked, Why have not these manifestations occurred before? Why has not God illumined ages past with these wonderful manifestations of His providence? The reason is obvious. When a little light has been from time to time thrown down, like the feeble rays of a far-off star across the gloom of night, men have shut it up in darkness! They have been enveloped in self and shrouded in scepticism! They think the age of miracles has ceased! Another cause why these things have not occurred in past ages was, the persecution of mediums—it was perceived that men would torture them. It alarmed the superstitious fears of the community. The mediums were charged with being witches, and in league with the Devil! I see them on trial, then taken to the scaffold and the stake, and I hear spirit foot-sounds accompanying them. The younger, more vigorous and more positive state of their accusers, under zeal for God and the good of his church, has made them admit themselves to be *what they were not.* Their defenceless, negative condition, makes them an easy prey to the will-power of their judges and accusers. Now, I perceive the sorrow of those spirits who were not sufficiently developed to foresee the catastrophe as the higher spirits did. They are comforting them in their last earthly agony; and, seeing the sad results of their attempt to communicate through physical manifestations, they have suspended the effort till a more favorable epoch.

"When men are told that spirits watch over them, it is not uncommon for them to say, 'Spirits should be in better business.' The truth is, that many men are so bad that they do not want their minds inspected; they do not wish to have it known how gross they are.

"A spirit wishes to express his idea of a hell. I see a mother with her children. She is training them in the path she herself has trodden. As she was ignorant and foolish, so are they. As her path has been beset with the briars and thorns which ignorance and folly engender, so is theirs. Now, I see her leave them and pass into the Spirit-world; but, impelled by the eternal and universal law of affinity, she still watches over them. Oh, the pangs of her spirit, for the wrong she has done, for the misery she has caused! Yet she fol lows them through all their devious windings through darkness and through crime, and is it not hell enough? Oh, is it not hell enough!

"Again the scene changes, and I see what caused the sin of the mother: A drunken man presents himself—his children, comparatively pure and unsullied, seek associates; for all must have such; they would gladly choose the pure and the good, but they are the drunkard's children, and are spurned from the doors of the intelligent and cultivated. So they are driven back to darkness and ignorance, to glean from the great law of association the happiness for which every human being pants. They could not seek it where they *would*, they must get it where they *can*. Thus, with minds soured by the repulse they have met with, and their darker passions stimulated by the desire of revenge for injuries received, they plod along their devious and uncertain way—the prison their asylum—the halter their inheritance—the constable and sheriff their administering angels. They asked society for meat; it gave them a *scorpion*—for bread; they got a *stone*. Oh, that men could see the *cause* of crime!—they would love and pity.

"If one tree is blighted so that it cannot bear wholesome fruit, should the other trees call it evil? That which is evil cannot become good, but the undeveloped may progress to development. The tree whose root is rotten cannot grow; but if it has been merely scathed, it may. So with the spirit—though a long time may elapse. The bud, placed in the sunlight, does not blossom in a day—if placed in darkness, not for weeks. A spirit, after it has left the body, will have to throw off all the perversion that remains. After that is done, progression goes on without hinderance.

"Be not wise in your own conceit. Let him that standeth in the light of truth, take heed lest he fall through the darkness of his own wisdom."

"Dr. Hallock related some remarkable personal descriptions of spirits through Mr. Home, occurring on the same evening. One spirit was described as having been known here by the name of 'Elizabeth.' Her person was described, and her prominent traits of character as well as the disease of which she died, with such accuracy, that a gentleman present knew her at once from the description. The only inaccuracy that he could point out, being the color of her hair, which had been described as brown, when in fact it was rather a light auburn. In explanation of which Mr. Home said, 'When I look at the forehead, which is very white, (which was the fact,) the hair looks brown to me.'

"The gentleman (a clergyman) declared that he was not thinking of her at all, and she was brought to his recollection solely by the accuracy of the description given.

"Mr. Home then said, 'I see an old woman, and her name is Abigail; they called her 'Aunt Abby.' To the question how did she look? he commenced by compressing the lips and cheeks in such a way as to indicate a person who had lost her teeth. This at once brought to his mind an old lady of that name, called by the whole family, 'Aunt Abby,' who died in the spring of 1817, when he was some eleven years of age. The appearance assumed by the medium was that of the last impression left upon his mind. She was an old woman; had prominent features, had lost her teeth for many years, was much emaciated by her last illness, and as her body lay in its grave-clothes, the thought of his young mind, as he stood gazing upon it, was that very peculiarity first indicated by the medium. Her nose and chin nearly met, so acute was the angle formed by her attenuated gums and shrunken lips.

"Many other facts were given, going to show the identity of the two individuals in question. But one great object seemed to be to teach us, by taking per sons not thought of at the time, (in the last case not thought of for many years), that it was no psychological impression from our own minds, as some have supposed; for there was no known impression of the kind existing at the time, and the memory was only awakened by the accuracy of the pictures which the medium had presented.

"Another equally interesting and accurate description of a spirit, who said his name was William, was given. Previous to the announcement of his presence and name by Mr. Home, and while he was engaged in the other delineation, a lady of high clairvoyant powers, through whose mediumship some of the most sublime lessons of truth and wisdom have been from time to time communicated, had written and shown to a gentleman sitting by her, the following sentence: 'I am impressed that my father is here and standing by my side; I feel his presence distinctly.' When Mr. Home had said, 'there is a spirit present and his name is William,' he asked, as if to gratify his own curiosity, 'Who is William?' and then immediately said, 'O, he says, Eliza knows me.' The lady's name was Eliza, and the spirit was her father. His appearance and prominent traits of character were delineated with great accuracy." Here at New York I made the acquaintance of Dr. Gray, one of the most eminent physicians there, and for whom I have ever had the deepest affection and esteem. He and his kind wife have given me counsel, and befriended me at all times, and under all circumstances. From his character and at tainments, he was eminently suitable as an investigator of phenomena, requiring a calm dispassionate judgment, and the testimony of such a man is, in itself, a sufficient answer to all the doubts of unthinking persons. I had also the pleasure of meeting Judge Edmonds, so well known as one of the judges of the Supreme Court. He investigated this subject in the most painstaking manner for three years, and was fully convinced, not only through the mediumship of others, but through his own and that of his daughter, a lady well known for her purity of mind and truthful nature. He was a frequent visitor to me, and saw all the phenomena which occurred in my presence. I was also acquainted with the late Professor Hare, the eminent chemist and electrician, and with Professor Mapes, so well known in agricultural chemistry. and for his acquaintance with this subject. A conference was formed at New York, which has met weekly for many years for the investigation of spiritual phenomena, and from its recorded transactions, I make the following extract:

"Friday Evening, June 18, 1852.

"Dr. Hallock related a case of physical manifestations which took place on the Friday evening previous at the house of Mr. Partridge, after the conference had adjourned. Mr. D. D. Home was the medium, and the circle consisted of Mr. Partridge, and his wife and daughter, Mr. W. Taylor and wife, Mr. S. B. Brittan, and himself. On the table around which we were seated, were loose papers, a lead pencil, two candles, and a glass of water. The table was used by the spirits in responding to our questions, and the first peculiarity we observed was, that however violently the table was moved, everything on it retained its position. When we had duly observed this, the table, which was mahogany and perfectly smooth, was elevated to an angle of thirty degrees, and held there, with every thing remaining on it as before. It was interesting to see a lead pencil retaining a position of perfect rest, on a polished surface inclined at such an angle. It remained as if glued to the table, and so of every thing else on it. The table was repeatedly made to resume its ordinary position, and then again its inclination as before, as if to fasten upon us the conviction that what we saw was no deception of the senses, but a veritable manifestation of spirit presence, and of spirit power. They were then requested to elevate the table to the same angle as before, and to detach the pencil, retaining every thing else in their stationary positions. This was complied with. The table was elevated, the pencil rolled off, and every thing else remained. They were then asked to repeat the experiment, retaining the pencil and every thing else upon the table stationary, except the glass tumbler, and to let that slide off. This also was assented to with the like result. All the articles retained their positions but the tumbler, which slid off and was caught in the hands of one of the party, as it fell from the lower edge of the table. Then the table, after being restored to the natural position, was moved strongly to and from Mr. Home, and to and from different individuals in the circle, as they requested.

"After this had been repeated several times, and while a corner of the table was inclined into his lap, Mr. Taylor asked if the spirits would lift it clear of the floor while it was in that inclined position. Assent was signified, and the table, after much apparent effort, was lifted clear of the floor as requested. Dr. Hallock said he was led to the conclusion that the effort was only apparent, because, while we were watching it closely, with a light upon the floor so as to see the slightest motion, the table in the meantime resting upon one castor on the floor and one corner of the leaf in Mr. Taylor's lap, was raised perhaps about one inch, after having been literally tumbled about the circle, sometimes upon one castor and sometimes upon two, the leaf resting first in one person's lap, and then in another. But when the foot of the table was finally raised, as described, he, to make sure that they were not mistaken in the fact, got down upon the floor to observe more closely. While looking, the foot of the table, instead of being raised a doubtful inch or so, was thrown up, clear of the floor, six or eight inches, as if all former attempts had been mere playful efforts. We then asked if they could move the table with a man on it. They replied, 'Yes, with twc men on it.' Mr. Partridge and myself then seated ourselves back to back upon the table. Our combined weight is a little over 350 pounds; but notwithstanding, the table was moved as easily as when nothing but the candlesticks and the other things were upon it. We were rocked backward and forward, to and from Mr. Home; the table was tipped from the medium and held stationary in that position, with us upon it—and finally we said playfully, 'when you get tired of rocking us, throw us off.' It was done—the table was tipped strongly and rapidly *from* Mr. Home, and we were thrown on the floor."

At the end of June I received the following letter from Dr. Hull:—

"Newburgh, Orange Co.
"On the Hudson.

"My dear Sir,

"I am desirous that you should make me a visit for myself and some intimate friends, at your first leisure, or freedom from present engagements.

"I will meet all your expenses from your place during your stay here, and for your return; and five dollars a day for ten days, *i.e.* fifty dollars.

"I do sincerely trust you will answer me promptly as to the time you can make me the desired visit; and if my proposition as to terms be not satisfactory, state what your terms are. All shall be made satisfactory to yourself.

"By addressing a letter to my direction—Newburgh, N. Y., it will soon reach me.

"I regretted I did not see more of you in New York, but I hope to have the pleasure fully made up here.

"Mr. Edward Fowler has promised to come up when you visit me.

"Very truly yours, &c.,

"A. Gerald Hull.

"D. D. Home, Esq."

In reply to this, I informed him that I was not a paid medium, but that I should be happy to visit him, as requested. I did so, and whilst with him manifestations of a very interesting character appeared to a family who had been deeply afflicted in the loss of their children. They and Dr. Hull took a great interest in my welfare—and feeling the importance of my completing my education, which from ill health had been much neglected, and of preserving me from the wearing excitement of the life I was then leading, they kindly proposed a home for me in their midst. I could not then avail myself of their offer, having promised to visit many friends during the autumn, but in the following year, as will be seen, I placed myself under their guidance.

In August, I went on a visit to Mr. Cheney, at South Manchester, Connecticut, and it was at his house that I was first lifted in the air, a manifestation which has since frequently occurred to me both in England and France.

The following is the description of the evening, in the words of a gentleman who was present.

"On the 8th instant, in company with three gentlemen from this city, the writer paid a visit to Ward Cheney, residing in Manchester, at whose house Mr. Daniel D. Home was temporarily stopping. A circle was formed, and the well-known vibrations on the table were soon loud and distinct. One of my friends had never seen any thing of the kind, and he accordingy looked under the table to make sure that no one touched it. Answers of a personal character, such as tests of identity, were given very freely. Mr. Home was then thrown into a spiritually magnetic state, discovering great rigidity of muscle, and the ordinary phenomena of the psycho-magnetic condition, including a magnetic locking of the jaws, in which an iron-like hardness of the muscles was apparent. He then spelt out (with his eyes closely bandaged) some remarkable and interesting messages to one or two of the company, the personal nature of which precludes their publication, but which were declared by those interested to be perfect tests. He did this by pointing with almost incredible rapidity to the different letters of an alphabet arranged on a seven by nine card—and thus spelling out the necessary words. A rapid writer had difficulty in keeping up with him, and when a word or a sentence was partially finished, a suggestion from any of the company as to what was intended to be spelt, would, if correct, be answered by eager and vehement rappings in various parts of the table. Among others, (all remarkable,) came a message from two sailors lost at sea, relatives of one of the company—a stranger to most of the company. These spirits announced themselves, somewhat unexpectedly, by canting over the solid and ponderous table, and roll ing it in the manner of a vessel in a violent tempest. Accompanying this demonstration came a violent *creaking* as of the cables of a ship in a storm at sea—and the creaking of the timbers and masts as the vessel surged to one side or the other, was distinctly heard by all. Next came the regular, sullen shocks of the waves as they struck the bows of the doomed vessel. All this time the table kept up the rocking motion. And now the large table was *capsized* on the floor! All this was done with no one touching the table, as a close and constant scrutiny was kept up by two, at least, of our party. These two sailors, whose names and ages were given, it seems lost their lives by the capsizing of a vessel as represented, although this fact, I have the best of reasons for knowing, could not previously be known to Mr. Home, or to any of the company excepting myself.

"Demonstrations now increased in force and number. Several tunes were rocked out by the table when no one touched it, the circle being seated a couple of feet, at least, from it. The swing or motion of the table was full three feet from the floor at each elevation, and the tune was kept with singular accuracy. A simultaneous expression from all the members of the circle attested their recognition of the several tunes as they were thus performed for our satisfaction.

"The table was actually lifted up from the floor, without the application of a human hand or foot!—A table weighing, I should judge, one hundred pounds, was lifted up a foot from the floor, the legs touching nothing. I jumped upon it, and it came up again! It then commenced rocking, without, however, allowing me to slide off, although it canted at least to an angle of forty-five degrees! Finally, an almost perpendicular inclination slid me off, and another of the company tried it with the same results.— These things all happened in a room which was light enough to allow of our seeing under and over, and all around the table, which was touched by no one except the two persons who respectively got upon it to keep it down!

"We went into a darkened room to see the spiritual flashes of light said to have been vouchsafed to some investigators. Instead of this we were greeted with tremendous rappings all around us. Some of the blows on the walls, floor, and table, within three inches of myself, were astounding. I could hardly produce snch violent demonstrations with my fist, though I struck with all my might. The very walls shook.— Answers to questions were given by concussions of varying force and intonation, according to the character of the spirits communicating. A favorite little daughter of one of the gentlemen present, a stranger from a remote State, who had left the earth almost in infancy, announced her presence by a thick-pattering *rain* of eager and joyful little raps; and in answer to an inward request of her father, she laid her baby hand upon his forehead! This was a man who was *not* a believer in these things—he had never before seen them, but he could not mistake the thrilling feeling of that spirit touch. I also had a similar manifestation, in the character of which I am not deceived.

"Suddenly, and without any expectation on the

part of the company, Mr. Home was taken up in the air! I had hold of his hand at the time, and I and others felt his feet—they were lifted a foot from the floor! He palpitated from head to foot apparently with the contending emotions of joy and fear which choked his utterance. Again and again he was taken from the floor, and the third time he was carried to the lofty ceiling of the apartment, with which his hand and head came in gentle contact.

"I omitted to state that these latter demonstrations were made in response to a request of mine that the spirits would give us something that would satisfy every one in the room of their presence. The medium was much astonished, and more alarmed than any of the rest, who, I may add, took the matter calmly, though they were intensely interested."

During these elevations, or levitations, I usually experience in my body no particular sensations than what I can only describe as an electrical fullness about the feet. I feel no hands supporting me, and since the first time, above described, I have never felt fear, though should I have fallen from the ceiling of some rooms in which I have been raised, I could not have escaped serious injury. I am generally lifted up perpendicularly ; my arms frequently become rigid and drawn above my head, as if I were grasping the unseen power which slowly raises me from the floor. At times when I reach the ceiling, my feet are brought on a level with my face, and I am as it were in a reclining position. I have frequently been kept so suspended four or five minutes, an instance of which will be seen in an account which is given of occurrences in the year 1857, at a chateau near Bordeaux. I have been lifted in the light of day upon only one occasion, and that was in America. I have been lifted in a room in Sloane Street, London, with four gas-lights brightly burning, with five gentlemen present, who are willing to testify to what they saw, if need be, beyond the many testimonies which I shall hereafter adduce. On some occasions the rigidity of my arms relaxes, and I have with a pencil made letters and signs on the ceiling, some of which now exist in London.

During this autumn and winter, I visited private families with whom I had become acquainted,—and never a day passed without some manifestations occurring. These are for the greater part of a private nature, appealing to the sympathies of relatives and friends, and could not properly be given to the world. They are to me, however, as to them, a dear reminiscence of the loving guidance of departed friends, who find their highest happiness in ministering to and consoling those who remain to fulfil their pilgrimage here. They ever say that God in his loving-kindness allows this, and that as he is an everywhere present God, and can bear with our shortcomings, they having been mortals like ourselves, can the more readily undesstand the weaknesses of our human nature. During the time I have already spoken of as my public life, I have met with thousands, many of whom disbelieved even the existence of the soul after death, and some who denied the existence of a God. Amongst these were even clergymen, who told me that though they had preached the Gospel, they themselves had never been fully convinced of existence in an after life. From the letters of a friend, an Episcopal bishop, I make the following extract. "You have the pleasant assurance of having been the instrument of conveying incalculable joy and comfort to the hearts of many people; in the case of sorrow you have changed the whole aspect of their existence, and you have made dwelling places light, that were dark before."

I went from Hartford to Springfield, to spend a few days with Mr. Elmer, and although at this time I did not hold séances, still the power was constantly with me in some form or other, as will be seen from the following.

"While Mr. Alderson was at my house, Mr. Home called to see us, having been absent a long time.—Soon after he arrived, he was taken with severe sickness, from which A. attempted relief by bathing his head. During the process, Mr. Home was thrown into the spiritual condition, and described Mr. A.'s father and sister; spoke their names and that of his mother; and the spirit of the father, while addressing his son, called him correctly by his christian name, which Mr. Home had no means of knowing—neither did he know the names of Mr. A.'s parents, which, he assured us, were known only to himself, as he had not mentioned them this side of Baltimore!"

On going to Boston my power returned, and with it the more impressive manifestations of music, without any earthly instrument. At night, when I was asleep, my room would be filled as it were, with sounds of harmony, and these gradually grew louder, till persons in other parts of the house could hear them distinctly. If by chance I awakened, the music would instantaneously cease.

CHAPTER III.

FURTHER MANIFESTATIONS IN AMERICA.

THE year 1853 was spent under the guidance of three friends, and during the summer months I resided at Newburgh, on the Hudson river, where my time was passed in the completion of my studies. I was at the Theological Institute, but only as a boarder, and in no way included in the theological classes. While here, I had an extraordinary vision, which is still so vivid that I remember it in all its details.

The institute was built on an eminence, commanding a view of peculiar beauty. Below lay the city; on the right, the river was lost in its windings among the rocky hills surrounding West Point; on the left, it lay in expanse, and could be traced for a distance of many miles; behind, spread out the country, with its pretty little farm-houses dotted here and there. I have sat for hours of an evening, watching the feeble flickering lights, and endeavoring to picture in my imagination the life-emotions which must from time to time have crossed those thresholds. Now, fancy pictured to me a young girl, on whose form time and care had passed but as an evening breeze; and a little further off it was, perchance, a mother whose little one was suffering, and every beat of whose feeble pulse she had counted, with that hope which only a mother may know, as she prays God to spare the pure, gentle, and loving little one, whom He has given her. Anon, it was one bowed down with age and sorrow; all that he had loved had gone to their rest, and he was alone in the world. Bright pictures of his youth flitted before him, but these only augmented his loneliness, for the light of the past had brought out in deeper contrast the shadows of the present.

These and similar trains of thought often occupied my idle hours; and, at times, these fancied scenes became as it were real, and furnished ample resource to a mind naturally inclined to dwell on subjects beyond the little narrow circle of every-day life.

One evening, I had been pondering deeply on that change which the world calls death, and on the eternity that lies beyond, until, wearied, I found relief in prayer, and then in sleep. My last waking consciousness had been that of perfect trust in God, and a sense of gratitude to Him for the enjoyment I received from contemplating the beauties of the material creation. It might have been that my mind was led to this by the fact of my having watched a beautiful star as it shone and twinkled in the profound stillness of the night. Be this as it may, it appeared to me that, as I closed my eyes to earthly things, an inner perception was quickened within me, till at last reason was as active as when I was awake. I, with vivid distinctness, remember asking myself the question, whether I was asleep or no? when, to my amazement, I heard a voice which seemed so natural, that my heart bounded with joy as I recognized it as the voice of one who, while on earth, was far too pure for such a world as ours, and who, in passing to that brighter home, had promised to watch over and protect me. And, although I well knew she would do so, it was the first time I had heard her voice, with that nearness and natural tone. She said, "Fear not, Daniel, I am near you; the vision you are about to have is that of death, yet you will not die. Your spirit must again return to the body in a few hours. Trust in God and his good angels: all will be well." Here the voice became lost, and I felt as one who at noonday is struck blind; as he would cling even to the last memories of the sunlight, so I would fain have clung to material existence—not that I felt any dread of passing away, nor that I doubted for an instant the words of my guardian angel, but I feared I had been over-presumptuous in desiring knowledge, the very memory of which might disturb my future life. This was but momentary, for almost instantaneously came rushing with a fearful rapidity memories of the past; my thoughts bore the semblance of realities, and every action appeared as an eternity of existence. During the whole time, I was aware of a benumbing and chilling sensation which stole over my body, but the more inactive my nervous system became, the more active was my mind, till at length I felt as if I had fallen from the brink of some fearful precipice, and as I fell, all became obscure, and my whole body became one dizzy mass, only kept alive by a feeling of terror, until sensation and thought simultaneously ceased, and I knew no more. How long I had lain thus I know not, but soon I felt that I was about to awaken in a most dense obscurity; terror had now given place to a pleasurable feeling, accompanied by a certitude of some one dearly loved being near me, yet invisible: it then occurred to me that the light of the spheres must necessarily be more effulgent than our own, and I pondered whether or not the sudden change from darkness to light might not prove painful, for instinctively I realized that beyond the surrounding obscurity lay an ocean of silver-toned light. I was at this instant brought to a consciousness of light, by seeing the whole of my nervous system, as it were, composed of thousands of electrical scintillations, which here and there, as in the created nerve, took the form of currents, darting their rayons over the whole body in a manner most marvellous; still, this was but a cold electrical light, and besides, it was external. Gradually, however, I saw that the extremities were less luminous, and the finer membranes surronnding the brain became as it were glowing, and I felt that thought and action were no longer connected with the earthly tenement, but that they were in a spirit-body in every respect similar to the body which I knew to have been mine, and which I now saw lying motionless before me on the bed. The only link which held the two forms together seemed to be a silvery-like light, which proceeded from the brain; and, as if it were a response to my earlier waking thoughts, the same voice, only that it was now more musical than before, said, "Death is but a second birth, corresponding in every respect to the natural birth, and should the uniting link now be severed, you could never again enter the body. As I told you, how ever, this will not be. You did wrong to doubt, even for an instant, for this was the cause of your having suffered, and this very want of faith is the source of every evil on your earth. God is love; and still His children ever doubt Him. Has He not said, 'Knock, and it shall be opened unto you: seek, and ye shall find?' His words must be taken as they were spoken. It is not for men to give any interpretation they may believe, or desire to believe, to what God has said. Be very calm, for in a few moments you will see us all, but do not touch us; be guided by the one who is appointed to go with you, for I must remain near your body."

It now appeared to me that I was waking from a dream of darkness to a sense of light; but such a glorious light! Never did earthly sun shed such rays, strong in beauty, soft in love, warm in life-giving glow, and as my last idea of earthly light had been the reflex of my own body, so now this heavenly light came from those I saw standing about me. Yet the light was not of their creating, but was shed on them from a higher and purer source, which only seemed the more adorably beautiful in the invisibility of its holy love and mercy,—thus to shower every blessing on the creatures of its creation; and now I was bathed in light, and about me were those for whom I had sorrowed, for although I well knew that they existed, and loved and cared for me, nevertheless their earthly presence was not visible. One that I had never known on earth then drew near and said, 'You will come with me, Daniel.' I could only reply, that it was impossible to move inasmuch as I could not feel that my nature had a power over my new spirit-body. To this he replied, 'Desire and you will accomplish your desires which are not sinful, desires being as prayers to the Divinity, and He answereth the every prayer of His children.'

For the first time I now looked to see what sustained my body, and I found that it was but a purple tinted cloud, and that as I desired to go onward with my guide, the cloud appeared as if disturbed by a gentle breeze, and in its movements I found I was wafted upward until I saw the earth, as a vision, far, far below us. Soon I found that we had drawn nearer, and were just hovering over a cottage that I had never seen; and I also saw the inmates, but had never met them in life. The walls of the cottage were not the least obstruction to my sight, they were only as if constructed of a dense body of air, yet perfectly transparent, and the same might be said of every article of furniture. I perceived that the inmates were asleep, and I saw the various spirits who were watching over the sleepers. One of these was endeavoring to impress his son where to find a lost relic of him which the son much prized, and the loss of which had greatly grieved him. And I saw that the son awoke and thought it but an idle dream, and three times this impression was repeated by the spirit; and I knew that when morning came, the young man would go, out of curiosity where he had been impressed to go, and that he would there find what he sought for. In an adjoining room I saw one who was tormented by dreams, but they were but the production of a diseased body.

I was most deeply interested in all this, when my guide said, "We must now return." When I found myself near my body, I turned to the one who had remained near my bed, and said, "Why must I return so soon, for it can be but a few moments I have been with you, and I would fain see more, and remain near you longer?" She replied, "It is now many hours since you came to us; but here we take no cognizance of time, and as you are here in spirit, you too have lost this knowledge; we would have you with us, but this must not be at present. Return to earth, love your fellow-creatures, love truth, and in so doing, you will serve the God of infinite love, who careth for and loveth all. May the Father of mercies bless you, Daniel!"

I heard no more, but seemed to sink as in a swoon, until consciousness was merged into a feeling that earth with its trials lay before me—and that I, as well as every human being, must bear my cross. And when I opened my eyes to material things, I found that the little star had given way to the sun, which had been above the horizon about four hours; making in all about eleven hours that this vision had lasted. My limbs were so dead, that at least half an hour elapsed before I could reach the bell rope, to bring any one to my assistance, and it was only by continued friction that, at the end of an hour, I had sufficient force to enable me to stand upright.

I merely give these facts as they occurred; let others comment on them as they may. I have only to add, that nothing could ever convince me that this was an illusion or a delusion; and the remembrance of those hours is as fresh in my mind now, as at the moment they took place.

In the autumn I returned to New York, with the intention of beginning a course of medical studies, but a chain of untoward circumstances seemed strangely to link themselves together, and to prevent my carrying out my intention. At that time I could not well comprehend why this should be; but since then I have often had occasion to thank God that it was so ordered. The kind friends who were doing what they thought to be best, in preventing others from seeing the manifestations, did not take into consideration that the phenomena which had been a source of information and consolation to them, were God-given, and that we had no right to conceal the light from any. As what was intended for me could only be brought about by my own decision, I acted as I felt would be for the best, and so it afterwards proved to be.

Previous, however, to my taking the step, I had another vision of great distinctness. I had been with some friends to dine at the house of a mutual acquaintance, and on returning, it was necessary to cross from Brooklyn to New York in the ferry-boat. The gatekeeper allowed our carriage to enter, and we were going down the inclined plane which led to the boat, when one of the men caught the horses by the bit, telling the coachman as he did so, that there was no room for us on the ferry-boat. Not only was this so, but the chains were already down, and the boat was in the act of leaving. There we were on a steep inclined plane, with restive horses, and the deep waters within a foot of them, the only barrier being a chain not over strong. Mrs. C—— begged to alight, and I jumped from the carriage and gave her my hand to assist her. As her hand touched mine, with the instantaneous sensation of contact, I saw with most perfect distinctness, that a little sister of mine had passed from earth. I was not aware that the child had been ill, and her illness being apparently but slight, my relatives had not thought it necessary to write to me about her. It was a strange transition; there I stood in the cold night air, and I heard the impatient pawing of the horses on the worn deal boards; I heard the waters as they broke against the side piles of the ferry; I felt a life-warm hand in mine, yet there, shielding her from the cold, beyond all fear, and where harm could not come, I saw my mother, with one of the three children she had left me to care for on earth. The child was close pressed to her heart, and her long silky hair lay scattered in profusion over my mother's shoulder. I saw also my spirit-sister Mary, who seemed anxious to soothe the child-like wonderment of her newly arrived sister. It was but for a moment, yet I saw it all, and I knew that God had given me another guardian angel. The next day letters came to announce what I thus already knew.

January of 1854 was the beginning of severer trials, for I had been so left to myself in solitude and study the whole winter, that mind and body were alike disturbed, and I wrote to my friends saying that I could not think of continuing the life I then led; and after many letters had passed between us, I was again left to myself to decide as to my future course. I had friends in Boston, who as soon as they knew what my intentions were, generously offered to do all that my other friends had been doing, and to allow me perfect liberty to see whom I might please. My health had suffered from the nervous anxiety of my solitary life and studies, and now the medical men whom I consulted, pronounced my left lung to be diseased. My spirit friends said that they were correct in their diagnosis, but that I would not yet pass from earth, as my mission was incomplete, and there was much yet for me to do.

I went from New York to Hartford, but I saw no strangers for a few weeks. From here I again went to Springfield, and Dr. Gardner of Boston, in a letter, dated March 1st, 1854, describes what he saw at this time, and though in some respects similar to what has been already described, will help to show the character of the manifestations at different periods of my life.

Dr. Gardner says, "I am induced to offer you the following facts, which I in company with several other persons witnessed at the house of Mr. Rufus Elmer in this city, on the evening of the 28th of February, 1854. Nine persons besides Mr. Home, were seated round a common cherry table, when the following phenomena occurred: The table commenced a trembling, vibratory motion, sounds were heard on the floor and table, some of which were very loud, then the table was rocked with great force, then raised nearly if not quite two feet from the floor, and it was held supported in mid air with a waving motion, as if floating on the agitated waters of the sea, for considerable time. This was repeated for several times. Then we were directed to place the dinner-bell (weighing one lb. one oz.) under the table on the floor, where it was rung with great violence many times; questions were answered by the raps upon it, and with it every individual in the circle was touched in such a manner that there could could be no mistake about it. We then requested the spirits to pass the bell from the floor, and to place it into our hands, which was done to each individual separately; and, again at our request, it was taken from our hands, and carefully deposited on the floor. Again, while we sung the hymn, 'Whilst shepherds watch,' the bell was raised from the floor, and rung in perfect time with the measure of the tune sung, after which another tune was drummed out by the bell against the underside of the table, the sound resembling the roll of drum-sticks in the hands of a skilful performer upon a tenor drum. This was continued for several minutes.

"All the above I know was performed without human agency; the hands of each person present during the whole performance above described being on the top of the table, with the room well lighted, and in full view of every person present; and this was also the case during the whole performance. During the whole of the various performances with the bell, as well as before and after it, our clothes were pulled almost constantly, two handkerchiefs were firmly knotted together while lying in the laps of the owners, we were many times touched more or less forcibly, producing a peculiar and indescribable sensation, some of us had our limbs grasped with considerable force, and distinctly felt the form of the spirit hand, a soft, delicate, elastic, yet powerful touch, which cannot be described, but must be felt to be appreciated. The reader will bear in mind that the hands of every person present were in plain view on the top of the table.

"During the evening, responses to questions asked,

were made by the invisible intelligence with the bell-handle, so heavy as to leave indentations on the table, which may be seen by any person who doubts. Many other manifestations were made, but the above are sufficsent to convey some idea of the wonderful invisible power there manifestod; and the many beautiful and sublime moral teachings there given by our heavenly visitants, through the medium while entranced, I trust will long be remembered and made a rule of life by those who heard them."

I next went to Boston, and while here the power seemed to increase in a manner, which surprised me not less than other witnesses of it. On several occasions spirits were seen distinctly by all present in the room, and more than once they kissed persons present so as to be both felt and heard. During the summer months my health gradually improved, and I once more thought that I would now be enabled to pursue a course of studies which would enable me to take my diploma as a medical man. But no! again a series of unforeseen circumstances combined to prevent me. In September, I returned to Springfield, and the letter I here insert is taken from "The Republiccn" and describes some phenomena witnessed by Mr. F. C. Andrue.

"On Monday last, September 25, 1854, I called after tea at the house of my friend, Mr. Elmer, for the purpose of returning a book which I had borrowed. Unexpectedly, I met there Mr. D. D. Home, who had just arrived from Boston. After conversing an hour or two, Mr. Elmer having to leave on the morrow on business, proposed a 'circle' that evening. We accordingly sat down—Mr. Elmer's family, Mr. Home and I being the only persons present. The occurrences, though very extraordinary, were similar to those already published. We were all touched by unseen hands, the room being well lighted with gas, a large bell was passed into our hands, &c. These things were not new to me, and are not to the public. I will therefore pass them by.

"Knowing that still more extraordinary 'manifestations' at times occurred to Mr. Home during the night, I mentioned that I would like to witness some of them. They urged me to stay and spend the night, and I did so.

"After leisurely undressing, putting out the light and retiring to bed, we soon began to hear faint raps, which rapidly increased in power and number, till the walls, floor, and bedstead fairly shook with strokes. They came like a shower. Soon came other noises, and then tho bed began to move across the floor. This seemed rather dangerous locomotion. It was the only thing that gave me any uneasiness. Having before witnessed so many wonders, I was not frightened, though Mr. Home seemed to be so, holding on to me with both hands, and begging with all his might that the bedstead should be stopped. *They* complied with his request, but only to come in a more tangible form.

Soon I began to feel some one stepping on my feet and ancles, over the bed-clothes, but with a pressure different from that produced by any hard substance. Directly after there came a hand on my head and forehead, *as much like flesh and blood* as any I ever felt, *only somewhat cold.* I began to ask questions, the fingers patting me on my forehead in answer. Several hands, touching me at the same time, claimed to be those of relatives of mine.

"A strong hand came, stated to be that of my grandfather. I asked, how am I to know that this is my grandfather? The hand moved from my forehead to my temple, over my eyebrow and eye, and then passed down over my face—the fingers patting me in the most gentle manner possible. At another time, at my request, hands patted my forehead with such force that the *sound* could be heard, I am confident, in any part of the room.

"I wish, before I close, to add a few words. To religious minds (which are strangely the most sceptical in this matter) I have this to say: By what process of reasoning can you bring yourselves to disbelieve, *my* testimony of what I *know* and *have seen*, and to believe the testimony of what John, Peter or Paul saw? I speak with all reverence—I doubt not their testimony; on the contrary I believe it *now* more than ever. But I know of no reason, (my veracity being unimpeached) why my testimony of what I *know* and *see* is not as good as that of any other man, living or dead. And there are thousands who know these things to be so, as well as I.

"To our *wise* men, whose hobby is scientific investigation, I would say: Of what use is it to those who have gone through what I have, to read Dr. Dodd's book, Dr. Rogers' theory, or to marvel over Professor Faraday's discoveries? who only proved that when he pushed, he pushed."

Early in November, I returned to New York, and

resumed my medical studies. I held séances two or three times a week, at my own rooms, and was in the habit of going amongst the poorer classes for the purpose of speaking to them of this most cheering truth. I have always found them to be the most candid and thorough in their investigations; and when they were in reality convinced, they were the most thankful to God in allowing such proofs of spiritual beings and forces to exist. I have seen many a poor heart-broken mother consoled with the thought that the fair young child, given her by God as a hope-star to cheer her as she toiled for her daily bread, but who had pined and gone for ever from her sight, was still living and loving her and her God-sent ministering angel. I well remember a poor man being present one evening, and the spirit of a little girl coming with the following message. "Father, dear, your little Mary was present last Wednesday, and God gave her power to prevent you from doing what you wished. If you were ever to do that, you could not come where your own Mary and her mother are. Promise me you will never think of such an awful thing again." We all looked astonished, but could not understand to what she alluded. Still it was evident the poor father knew too well, for throwing himself on his knees, he said, as the tears rolled down his cheeks, "Indeed, it is but too true, that on Wednesday last I decided to cut my throat; but as I took the razor to do it, I felt that had my child been alive, she would have shrunk from me with horror, and this very thought was the saving of me."

My frequent séances were attended by persons who

were introduced to me by friends, and I met at this time many hundreds. One of these séances is spoken of in the "New York Conference," of December 26, 1854, and may serve to give an idea of my mediumship at this time.

"A gentleman present related the facts of a circle which met on Wednesday evening last. Mr. Home was the medium. When seated, the first thing noticed was an undulating motion on the table, which was followed by its being lifted entirely clear off the floor. This was repeated several times. Once or twice it was raised as high as the chins of the party sitting at it, the hands of every person in the room being upon the table. A guitar in its case standing in one corner of the room was heard to move, and on examination, the end resting upon the floor was found to have moved several inches. Loud raps were heard in its vicinity while this was being done, and a closet door opening upon the room in which they were seated, was shut with considerable force. The circle during these occurrences remained seated at the table, and some six or eight feet from where they took place. The guitar case was then unlocked, and the instrument placed under the table. In this position it was played upon repeatedly, not, to be sure, in the highest grade of the art, but with very fair average skill. The hands of the party during this performance were all upon the table in plain sight of every one. There was no chance for trick, the room being sufficiently light for all to see the exact position of every person and thing in the room. The guitar was then placed in the lap of each member of the circle in rotation. Each one took hold of the end presented, and held on until the instrument was removed by the invisible agency. The table, the chair, in which they were seated, and the floor of the room itself, were made each in turn to exhibit a tremulous motion sensible to all. The large rocking-chair in which Mr. Home was seated, was next rocked forcibly. Then, by direction through the alphabet, the whole party of ten persons, in rotation, took the same chair, and were rocked in the same way. The application of the power was as though a person had hold of the upper part of the back of the chair with one hand, and the other on its arm The application of the force at these points could be felt distinctly at every vibration; and the force necessary to produce them may be appreciated by stating that the feet of the sitter were held out straight, and were frequently made to strike the under side of the top of the table. Every one was touched in turn as by human hands, some large and some small. A lady present who had been touched with what purported to be the hands of her little daughter, asked if she could take the handkerchief out of her lap? Very soon it was seen to move slowly from her lap, and disappear beneath the table. In a few minutes, raps indicating the alphabet were heard, and this sentence was received: "Mother, now look and see what we have done." On looking, the handkerchief was found knotted and twisted into the form of a *doll-baby*, not very symmetrical, but sufficiently like to show the evident design, as well as ingenuity and power to execute. Several other interesting facts occurred during the evening.

"Dr. Hallock said he was present when the facts

just narrated occurred. The point which he particularly wished to illustrate was the open character, so to speak, of these manifestations. When an important fact is stated, accompanied with the explanation that it occurred in a dark room, it naturally raises the question of deception in the mind of the hearer, which the most elaborate statement of particulars cannot eradicate. From beginning to end these manifestations were free from that objection. Every person in the circle, Mr. Home included, was in full view. When the guitar was played, all our hands were *seen* to be on the table. A man could not have touched the strings of that instrument with the toe of his boot even, much less with his hand, without detection. So of all the other facts of the evening. In one instance, after several unsuccessful attempts to retain a sheet of paper upon the smooth surface of the table when elevated to a considerable angle, the table with the sheet of paper on it was turned so as to rest *on its edge*, the top being vertical, and the paper still retaining its position, until it was suffered to fall at the request of one of the gentlemen present. The exhibition of power and intelligence manifested on that evening, were done *for us*, and not *by us*—if ten pairs of eyes, with the remaining complement of senses, are to be taken as evidence."

In January, 1851, the weather was more than usually cold and severe, and my cough had so increased, with other symptoms of a more alarming nature, that all idea of completing my medical studies had to be abandoned entirely. The medical men whom I consulted, all coincided in saying that my only hope of having my life prolonged, was to visit Europe. This was to me a hard struggle, in being thus separated from those who would have tended me with every affection, and to be thrown as it were a stranger in what was now to me a strange land. My family had by this time all been residents of America for some time, and I knew no friend in all England. I would not have heeded the advice of my medical men, and I should have remained where I was to pass from earth; but my spirit friends told me that I must go, and their counsels could not be unheeded. I accordingly went to pay a series of farewell visits to those friends who had been so kind to me; they as well as I feeling that in all probability it was the last time we should meet "in the flesh." While at Hartford in March, on one of these visits the séance here alluded to took place.

"The following occurrences transpired in this city on the evening of the 14th ultimo: A small party were seated with Mr. D. D. Home, who is probably the most remarkable of modern mediums for spirit-manifestations of a physical or tangible order. It was intimated that if we would procure a table-cloth and place it upon the table, the unseen presences would manifest themselves by lifting up the cloth. The cover was accordingly procured, when we placed it upon the table, put the lamp upon it, and drew back far enough to prevent the possibility of any one of the party touching it, unless by stretching forward; and the slightest movement of the kind by any one present would have been instantly detected. In a moment more the table-cloth was plainly *lifted up*, on the side opposite to the medium, and in the full light of the lamp. It present ed the appearance of something under it, for it *moved about* under the cloth, going first to one side of the table and then to the other. Presently it *reached out*, lifting the sides of the cloth, *towards each one present*, in succession. In this manner the force, or substance (for it was a substantial thing, resembling a hand), reached out and *shook hands* with the company. It felt, through the cloth, like a hand; but on retaining it for a closer inspection, it seemed to *evaporate* or *dissolve*, and was rapidly lost. In its nature and composition it resembled, apparently, the hand and arm seen on a previous occasion by a party of six, and described in a former article.

"Soon after this, the thing (whatever it was), again lifted up the table-cloth, moving apparently all about the table, and raising the cloth as it moved. In a moment more it reached forward and *touched* one of the party; then drew back and again reached out and touched another. Different parts of the person were thus touched; and presently the hand, if it was a hand, *left* its protection of the table-cloth, and commenced *touching* the party in succession, some in one place, and others in another. But nothing could be *seen!* If requested to touch, for instance, the right shoulder, the hand would unexpectedly respond by touching the *left;* or if asked to touch the leg, perhaps the breast or hand of the one asking would be touched—seemingly with a view to indicate in the clearest manner that the power and the intelligence was separate from the mind of the party. The invisible agency thus operating touched the writer at first on the knee, and, gradually advancing upwards, finally took him by the hand; but, although this was in a pretty good light (a little below the edge of the table), no traces of the hand that was palpably touching mine could be seen.

"A guitar, of a size and weight somewhat unusual, had been placed beneath the table, in the hope of getting some *music* from the spirits. I placed also a quire of letter paper and a pencil upon the instrument, that they might, if able and so disposed, give us a sample of *writing* without mortal hands. (Both of these performances have been witnessed at circles in New York, and elsewhere.) As soon as we were again seated and quiet, the guitar was sounded, and then *played upon*, evidently by real, substantial fingers, for the touches on the strings were strong and distinct. Presently the quire of paper was thrown from the instrument upon the floor, a distance of some three or four feet, and the music was again produced, louder than before. Next, the guitar, large and heavy as it was, was *dragged out* from its place, and *carried away to a door*, a distance of five feet from the table, and there the music recommenced, stronger and clearer than ever. This had all been done while the party sat quietly at the table. At this juncture, in order to see the performance going on at that distance, the writer leaned forward towards it, and in so doing, accidentally extinguished the lamp on the table; but as a good light was reflected upon all of us from a grate of glowing coals directly in front of the party, it was decided not to break the circle to relight the lamp, and the manifestations went on.

"While we sat thus, *the guitar, at the distance of five or six feet from the party, was played upon exqui sitely*, and for several minutes, by some power other than that of any one bodily present. The instrument was partially in shadow, and the hand that swept its strings could not be seen; but the *music* was surpassingly beautiful. It was of a character entirely new to those who listened, and was sweeter, softer, and more harmonious than anything I have ever heard. Portions of it were filled with a certain soft and wild melody that seemed to be the echo of other music far away, and for the exquisite sweetness of which there are no words. It was of that

———" 'Music that softer falls
Than petals from blown roses on the grass,
Or night dews on still waters between walls
Of shadowy granite in a gleaming pass.'

Anon it changed, and rose to a 'full orb' of strong, tempestuous melody, filling the house with its sounds. It was heard by a lady residing in another part of the house, who inquired about it the next day; thus proving the strength and the *reality* of this immortal music.

"It was asked by one of the circle, 'Can you strike on all the chords at once?' *Ans.* (by responses on the strings)—'Yes,' and this was actually done.

"The guitar was then removed to a corner of the room, still farther off; and as soon as all were seated, it was again played upon, at that distance, for some time; then it was brought back by invisible means and placed near the table. Mr. Home remarked, that all this transcended anything of the kind in his previous experience, and he proposed to 'see what they *could* do,' taking the guitar to the most distant corner of the room. It was suggested to him by us that this would be useless, as they could do nothing at that distance from himself; but upon his taking his seat again the spirits began playing the instrument in that farthest corner!—at a distance (as ascertained by subsequent measurement) of nearly *eleven feet* from circle or the medium! Then the guitar was moved from its place by the spirits and brought towards the circle; but, encountering a heavy mahogany chair on the way, *the instrument was laid down and the chair dragged several feet* out of the way; after which the guitar was taken up and carried all *around the circle* by the invisibles, and at length deposited in the *opposite* corner! In a few moments more the writer saw it *poised in the air*, top upwards, and nearly over his head! The remark was made, "Well, if I did not *see* this myself, I wouldn't believe it on other testimony"—whereupon the instrument *reached forward and playfully tapped the speaker three times upon the shoulder.* Then it was passed across the table (over his head) towards Mr. Home, whom it lightly touched several times upon the head! Being close to it during this performance, I watched it narrowly by the aid of the fire-light. The bottom end of the instrument was very near my face, while the opposite end was thus being used; it was not, in fact, six inches above my head, and just in front of me. *The indistinct outline of a human hand could be seen grasping the instrument just below its centre.*

"Reaching up, I grasped the instrument firmly in both hands and held it above my head, requesting at the same time that the one who had been performing would *now* play it if possible. *Immediately the strings were touched* as if by human fingers, though now invisible, and the guitar was played as well while thus held in the air as it had been while on the floor!

"The *quire of paper* before spoken of was *taken from the floor, slowly lifted up, and placed upon the table,* as I can affirm, without the aid of a human hand. Sitting at that end of the table where this was done, I was enabled to see the whole of this proceeding. The quire of paper was placed upon the edge of the table, and so near my hand as to touch it. This was done slowly and deliberately, and this time at least I was permitted to see plainly and clearly *the hand that had hold of it.* It was evidently a *lady's hand*—very thin, very pale, and remarkably attenuated. The *conformation* of this hand was peculiar. The fingers were of an almost preternatural *length,* and seemed to be set *wide apart.* The extreme *pallor* of the entire hand was also remarkable. But perhaps the most noticeable thing about it was the shape of the fingers, which, in addition to their length and thinness, were unusually *pointed* at the ends; they tapered rapidly and evenly toward the tips.* The hand also *narrowed* from the lower knuckles to the wrist, *where it ended.* All this could be seen by such light as was in the room, while the hand was for a few moments holding the paper upon the edge of the table. It sud-

* The writer has since been shown a daguerreotype taken from a picture of the lady whose name was written as above described, and whose disease was consumption. The portrait was taken just before her death, and the hands and fingers in the daguerreotype, although rather indistinct, bear a most close and remarkable resemblance to the hand described above.

denly disappeared, and in a moment the *pencil* was thrown from some quarter, and fell upon the table, where the hand again appeared, took it, and *began to write.* This was in plain sight, being only shaded by one of the circle who was sitting between the paper on he table and the fire. The hands of each one present were upon the table, in full view, so that it *could* not have been one of the party who was thus writing. Being the nearest one to the hand, I bent down close to it as it wrote, to see the whole of it. It extended no farther than *the wrist.* With a feeling of curiosity natural under the circumstances, I brought my face *close* to it in the endeavor to see exactly what it was, and, in so doing, probably destroyed the electric or magnetic influence by which it was working ; for the pencil dropped and the hand vanished. The writing was afterwards examined, and proved to be *the name, in her own proper handwriting, of a relative* and intimate lady friend of one in the circle, who passed away some years since. Other marks were also made, and the word 'Dear' had been written just as the pencil dropped. This writing has been preserved, and remains as an evidence of the reality of the fact. That it was produced by no hand of any one bodily in that room I *know* and affirm.

"The hand afterwards came and *shook hands* with each one present. I felt it minutely. It was tolerably well and symmetrically made, though not perfect; and it was *soft* and slightly *warm.* IT ENDED AT THE WRIST."

CHAPTER IV.

IN ENGLAND.

On the 31st of March, 1855, I sailed from Boston for England in the 'Africa,' the late Captain Harrison being the captain of the ship. On the ninth day of our voyage we neared England, and the signal cannon was fired. I never can forget my feelings as I looked around me, and saw only joy beaming on the faces of my fellow-passengers; some there were who were about to reach their home, and the thought of kind friends waiting to welcome them brought the smile of joy on their countenances. Others were travellers who saw the Old World with all her art treasures spread before them, and the monotony of a sea voyage so near its termination. I stood there alone, with not one friend to welcome me, broken down in health, and my hopes and fairest dreams of youth, all, as I thought, for ever fled. The only prospect I had was that of a few months' suffering, and then to pass from earth. I had this strange power also, which made a few look with pity on me as a poor deluded being, only devil-sent, to lure souls to destruction, while others were not chary in treating me as a base impostor. I stood there on the ship's deck amongst the crowd of passengers, and a sense of utter loneliness crept over me, until my very heart seemed too heavy for me to bear up against it. I sought my cabin, and prayed to God to vouchsafe one ray of hope to cheer me. In a few moments I felt a sense of joy come over me and when I rose, was as happy as the happiest of the throng.

I reached Cox's Hotel in Jermyn Street on the evening of the 9th of April; and as soon as Mr. Cox knew who I was, he welcomed me more as a father would welcome a son, than as a stranger whom he had never seen, and from that time to this he has been to me the most sincere and generous friend.

It soon became known that I was in England, and in less than a month I had more engagements than I could well fulfil. While at Cox's Hotel, Lord Brougham expressed a desire to see me for the purpose of investigating the phenomena, and as his lordship's evenings were fully occupied, I appointed an early afternoon. Accordingly his Lordship came accompanied by Sir David Brewster, with whom and Mr. Cox I had a séance, which shortly afterwards, in consequence of the misrepresentations and evasions of Sir David Brewster, became of considerable public interest, inasmuch as it was made the means of a general discussion in the newspapers on the subject of the spiritual phenomena. There are few matters in which Sir David Brewster has come before the public which have brought more shame upon him, than his conduct and assertions on this occasion, in which he manifested not only a disregard for truth, but also a disloyalty to scientific observation, and to the use of his own eyesight and natural faculties. In order that Lord Brougham might not be compelled to deny Sir David's statements, he found it necessary that he should be silent, and I have some reason to complain that his Lordship preferred sacrificing me to his desire not to immolate his friend, since his silence was by many misconstrued to my disadvantage. The correspondence which ensued was so interesting and characteristic, and is moreover so useful as being the first great occasion on which one of the pretended magnates of science has come forward on the subject of these phenomena, that I have thought it well to give the substance of it, with some pertinent remarks on Sir David Brewster's conduct in an Appendix. It will be a means whereby his character may be the better known, not only for his untruthful dealing with this subject, but also in his own domain of science in which the same unfaithfulness to truth will be seen to be the characteristic of his mind.

The immediate effect, however, of this ventilation of the subject was, as I have invariably found it, to excite only the greater interest in the phenomena, and it was thereby the means of convincing numbers of all classes who visited me. My time was fully occupied, notwithstanding my delicate health, in giving séances to anxious enquirers of all ranks and classes, from the peer to the artizan, and including men of all the professions high in art, science, and literature, who were both more competent and truthful than I found Sir David Brewster to be to form a correct conclusion.

After some time in Jermyn Street, I went to stay with a friend at Ealing, who was deeply interested in the subject, and his house was, during the greater part of my stay, almost besieged by persons wishing to witness the phenomena. Hundreds had their wishes gratified, and saw what has proved enough to be the turning point of their lives, and what rendered no longer possible those materialistic and sceptical notions, which are still unhappily so rife amongst the most highly educated classes at this day. Many interesting incidents occurred during my stay at Ealing, and the hands and once or twice the head of the spirit form were repeatedly seen by many, who publicly testified to the fact. But although I was apparently wearing out my life by the fatigue and excitement which these constant séances caused to me, I was not allowed to become proud of my position, for the good clergyman of Ealing found it his duty to publicly preach against me, and to attribute the manifestations to the devil. The position which is taken up by many of the clergy, is to me, in itself, an extraordinary manifestation, for certainly these phenomena, whether from God or from the devil, have in ten years caused more converts to the great truths of immortality and angel communion, with all that flows from these great facts, than all the sects in Christendom have made during the same period. Indeed, whilst the churches are losing their adherents, the belief in spiritual laws caused by these external manifestations, is becoming widely spread through the sceptical masses. It is not at all improbable that in pursuing their new studies, these last may be the means in their turn of converting the clergy to a belief in spiritual laws.

Whilst I was at Ealing, a distinguished novelist, accompanied by his son attended a séance, at which some very remarkable manifestations occurred, and which were chiefly directed to him. The rappings on the table suddenly became unusually firm and loud. He asked "what spirit is present?" the alphabet was called over, and the response was, "I am the spirit who influenced you to write Z——!" "Indeed," said he, "I wish you would give me some tangible proof of your presence." "What proof? will you take my hand?" "Yes," and putting his hand beneath the surface of the table, it was immediately seized by a powerful grasp, which made him start to his feet in evident trepidation, exhibiting a momentary suspicion that a trick had been played upon him; seeing, however, that all the persons around him were sitting with their hands quietly reposing on the table, he recovered his composure, and offering an apology for the uncontrollable excitement caused by such an unexpected demonstration, he resumed his seat.

The following words were then spelt out, "We wish you to believe in the ——" and then stopped. It was asked of the spirit: "In what am I to believe? in the medium?" "No." "In the manifestations?" "No." At that moment he was gently tapped on the knee, and putting his hand down, a cross was placed there by the spirit, which significantly finished the sentence.

The cross was made of card-board, and had been lying on a small table with other ornamental articles in a distant part of the large room in which the party were seated. The investigator, apparently much impressed with the incident, turned to Mrs. Rymer, and asked permission to retain the cross as a souvenir, to which she assented, saying that its only value to her was that it had been made by her boy, then recently deceased, but she could have no objections to him keeping it, if he would remember the injunction. He bowed his assent, and placing the souvenir in his breast pocket, carried the cross away with him.

On another occasion the children had been playing in the garden with some fresh-gathered flowers, out of which they had former a wreath. A séance was proposed. It was a calm summer's evening, with the full moon just rising. A large circular-shaped table was selected in the drawing room, which room was on a level with the garden lawn, the French windows extending to the ground, and the moonlight-twilight shone through them sufficiently to make everything in the room visible.

The party seated themselves around the half circle of the table, leaving the other half nearest to the garden window vacant After several minor incidents had occcured, the table rose slowly from the ground, and ascended to the ceiling of the room. out of the reach of all but Mr. Coleman, who was tall enough to just touch its rim. It then descended steadily and settled on the floor with no more sound than if it had been a feather's weight.

Having taken their seats again, a beautifully-formed feminine hand became distinctly visible to all the party present. It came up from the vacant side of the table, and made an unavailing effort, at first, to reach a hand-bell which had been placed there. In a short time, the fleshy and delicately-formed arm became visible up to the elbow, and was enveloped in what appeared to be a gauze sleeve, through which it was transparently seen. The fingers then took up the bell, held it suspended for a moment, rung it, and slowly carried it, ringing, beneath the table. Mr. Coleman finding the bell jingling against his knee, put down his hand, received it, and placed it on the table. He then asked if he might feel the hand, which was neither warm nor cold, but of velvety softness, and it was placed with a gentle pressure in his.

When the hand first appeared, all in the circle had hold of each other's hand, I having, at Mr. Coleman's request, placed both my hands in Mr. Coleman's grasp.

Whilst seated in this position, the wreath of flowers, which had been made by the children, was seen by all to be lifted from my head, where it had been playfully placed a short time previously. No hand was visible. The wreath then descended to within an inch of the surface of the table. It then slowly traversed round the circle and back again to Mr. Coleman, who took it, and retained it at home until the flowers withered.

At another sitting, each person in the circle who wore a ring had it gently removed by a spirit hand, the hand being seen afterwards with all the rings on its fingers, and after displaying itself by turning about, showing the back and palm two or three times, inverted itself, and cast the rings upon the table.

One evening at Ealing, Sir David Brewster, Mrs. Trollope the authoress, and her son Mr. Thomas Trollope, and several others were present. The table at which the party sat was a long telescopic dining table, having two legs at each end and none in the centre.—One end of it was occupied by Mr. Trollope, Sir David Brewster, and a lady. I sat about the centre of one side, having Mrs. Trollope on my left; the others present occupying the remainder of the table. There was no cloth or drapery of any kind. Sir David was invited to look under the table and make every investigation, and he did most properly avail himself of the opportunity afforded him by carefully looking under the table, both before sounds were heard and during the time they were being made. On this occasion Sir David tried to lift the table—sometimes he could not, at other times he could—or, as Sir David said, "the table was made light and heavy at command."

An accordeon was called for—hymns and tunes were played, and without any visible agency. After the party broke up, Sir David, in the course of conversation, said, "I should have liked if we had been all standing when the table lifted." Sir David, Mr. Trollope, and Mr. Rymer then sat down to see if it were possible to move the table or to raise it by their feet, but it could not be raised by the united efforts of the feet of all three. Sir David was invited to come the next evening for the purpose of complying with his request of standing at the table, but he could not come, having a pre-engagement.

This table, which was twelve feet long, has been sometimes completely turned over, replaced, and again turned over, all our hands being on the surface. Occasionally it has been moved while we were all standing—without any one touching it, even with their hands.

Mr. Trollope came on the following evening—we sat round the same table as on the previous evening—the alphabet was called for, and three of us were told to go into another room, to get a smaller table, and stand. We were not to sit, but to stand. We did so—and a heavy card table, on pillar and claws, and which was brought from another room, and at which we had never sat before, was repeatedly lifted off the ground, at least twenty inches.

One evening a gentleman was present when it was intimated to him through the alphabet by knocks on the table that his aunt *Dorothy* was present; he was surprised, and assured us that could not be so, for he never had an aunt; he afterwards wrote to his sister, who was residing in the north of England, and this was her reply:—

"I never heard of our father having a sister—there were four sons, and their father died when they were all very young; but I expect to see my elder sister, who knows more of our family, and I will ask her.

"P.S.—She has just come, and I find *our father had a sister*—our grandfather was twice married; by his first wife he had one daughter, whose name was Dorothy, and who died an infant—and who, of course, was our aunt."

One evening as Mr. Rymer was passing through the room he stood for a few moments at the end of the table. His attention was arrested by the sounds, and it was stated to be his little boy, who had passed away some years before. He asked if he recollected how pleased he was when on earth to place him a chair on his return home—the chair was immediately moved round the corner of the table, by no visible agency.—It was placed behind him, and he sat down upon it.

This was in the presence of five persons, one of

whom was the editor of a well-known work on the "Occult Sciences." All at the table saw the chair moved to where the father was standing. The hands of all were on the table—no one knew that he intended to ask for a chair, and until that instant, he said, that he did not know it himself.

Another evening we were told through the alphabet that the same litttle boy was present in spirit. It was asked if he could write as on earth, and he answered that he would try. A sheet of note paper, clean, and without any writing of any description was taken, and placed on the cloth. The brass fastenings of the table were then displaced one by one and fell to the ground; the table was opened or pulled out by no human agency—every one in the room was seated at the table and had their hands on its surface. It was then asked if the paper and pencil should be placed on the table near the opening of the cloth; three sounds, "Yes." Immediately the form of a small hand was seen under the cloth. It was felt by some who placed their hands upon it. The paper and pencil were then removed, the form of the hand disappearing at the same time. In a few minutes the same form of hand was again seen replacing the paper and the pencil, the alphabet was called for: "*Dear papa, I have really done my best.*" The father removed the paper and pencil, and on that paper was written—"Dear papa, dear mamma," and signed "Wat." Watty was the name of the child. No one was previously aware that it was intended to ask for this to be done.

At Sandgate in Kent, where I stayed for some time,

at a séance, we numbered thirteen. The table was elevated at least two feet, and the accordeon was played. The tune was not known to any of us. We asked the name, and were told that it was the "Song of the Sea." A hand and arm in white drapery appeared—it was seen by all at the table on several occasions during the evening, and they had every opportunity of carefully examining it.

A few evenings afterwards the table was near the window. It was twilight. Songs were heard on the accordeon. The tune was new to us, and we were told that it was the "Song of the Angels to the Mourners." It was followed by a hymn which had been frequently played before. It was spelt out by sounds on the table, *some will show you their hands to-night.* The table was gently raised and lifted up several times, a hand appeared above the table, and took from the dress of one of the party a miniature brooch, and handed it to several at the table. Hands and arms were then distinctly seen by all at the table of different forms and sizes—sometimes crossed as in prayer, and at others pointing upwards. On another occasion sounds were heard, communications were made, and hands and arms in white drapery were again seen. A spirit hand took up a Bible which was on the table, and opened it. This was seen by all, and a leaf was folded down, the hand took a pencil and marked the two verses sixteen and seventeen of the thirteenth chapter of St. Matthew—"But blessed are your eyes, for they see: and your ears, for they hear. For I say unto you that many prophets and righteous men have desired to see things which ye see, and have not seen them; and to hear these things which ye hear, and have not heard them."

At this time hands and arms were frequently seen and they were repeatedly felt by all at the table as distinctly as though they were the hands and arms of living mortals, and frequently they shook hands with them as really and substantially as one man shakes hands with another.

Of all the accounts which have been given of the phenomena there has been none so good as that of Dr. J. J. G. Wilkinson, who towards the close of the Brewster controversy, wrote a letter to the "Morning Advertiser," under the signature of Verax. He had been frequently present at séances, and was eminently qualified not only for the investigation, but for a philosophical expression of their results and consequences—and I need offer no apology for giving at length his eloquent narration, which was entitled "Evenings with Mr. Home and the Spirits."

"The 'Great Wizard of the North' has roused attention to the subject of spiritual manifestations in such a manner that everybody is talking about them; and, moreover, the country papers are the battle-ground of letters *pro* and *con*, which debate the subject with some warmth; and, wherever a name can be got at, with a little personality. But, hitherto, I have seen no statement of the experience of any of the writers in regard to these manifestations. This is to be regretted, perhaps, because by bringing forward experiences and explanations, the subject might have been divested of some of that heat which is so bad a scientific medium. I will now endeavor, with your permission, to tell what

I saw and felt on three separate evenings, stating them in their order.

"It was late in the spring of this year that I was invited by a friend, well known in the literary world, to pay a visit to the lodgings of Mr. Daniel Dunglas Home, then recently arrived from America, for the purpose of witnessing certain remarkable phenomena alleged to be from supernatural causes. Many feelings prompted me to accept the invitation; as, also, did the knowledge that Mr. Home was familiarly known, as a plain, honest man, to Dr. Gray, the first homœopathic physician in New York, and for whose character I have the highest esteem.

"I went to his house in Jermyn-street, and introduced myself on the appointed evening to Mr. Home, who, I found, was a modest, intelligent youth of about twenty, in ill-health; and, indeed, as he himself informed me, and as, on inspection, I found to be the case, with the marks of consumption legible upon his frame. My wife accompanied me, and I met in Mr. H.'s rooms three friends, all of them men of talent and integrity. Bent upon narrative, and not upon defense or hostility, I will omit nothing; and so I here observe that we were, all of us, believers, beforehand, in the possibility of spiritual manifestations.

"Before sitting down in 'the circle,' I asked Mr. Home for some account of his antecedents. To the best of my recollection he gave the following particulars. He was born in Scotland, and was taken to America when a child. Very early in life he used to surprise those with whom he was, by spontaneously narrating, as scenes passing before his eyes, distant events, such as the death of friends and elatives; and these instances of second sight were found to be true telegraphy. It was not his fault—he could not help seeing them. Later on in his career, various noises were heard in the room beside him. This was about the time when the spiritual 'rapping' became known in America.

"He lived with an aunt, who was greatly scandalized at these circumstances. A member of the Presbyterian Church, these knockings even accompanied him to Divine worship; and, coming to the knowledge of his ecclesiastical overmen, he was adjudged to be the victim of satanic influences, and either excommunicated, or otherwise banished from the congregation. Afterwards he became a medical student; but ill-health forced him to abandon the idea of pursuing medicine as a calling. Such were the heads of what he told us, in answer to our enquiries, about himself.

"We were in a large upper room, rather bare of furniture; a sofa, a large round table, and a little buffet, together with a few chairs, were the fittings-up. One of the party had brought with him a hand-bell and an accordeon. We sat around the table, with the hands resting upon it. In a few minutes the table vibrated, or shuddered, as though actuated from within; it then became still, and instantly every one of us shook in his chair, not violently, but intimately, and like a jelly, so that objects 'dothered' before us. This effect ceased; and now the heavy table, with all our hands upon it, raised itself high up on its side, and rocked up and down; the raising proceeding from all different quarters, Mr. Home and all the rest of us (excepting our hands and arms, which were necessarily moved) sitting death-still. The lamp on the table seemed as if it must tumble off; but he assured us there was no danger of *that*—that it was held safely in its place. The hand-bell had been placed upon the wooden rim round the pedestal of the table, and it now began to ring, apparently under different parts of the circle. Mr. Home said that the spirits were carrying it to one of the party, and suggested myself. I was sitting nearly opposite to him, at about three feet distance. I put my hand down under the margin of the table, and, in perhaps a minute's time, I felt the lip of the bell poked up gently against the tips of my fingers, as if to say, 'I am here, take me.' This palpitation of the bell continued until I moved my fingers up its side to grasp it. When I came to the handle, I slid my fingers on rapidly, and now, every hand but my own being on the table, I distinctly felt the fingers, up to the palm, of a hand holding the bell. It was a soft, warm, fleshy, substantial hand, such as I should be glad to feel at the extremity of the friendship of my best friends. But I had no sooner grasped it momentarily, than it melted away, leaving my hand void, with the bell only in it. I now held the bell lightly, with the clapper downwards, and while it remained perfectly still, I could plainly feel fingers ringing it by the clapper. As a point of observation I will remark, that I should feel no more difficulty in swearing that the member I felt was a human hand of extraordinary life, and not Mr. Home's foot, than that the nose of the Apollo Belvidere is not a horse's ear. I dwell chiefly, because I can speak surely, on what happened to myself, though every one round the table had somewhat similar experiences. The bell was carried under the table to each, and rung in the hand of each. The accordeon was now placed beneath the table, and presently we heard it moving along. Mr. Home put down his hand to the margin, and the instrument was given to him. With one hand upon the table, and with the other grasping the white wood at the bottom of the accordeon, he held it bottom upwards, the keys hanging down over, and the instrument resting for support on his right knee. It played 'Home, sweet home,' and 'God save the Queen,' with a delicacy of tone which struck every one present: I never heard silence threaded with such silver lines. Afterwards, in the same way, we were favored with 'The Last Rose of Summer.' The accordeon was then taken to each member of the party in succession; we could hear it rustling on its way between our knees and the pedestal of the table; and in the hand of each person, a few notes, but no whole tunes were played. When in my own hand, I particularly noticed the great amount of force which was exerted by the player. It was difficult to hold the instrument from the strong downward pull, and had I not been somewhat prepared for this, the accordeon would have fallen upon the floor. In the course of the evening we all felt either a finger, fingers, or a whole hand, placed upon our knees, always with a pleasant impression at the time. A white cambric handkerchief was drawn slowly under the table, and in the course of a few minutes handed to another person, tied in two knots, and put as a boquet into the bell. And this experiment also was repeated for nearly all present. While these things were going on, rappings were heard in all parts of the room, in the table, in the floor, and the ceiling; and sometimes they were so loud that the medium requested the spirits to remember that he was only a lodger, and that these noises might disturb the people in the rooms above and below. They were very unlike the 'Great Wizard's' raps, and occurred indifferently, as I said before, in all places and corners of the chamber. Towards the end of the séance, five distinct raps were heard under the table, which number, Mr. Home said, was a call for the alphabet. Accordingly, an alphabet was made; and on Mr. Home asking if any spirit was present who wished to speak to one of the party, the following sentence was given by the alphabetic telegraph:—'My dear E—, Imortality is a great truth. Oh! how I wish my dear wife could have been present.—D.C.' It purported to be a near relation of one of those present, who died last year. The spelling 'imortality' surprised me at first; but I recollected that the deceased, whom I knew well, was constantly versed in black letter writing, which makes elisions in that way. This ended, the medium fell into an apparently mesmeric trance, from which he addressed some good words of exhortation to each of us; and told one of the party in particular, several details about deceased members of the family, which were not known in the circle at the time, but verified to the letter afterwards. These I forbear to mention, because they were of a strictly private nature. In his address, Mr. Home spoke, not as from himself, but as from the spirit assembly which was present; and he ended with a courteous 'Good night,' from them.

"Considering that it requites a large apparatus of

preparation for the greatest of wizards to effect the smallest part of what *we* saw on this evening, namely, a few raps, one might have suspected that Mr. Home would have had rather bulging pockets, to do what I have related, but I can assure your readers, that he was as meagre and unencumbered as the scantiest dresser need be: he had no assistants, and no screens. When, during the evening, I asked if the jugglers did their tricks by means similar to the agencies there present, the raps said 'No:' but in a pronounced manner they said 'Yes,' when the same question was put with regard to the 'Indian Jugglers.' We also asked Mr. Home why the effects generally took place *under* the table, and not upon it. He said that in habituated circles the results were easily obtained above board, visibly to all, but that at a first sitting it was not so. That scepticism was almost universal in men's intellects, and marred the forces at work; that the spirits accomplish what they do through our life-sphere, or atmosphere, which was permeated by our wills; and if the will was contrary, the sphere was unfit for being operated upon.

"It was perhaps a fortnight after this that Mr. Home came by invitation, to my own house, to sit in the circle of my family. He was brought to the door in a carriage by some friends, with whom he was staying, without any paraphernalia which would characterize a wizard's art. I watched him walk up the garden, and can aver that he had no magic wand up his trouser leg, nor any hunch in his dress that could betoken machinery or apparatus of any kind whatever. Arrived in the drawing-room, the 'raps' immediately commenced in all parts of it, and were also heard in the back drawing-room, which opens into the front by folding doors. The party assembled to constitute the 'circle' consisted of Mr. Home, my wife, my four children, and myself, and two domestics. We sat round a large and heavy loo table, which occupied the centre of the room. In a minute or two the same inward thrill went through the table as I have described in the first séance; and the chairs also, as before, thrilled under us so vividly, that my youngest daughter jumped up from hers, exclaiming, 'Oh! Papa, there's a heart in my chair,' which we all felt to be a correct expression of the sensation conveyed. From time to time the table manifested considerable movements, and after cracking, and apparently undulating in its place, with all our hands upon it, it suddenly rose from its place bodily some eight inches into the air, and floated waving in the atmosphere, maintaining its position above the ground for half a minute, or while we slowly counted twenty-nine. Its oscillations during this time were very beautiful, reminding us all of a flat disc of deal on an agitated surface of water. It then descended as rapidly as it rose, and so nicely was the descent managed, that it met the floor with no noise, and as though it would scarcely have broken an egg in its contact. Three times did it leave the floor of the room, and poise itself in mid air, always in the same manner. During these intervals the medium was in a state of the completest muscular repose; nor, indeed, had he the toe of Hercules for a lever could he have managed this effect, for he and all of us stood up each time, to follow the mounting table, and he stood with as complete absence of strain as the rest of us. It requires two strong men to lift the table to that height; one person might throw it over, but could by no means raise it from the floor.

"The travelling of the hand-bell under the table was also repeated for every one present, and this time they all felt the hand, or hands, either upon their knees, or other portions of their limbs. I put my hand down as previously, and was regularly stroked on the back of it by a soft palpable hand as before. Nay, I distinctly felt the whole against mine, and once grasped the hand, but it melted as on the first occasion; and immediately a call was made for the alphabet, there being something to communicate. The 'spirits' now spelt out through Mr. Home, who had known nothing of what I had done under the table, 'Do not grasp our hands.' I asked why, and Mr. Home said that they had great difficulty in presenting, and thus rapidly incarnating these hands out of the vital atmosphere of those present, and that their work was spoilt, and had to be recommenced, when they were interfered with, perhaps as a thought is sometimes broken in twain, and cannot easily be resumed on the irruption of a stranger. During the séance I had the border of a white cambric handkerchief just appearing out of the side pocket of my paletot, which was open; and though I could see no agency, I felt something twitching at the handkerchief, and very gradually drawing it from my pocket. Simultaneously with this, my eldest daughter, who sat opposite to me, exclaimed, 'Oh! I see phosphoric fingers at papa's pocket!' and, now visibly to all, the handkerchief was slowly pulled out, and drawn under the table; whilst, at the same time, I felt an arm that was doing it, but which was invisible to me. At this time I was at least three feet from Mr. Home, with a person between us, and he was absolutely passive. The feeling I had was of nudges, as distinct as ever I felt from a mortal limb, and that on my breast and arm, which were above the table; and yet, though the operation of abstracting my handkerchief was going on visibly to all, the rest of the circle, as well as myself, (all except my eldest daughter), could see nothing. I can swear that there was no machinery, unless the skin, bone, muscle, and tendons of an unseen hand, forearm and elbow deserve the name.

"While this was going on, and for about ten minutes, more or less, my wife felt the sleeve of her dress pulled frequently, and as she was sitting with her finger ends clasped and hands open, with palms semi-prone upon the table, she suddenly laughed involuntarily, and said, 'Oh! see, there is a little hand lying between mine; and, now, a larger hand has come beside it. The little hand is smaller than any baby's, and exquisitly perfect.' Our domestics, and two of the children, as well as my wife, all saw these hands, and watched them for between one and two minutes, when they disappeared. I now held my watch at the table side, the key in my hand, the chain and watch dangling from it, and I felt the weight of the watch gradually taken off, the chain being raised horizontally to my hand, and then the key, which I retained, was pulled laterally, and I let it go. It was taken under the table to my youngest daughter, and put on her knee. Whenever objects were thus removed from the hand, they were taken with a degree of physical power sufficient to suggest that the agent was capable of holding the object without letting it fall. An hour and three-quarters were occupied in these and similar manifestations, of which I have mentioned only the most striking, or those personal to myself; and now Mr. Home passed into the trance state, spoke of the spirit life, and the coming knowledge of it on earth, and said a few words apposite to each person present; dwelling also upon the spiritual attendants who were standing beside each. When he came to my wife he lifted up his hands in an ecstacy, and described a spirit with her, most tiny, but beautiful. He said it was a little sister who had gone away a long time. 'But,' she said, 'I never had such a sister.' 'Yes, you had, though she had no name on earth.' On inquiry in the family, an event, such as he alluded to, had happened. This is the chief part of what struck me in Séance No. 2.

"At 10 p.m., Mr. Home went away on his own legs, so limber that I never so much as thought of any explanation of pasteboard arms or electric batteries concealed about his person.

"The next séance which I shall describe took place about the third week in July, at the house of a valued friend in Ealing, who had become convinced of the genuineness of the phenomena which accompanied Mr. Home, and with whom that gentleman was now staying. The party sat down to the table with Mr. Home, in the dusk of a fine evening, and were nine or ten in number. Here again I am forced to chronicle chiefly what befel myself, in order that I may be no second-hand witness. The first thing I remarked was a gentle tremulous flash of light through the room, but what was the cause of it I am unable to determine. When we had sat a few minutes I felt a decided but gentle grasp of a large man's hand upon my right knee, and I said to Mr. H., 'There is a man's hand upon my knee.' 'Who is it?' he said. 'How should I know?' was my reply. 'Ask,' said he. 'But how shall I ask?' 'Think of somebody,' was his answer. I thought involuntarily of an intimate friend, once a Member of Parliment, and as much before the public as any man in his generation, and who died on the 30th of June last. And I said aloud, 'Is it ——?' Hearty affirmative slaps on the knee from the same hand which had remained fixed till then, were the reply to my question 'I am glad to be again in the same room with you,' said I. Again the same hearty greeting was repeated. 'Are you better?' I inquired. A still more joyous succession of slaps, or rather, if I may coin a word, of accussions; for the hand was cupped to fit my bent knee, and gently struck me in that form. 'Have you any message to your wife, whom I shall probably see in a few days?' Again, affirmative touches, five in number, therefore calling for the alphabet. Mr. Home now called over the alphabet. A B C D, and when he called T, my knee was struck; again when he said H and E, and so on, until this was spelled out: 'THE IMMORTAL LOVES.' I remember at the time thinking that this was rather a thin message; but the next time I saw Mrs. —— I told her the circumstances, and gave her the words. Her son was sitting with her, and said, 'That is very characteristic of my father, for it was a favorite subject with him, whether or not the *affections* survive the body; of the immortality of the soul itself he never doubted; but the words, the immortal *loves*, show that he has settled the problem of his life.' Suoh was the import which the family of the deceased quite unexpectedly to me conferred upon the phrase. To return to Ealing, and that evening, after the last stroke of the hand indicated the end of the sentence, I said, 'If it is really you, will you shake hands with me?' and I put my hand under the table, and now the same soft and capacious hand was placed in mine, and gave it a cordial shaking. I could not help exclaiming, 'This hand is a portrait. I know it from five years' constant intercourse, and from the daily grasp and holding of the last several months!' After this it left my knee; and when I asked if there was anything more, there was no response, and the agent appeared to be gone. But in two or three minutes more another hand, evidently also a man's, but small, thin, firm, and lively, was placed in the same position which the former had occupied; and after some preliminary questioning with Mr. Home, I said, 'Is it Mr. ——?' naming another valued friend, who, after twenty years of suffering, had departed this life almost on the same day as Mr. ——. With liveliest finger tips, the affirming hand danced up and down my leg, and upon my knee. I said, 'I am glad to find you so much better.' The playful hand beat 'yes' again. And this, in reply to renewed questions, for two or three minutes. Then I said, 'Have you any communication for your wife when I see her?' There was no response, and that agent then ceased to manifest himself. After another short pause, a totally different hand, a lady's, came to me, rested in my hand under the table, rubbed my hand, and allowed me at leisure to examine the deli cate, beautiful, and warmth-raying fingers. It was signified that it was Mrs. ——, whom I had known in life, and who wished to greet me. Between and during what happened to myself, many of the rest of the circle were touched; and described their impressions much as I have described mine. Some had merely a single finger put upon their knees. Mr. Home said that the presenting spirits could often make one finger where they could not make two: and two, where they could not form an entire hand; just as they could form a hand where they could not realize a whole human figure; and he also said that this was one reason why they did not show themselves aboveboard, because they did not like imperfect members to be seen.

"These phenomena occupied less than an hour; and now the circle was broken up, and reconstituted, nine persons, to the best of my recollection, being arranged at the table. The table was placed opposite a window, and the bright moonbeams streamed down upon ts side. There was no candle in the apartment. The space of table which fronted the window was not occupied by sitters; but the company sat round about three-fourths of it, leaving the rest vacant. The right wing of the party was terminated by Mr. Home; the left by the son of the host. In a few minutes' time, close beside the latter gentleman, there emerged into sight above the rim of the table, in the vacant space, a delicately beautiful female hand and part of the forearm, apparently of ghostly tenuity. As I was sitting exactly opposite the vacant space, I had a fair opportunity of watching this hand as it projected against the moonlight; it was a filmy-looking woman's hand, with the fingers drooping forwards from left to right as I sat. The hand curved up over the table margin, deliberately grasped a hand-bell placed near, and carrying it partly down, let it drop upon the floor. It then rose to sight again, and took away a cambric handkerchief also placed near, which was tied in two knots under the table, and presented to one of the company, who had been strongly moved from the time that this hand was first seen. I forbear to give the further details of this hand, because they seemed to be of a private nature; suffice it to say, that it caused no little emotion to a gentleman who seemed concerned. On its disappearance, another hand, large, strong, and with the fingers extended, and pushed bolt up in the moonlight, rose above the table near to Mr. Home. He cried out, 'Oh! keep me from that hand! it is so cold! Do not let it touch me!' Shortly it also vanished, and a third hand was seen at the other side of the vacant table edge: this hand was in a glove. Then, presently, a fourth hand ascended on the extreme left—a lady's hand, of beautiful proportions—and traversed the entire vacant space from left to right, rising, and displaying the forearm; and then, as it neared Mr. Home, the entire arm. When it reached him, the hand was level with his forehead, upon which it laid its palm, and with its fingers put his hair back, and played upon his brow for perhaps half a minute. I was sitting next but one to him, and leant forward past my intermediate neighbor, at the same time requesting that if the hand belonged to my friend Mrs. ——, it might also be laid on my forehead. This was deliberately done; and I felt its thrilling impression as the palm was laid flat upon my brow, where it remained for several seconds. It was warm and human, and made of no material but softest flesh. During the interval in which I felt it, I had abundant opportunity of examining most closely the arm and forearm. The forearm sleeve appeared to be of white cambric, plain and neat, and it shone like biscuit porcelain in the moonlight. The sleeve of the dress up the arm was darker, but I do not remember the color. And bending over, as I did, to the vacant rim of the table, I saw how the arm terminated—apparently in a graceful cascade of drapery; much as though an arm were put out through the peak of a snowy tent, the apex of which thus fell around the shoulder on every side. On leaving my forehead, the arm at once disappeared, and I watched it go. It was drawn into the same drapery; but so naturally, that I can only liken it to a fountain falling down again, and ceasing into the bosom of the water from which it rose. And I also saw the drapery itself vanish, apparently by the same dissipative process. And now the spirits spelt out 'Good night.'

"These events occurred in the house of one of my oldest friends, whose superior in integrity I have never known, and of whose talent and sagacity I never heard a doubt entertained until he endorsed these unpopular manifestations.

'Such is my experience. One hope I have in putting it forward is, that others who have seen Mr. Home may do the like, and thus make their contribution to the facts of the case.

"In conclusion, I will observe, that Sir David Brewster, and others almost as eminent, appear to me to make a scientific error in one respect—viz., in their estimate of the value of a man's character. They seem to think that charging a man of good antecedents, and with every appearance of a blameless life, with lying and imposture of the most systematic kind, is positively the easiest account that can be given of any rare phenomenon out of the pale of their own previous philosophy. I submit that this is not, for their own credit, the very first hypothesis of the case that ought to rush into their minds. Neither, parallel with this, is the other hypothesis that men of ability in all other things, and till then known to be shrewd and searching, are infatuated dupes, to be commended as a proper valuation of what is rare and valuable in the human species. The rule of law, that 'a man must be supposed innocent till proved guilty,' is also *the* rule in such scientific explorations. This rule loves facts, and hates slander. I differ, therefore, with Sir David Brewster in his mode of exploration, and also in his valuation of presumptive honesty and human testimony, which always hitherto has been the most substantial word in the world, and a pillar which Divine Providence has not disdained to use in supporting the canopy of his Revelations.

"This rule I would especially press upon the great Sir David Brewster, a man of position, wealth, worldly repute, great talents, a name no one dare assail, and withal, responsibility to Heaven and his generation, when he is dealing with the orphan, Home, a man apparently as blameless as himself, but with neither riches, nor health, nor station, nor any possession if not honesty, and a ruinous peculiarity of gift. It is not, I say, the easiest way out of a difficulty to call this youth a cheat. There are cheats of our own household, cheats in our own heads, sometimes called prejudices, which might be suspected *first*, without violating any rule of scientific inquest, or humane valuation.

"The experience of others in these matters has, perhaps, differed very widely from my own, and I desire to see this experience also brought forward. At other séances I have seen only a part of the phenomena which I have described as taking place on the three evenings which I have selected as being the fullest and best. And once or twice, when persons were sent whom it was most desirable to convince, almost nothing occurred. This, I submit, is one of the strongest arguments in Mr. Home's favor. Were the phenomena a trick, they might always be produced to order without variation. 'The Great Wizard' never fails. But as he himself says, the spiritualists always fail in his company. Let this suggest that there is a total difference between him and them. It does not surprise me that spirits and their gifts should retire to a great gulf distance from where the 'Great Wizard' is.

"It seems probable from experience as well as reason that, granting the phenomena to be spiritual, the presence of determined scoffers at, and disbelievers in them, should, in case the said persons be preponderant in their influence in the circle, render the manifestations imperfect or perhaps null. The known laws of human sympathy, and the operations of our own spirits when antipathetic persons are near us, may also be cited in proof of this. I conclude, then, that to the scoffer and the strongly prejudiced, who want no evidence, and to whom evidence has no appeal, evidence is, for the most part, not forthcoming. This simplifies the position; but what still remains is the peculiar Christian politesse of this century, viz., the necessity of good manners and the agreeing to differ. On the part of those who believe, this may be best secured by letting the other party be. Providence can convince *them*, too, as easily as ourselves, when the time and their function comes, but by snatching at them prematurely before they are ripe, we may evoke, on a great scale, two of the most formidable spirits of this world —WRATH AND FEAR.

"As a final remark, let me caution the public against being led by Sir David Brewster, Mr. Faraday, and other men of great names in their own departments, in this matter which is obviously not within their field. We hear much of not choosing Crimean generals on old Peninsular qualifications. But to select a Faraday or a Brewster for opinion on this case, is a far worse error; for all generals, past, present, and to come, are in the military line; but these great men are not, and never were, in the line upon which they have professed to decide. They are so alien to the subject, that they do not know the first condition of prosecuting it, namely, a gift of sympathy, and openness to conviction. Their very specialty of excellence in physical explorations, is against them in this new walk, which is combined spiritual and physical. The common observer with little in his mind, with no repute to support, and no case to uphold, may perchance be equipped by nature for these revolutionary sciences where the *savans* are stupid upon them. Twelve fishermen, and not the High Priests, are the everlasting resource of Providence. I therefore invite the unattached laity of all descriptions, the willing fishermen, to remember that they have no overmen in this department; that it is an untrodden field; and that by the grace of God, there is at least a freedom for us all from the pressure of big names; because 'the race is not to the swift, nor the battle to the strong.'"

The admirable narrative and reasoning of this letter leave nothing further to be said as to the manifestations during the remainder of my stay in England during the year, as I found it desirable to change the climate for that of Italy in the autumn. But I did not leave England without the satisfaction of having given opportunities to many hundreds of persons to investigate the phenomena for themselves, and through them the subject began to assume a form and importance which have made it the fear and the bugbear of those who had completed their circle of knowledge, and have no room in their philosophy for further facts. They are unfortunately many, whose minds have been in early life stereotyped in too hard and unyielding a material, to admit of either corrections or additions.

CHAPTER V.

AT FLORENCE, NAPLES, ROME, AND PARIS.

Early in the autnmn of 1855 I went to Florence accompanied by the son of the gentleman with whom I had been residing at Ealing. I remained in Florence till the month of February, 1856, and although some persons there did all they could to injure me by false statements, I was only the more cherished by those who best knew me. I met there many distinguished men and women, and a Prince of one of the Royal Houses became deeply interested in what he witnessed. The manifestations while I was at Florence were very strong. I remember on one occasion while the Countess O—— was seated at one of Erard's grand action pianos, it rose and balanced itself in the air during the whole time she was playing. She also, whilst we were seated at a table in the room, took up an album which chanced to be lying there, and said, "Now if this is in reality the spirit of my dear father, I know you would wish to convince me, you can do so if you will, write your name on this page." She opened the book and placed it on her knees, and held a lead pencil in her hand. In a moment the pencil was taken out of her hand, and the name of her father, the Count O——, was written. On examination she said, "There is a slight resemblance to your writing, but I would wish it to be more distinct." She placed the open book again on her knees, and again the writing came in the same way, and also the words, "My dear daughter ——." This last writing she cut from my album, leaving in it the words first written, where they still are; and on going home she showed it to an old friend of her father's, saying, "Do you know whose writing that is?" "Of course," he said, "it is your father's." When the Countess told him it had been written that very evening, he thought that to a certainty she had lost her senses, and on appealing to her husband, and finding that he corroborated her statement, he was equally alarmed for them both.

At the house of an English resident at Florence, I had many séances at which the power was very great, and she wrote a private account of some of the phenomena, which will show the reader the nature and extent of the manifestations at that time. I am very glad that I am able thus to give the results of the observations of others rather than my own unsupported statements. The lady says:

"The house in which I at present reside, and which, for some years past, has been my home, is a large, rambling, old-fashioned villa in the neighborhood of Florence, whose internal architecture gives evidence of its having been built at different periods—those periods probably distant from each other.

"The oldest parts of the house, judging from the ornaments of a chapel which forms part of it, must, I should say, have been constructed in the early part of the sixteenth century. The rooms which I occupy are almost immediately above the chapel, and communicate on one side with the lower part of the house by a narrow stone staircase. On first coming to reside here we learned that the villa had, in common with many others of the same description, the reputation of being haunted. Strange lights it was said had been issuing from the chapel windows, and unearthly noises heard in that part of the house to which I have alluded. Some friends passed the winter with us some five or six years since, and their servant occupied a small room on an *entresol* between the chapel and my rooms, but his rest became so broken, and he described the noises he heard as so peculiar, that he requested to be allowed to sleep elsewhere. I was formerly much in the habit of dismissing my maid early, and sitting up either reading or writing until a late hour. At such times I have been suddenly seized with a strange fearfulness, a kind of nervous dread, more easily imagined than described. In fact, it would be impossible to describe my sensations at those moments, further than by saying that I felt I was no longer *alone*. This feeling usually lasted from five to ten minutes, and invariably left a painful impression on my spirits. I also often heard a peculiar rustling sound in my room, and around my bed, as though some one were agitating the bed curtains, and this sound was invariably accompanied by a chilliness, as if a door had been suddenly opened, and a strong current of cold wind had rushed with violence into the room.

"These sounds and the other painful sensations

which I have described, and which I was totally unable to explain, continued at intervals with greater or lesser degrees of intensity until the month of October, 1855, when much sensation was created in Florence by the arrival of Mr. Home, whose reputation as a spirit medium had rendered him celebrated. A short time after his arrival in Florence, the sounds in my room became more distinct and more frequent, and the very peculiar nervous feelings of which I have spoken, were not confined so exclusively to myself, but were frequently shared by my sister, if she remained any time in my room. My rest at length became so broken, and in consequence my health so impaired, that I had my bed moved into a room adjoining the one in which I had been in the habit of sleeping, hoping that the change would bring me quiet.

"The first night was undisturbed, but the next and succeeding nights were so painful that I frequently lay awake until morning. In the meantime, we made Mr. Home's acquaintance, and having been a witness of effects so wonderful as only to be ascribed to a supernatural cause, I determined to discover, if possible, the real secret of my haunted rooms.

"Mr. Home having been invited to make a stay of a few days in our house, was on the first day of his arrival made acquainted with the mystery of my rooms, nd he proposed that a séance should be held in them for the purpose of endeavoring to ascertain whether or not the strange sounds which disturbed me were to be attributed to supernatural agency. Accordingly about eleven o'clock on that same evening, my sister, Mr. Home and myself repaired to my room, and placed ourselves at a small round table in front of, and very near the fire-place. We were warmly covered, and the fire was blazing brightly; yet the cold that pervaded the room was intense, penetrating to the very bones. I should mention that for many previous days, I had suffered from what appeared to be a cold air, which was quite independent of the atmospheric temperature, blowing over my body, especially the lower limbs. This feeling never left me, and all artificial means failed in destroying the sensation of chilliness. This same cold air was now felt by both my sister and Mr. Home to such a degree as to be painful to them also. I have since found that it is a frequent accompaniment of the manifestations.

"Previously to placing himself at the table, Mr. Home had descended to the chapel, where, however, all was quiet. On reascending the stairs, he heard a sound as of a muffled bell tolling in the chapel. We had scarcely sat a moment at the table, when it began slowly to move about in different directions, generally inclining towards the side on which I sat. Presently the movements became more violent, and assumed, if I may be allowed the expression, an angry appearance. We asked if a spirit were present, and the table replied by making the three usual affirmative movements.

"We then further inquired whether the spirit present was a good one, and were answered in the negative. We spoke in harsh terms, which seemed to irritate the spirit, for the demonstrations became very angry. A high backed old fashioned chair, which stood at a little distance from the table was suddenly and without human contact, drawn close to it, as though some one, in sitting down, had so drawn it. Nothing was, however, visible. Mr. Home proposed that we should move into the next room, my bed-room, and try whether any further manifestations would be made there. We did so: but all remained quiet. We then returned to the room we had just quitted, and sat at another table covered with a cloth. We had previously heard a rustling sound about, and under the tables, such a sound as would be made by a person moving about in a heavy garment. This noise was accompanied by a scratching on the wood of the table, as though some one were scraping it with his nails. We then distinctly saw the cloth on the side of the table next to me move up, as though a hand raised it from beneath. The hand appeared to be in a menacing attitude. Mr. Home was also often touched on the knee, and he described the touch as peculiarly strong and disagreeable.

"We then entreated the spirit to leave us, requiring it should return on the following evening, and declare its purpose in thus tormenting us. This it promised, and on being further adjured in the name of the Holy Trinity to leave us, the demonstrations ceased.

"The night was very unquiet. The sensation of cold, of which I have before spoken, accompanied me every where, and I heard a frequent scratching under my pillow, and on my bed. On the next evening we met again in my room, and were joined by two other persons, one a member of our family, the other, a gentleman known to Mr. Home, and who was then investigating this phenomenon, both men of strong nerve and dispassionate judgment. The usual cold was felt, and the table became much agitated. A small stiletto, which I use as a paper-knife, was taken from the table as by an invisible hand, and drawn from the sheath. The table was then lifted from the ground, and was violently pushed across the room. It stopped opposite a door leading to the staircase, and we resumed our places.

"A small hand-bell was taken from off the table, and violently rung in different directions. The dagger was thrown about under the table, and rubbed against Mr. Home's knees. My elbow was violently grasped by a hand, the fingers of which I distinctly saw—they were long, yellow and shining. Other persons present, who felt its grasp, described its touch as clammy and horrible. I spoke gently to the spirit, who, in answer to my questions, said he was unhappy, and that perhaps I might be of some use to him. He promised to return and speak farther on the following evening, and after lifting the table several times high above our heads, he left us.

"The whole of the next day I was more or less tormented by the cold air, which blew over my face and limbs, especially in the evening, a short time before the hour appointed for the séance. This wind then became very strong, and again a hand raised the cloth of the table on which I was leaning, and touched my arm as if to remind me of my engagement. We repaired to my room, one member only of my family being present, my sister having suffered too much from alarm on the previous evening to join us.

"The demonstrations of the table immediately began, but in a quieter manner than on former occasions. I immediately spoke (I should say that Italian was the only language used*), in a soothing manner. In reply to many questions the spirit told me he was unhappy, and had wandered about the house for many many years, that his name was Giannana, that he had been a monk, and had died in the room which I then occupied. I desired to know whether I should have masses said for the peace of his soul. He answered in the negative, but requested that I should pray that it might find some repose. I further begged him to tell me why on the previous evening he had made so much use of the little dagger, and he answered that in life he had but too well known how to employ it. He then promised me never again to return to my rooms; and since that evening those painful sensations and strange noises, of which I have spoken so much, have left me, and never have returned. Frequent séances, where good and loving spirits have given us comforting communications, have been since held by their own special request in my room. The dagger has by them been drawn from its sheath, and the bell rung, as though the touch of holy hands were needful in order to destroy any painful recollections in my mind connected with these articles, or any reluctance I might feel to again make use of them. In fact my rooms seem to have undergone a complete *purification*, and I feel that whatever painful influence did once ex-

* Here the writer omits a rather curious circumstance. The Italian, she observed, was incorrectly spelled; but, on afterwards comparing it with the state of the language in the sixteenth century, it was found to be correct.

ist there, it has disappeared wholly, and I trust for ever."

The above was written shortly after the strange event it records. On the 3d of April, 1860, being then in London, I received a letter from the same lady, dated Florence, 27th March, of which the following is an extract:

"I believe I told you that the noises at the Villa are worse than ever, and the new proprietor is dreadfully disturbed by them. The house has been exorcised, but without effect. My own rooms are the most disturbed."

On the 5th of December, 1855, whilst I was returning to my rooms late at night in Florence, the streets being deserted, I observed a man stepping from the doorway of the adjoining house. I was on the step leading to my own door, and was looking up at the window to see if the servant was still up, when I received a violent blow on my left side, the force of which and the emotion caused by it, threw me forward breathless in the corner of the doorway. The blow was again repeated on my stomach, and then another blow on the same place, and the attempted assassin cried out, "Dio mio, Dio mio," and turning with his arm outstretched, he ran. I distinctly saw the gleam of his poignard, and as he turned, the light of the lamp also fell full on his face, but I did not recognize his features. I was perfectly powerless, and could not cry out or make any alarm, and I stood thus for at least two minutes, after which I groped my way along the wall to the door of a neighbor, where I was admitted. I thought I must have received some serious in jury, but on examining myself I found that the first blow had struck the door key, which I happened to have in my breast pocket, immediately over the region of my heart. I wore a fur coat, and this had chanced to be twice doubled in front. The second blow had gone through the four folds of it, through a corner of my dress coat, my waistcoat, and the band of my trousers, without inflicting any wound. The third blow had penetrated the four folds of my coat, and al so my trousers and linen, and made a slight incision, which bled, but not freely.

I had that morning received from a dear friend, who had in his house a clairvoyant of remarkable powers, a letter begging me not to go out that evening, as she had received a warning of impending danger—but to this I paid no attention. I never discovered the perpetrator, nor the cause of my life being attacked. Many reasons were assigned—amongst them robbery, mistaken identity, and religious intolerance.

In the month of January, Signor Landucci, then Minister of the Interior to the Grand Duke of Tuscany, sent to me to request that I would not walk about the house at night between the lights and the window, or go out in the streets in the daytime, giving as a reason that some of my enemies had been playing upon the superstitions of the peasantry, and telling them that it was my practice to administer the seven sacraments of the Catholic church to toads, in order by spells and incantations to raise the dead. This had so enraged and excited them that they were fully bent on taking my life, and for that purpose were concealed about the neighborhood with fire arms.

I met at this time a Polish nobleman, who with his family was about to visit Naples and Rome, and who most kindly pressed me to accompany them. I was left in Florence without money, and my friends in England having their credulity imposed upon by some scandalmongers, and thinking me to be leading a most dissolute life, refused to send me even money of my own which had been entrusted to their care. I told the Count B——— that I would travel with him, and the very day I gave this assent, the spirits told me that my power would leave me for a year. This was on the evening of the 10th of February, 1856. Feeling that the Count and his family must have felt an interest in me, arising only from the singular phenomena which they had witnessed in my presence, and that this cause being removed, their interest in me would have diminished, I wrote the following morning to inform them of what I was told, and say that I could no longer entertain the idea of joining them. They at once told me that it was for myself, even more than for the strange gift I possessed, that they had become interested in me. I went to them, and in a day or two we left Florence for Naples. While here, although my powers had left me, still my presence seemed to develope the power in others; for I met, at his own residence, the Hon. Robert Dale Owen, who was the American Minister to the Court of Naples, and it was in the presence of one of the Royal Princes of that family, himself a medium, that he was first convinced. Mr. Owen has since written a most able and carefully arranged book of authentic facts, entitled, "Footfalls on the Boundaries of another World," in which he has brought together both the facts and the philosophy of this great subject. We remained in Naples nearly six weeks, and then proceeded to Rome. Here in the absence of the power, my mind sought in the natural world for that consolation which it had hitherto found in the spiritual, and now this being withdrawn, life seemed to me a blank. I read with intense eagerness all the books I could find relating to the doctrines of the Romish church, and finding them expressive of so many facts which I had found coincident in my own experience, I thought that all contending and contradictory beliefs would be for ever set at rest, could I but be received as a member of that body. My experiences of life and its falsity had already left so indelible a mark on my soul, from my recent experiences of it at Florence, that I wished to shun everything which pertained to this world, and I determined to enter a monastery.

After two or three weeks of serious deliberations on the part of the authorities, it was decided that I should be received as a member of the church, and I was confirmed. The Princess O—— was my godmother, and the Count B—— my godfather on the occasion. I was most kindly received by the Pope, who questioned me much regarding my past life. He pointed to a crucifix which stood near to us, and said, "My child, it is upon what is on that table that we place our faith." He also gave me a large silver medal, which it has since been my misfortune to lose.

It has since been frequently said of me that at this

interview with the Pope, I had promised him that I would not have any more manifestations ; but it is hardly necessary, after what I have narrated, to say that I could not have made any such promise, nor did he ask any such promise to be made.

In June, 1856, I went to Paris, and, as I had been advised to do by the Pope, I sought the counsel of the Père de Ravignan, one of the most learned and excellent men of the day. The purpose of my remaining in France was to acquire a facility in the language. During the winter I again fell ill, and Dr. Louis, one of the most celebrated physicians in France for consumptive cases, decided on auscultation that my left lung was diseased, and advised a more genial climate. This could not, however, be accomplished, and for some time I was confined to my bed. The time was fast drawing nigh when the year would expire, during which my power was to be suspended. The Père de Ravignan always assured me that as I was now a member of the Catholic Church it would not return to me. For myself I had no opinion on the subject, as I was quite without data except his assurance on the point.

On the night of the 10th of February, 1857, as the clock struck twelve, I was in bed, to which I had been confined, when there came loud rappings in my room, a hand was placed gently upon my brow, and a voice said, "Be of good cheer, Daniel, you will soon be well." But a few minutes had elapsed before I sank into a quiet sleep, and I awakened in the morning feeling more refreshed than I had done for a long time. I wrote to the Père de Ravignan, telling him what had occurred, and the same afternoon he came to see me

During the conversation loud rappings were heard on the ceiling and on the floor, and as he was about to give me his benediction before leaving, loud raps came on the bedstead. He left me without expressing any opinion whatever on the subject of the phenomena.

The following day I had sufficiently recovered to take a drive, and on Friday the 13th, I was presented to their Majesties at the Tuileries, where manifestations of an extraordinary nature occurred. The following morning, I called on the Père de Ravignan to inform him of this. He expressed great dissatisfaction at my being the subject of such visitations, and said that he would not give me absolution unless I should at once return to my room, shut myself up there, and not listen to any rappings, or pay the slightest attention to whatever phenomena might occur in my presence. I wished to reason with him, and to explain that I could not prevent myself from hearing and seeing, for that God having blessed me with the two faculties, it was not in my power to ignore them. As for shutting myself up, I did not think, from having before tried the experiment, that it was consistent with my nervous temperament, and that the strain on my system would be too great if I were thus isolated. He would not listen to me, and told me I had no right to reason, "Do as I bid you, otherwise bear the consequences." I left him in great distress of mind. I wished not to be disobedient, and yet I felt that God is greater than man, and that *He* having bestowed the power of reason on me, I could not see why I should be thus deprived of it. On reaching my room, I found there a very dear and valued friend, the Count de K——. He observed my agitation, and questioned me as to the cause. I told him all, and he said, "There is but one thing to do, come home with me, and we will send for the Abbé de C——, and consult him." The Abbé came, and after hearing my story, he said, "That they might as well put me in my grave alive, as to carry out what had been ordered," adding, "I would like very much to witness some of these wonderful things." Most fortunately my emotion had not destroyed the power, as is usually the case when I am agitated, for while we were together several interesting phenomena occurred. His words were, "Let this power be what it will, it is in no way of your making." He recommended me to seek another spiritual adviser, and added, "I myself would gladly be your adviser, but as it would be known, I should only be persecuted." He gave me the name of one of the most eloquent preachers of the day, and I introduced myself to him, and remained under his guidance during the few weeks of my stay in Paris previous to my going to America to bring back my sister. During my absence, the curiosity had become very great to find out who was my confessor, and the Countess L——, having heard that he was a distinguished man, called upon several of the most noted in Paris, and after a short conversation, she abruptly said to each, "So you are Mr. Home's confessor." Most naturally on one such occasion, she chanced to find the right one, and his look of surprise betrayed him. His surprise was that I should have revealed his name, and this he expressed to the Countess, who told him that I had not betrayed him, but that she had used that artifice to ascertain the fact. This was the cause of my not continuing with him longer as my confessor.

The extract I here give is one from the recently published life of the great confessor, the Père de Ravignan, who had been recommended to me by the Pope, and I can only regret he is no longer here to contradict, with his own pen, the false statements concerning me, made by his biographer, the Jesuit, Father A. de Poulevoy. At the termination of Chapter XXIV, this person says, "We could not close this chapter without making mention of that famous American medium, who had the sad talent of turning other things than the tables, and invoking the dead to amuse the living. A great deal has been said, even in the papers, of his acquaintance, religiously and intimately, with Father de Ravignan, and they have seemed to wish, under the passport of a creditable name, to introduce and establish in France these fine discoveries of the New World. Here is the fact in all its simplicity. It is very true, that the young foreigner, after his conversion in Italy, was recommended from Rome to the Father de Ravignan, but at that period, in abjuring Protestantism, he also repudiated magic, and he was received with that interest that a priest owes to every soul ransomed by the blood of Jesus Christ, and more, perhaps, to a soul which has been converted, and brought to the bosom of the church. On his arriva in Paris, all his old practices were again absolutely forbidden. The Father de Ravignac, according to all the principles of the faith, which forbids superstition, forbade, under the most severe penalties he could inflict, that he should be an actor in, or even witness of, these dangerous scenes, which are sometimes criminal. One day the unhappy medium, tempted by I know not what, man or demon, violated his promise ; he was re taken with a rigor which overwhelmed him. Coming in then by chance, I saw him rolling on the ground, and drawing himself like a worm to the feet of the priest, who was in saintly anger. The Father, however, touched by his convulsive repentance, lifted him up, forgave him, and sent him away, after having exacted, by writing this time, a promise under oath. But soon there was backsliding which made much noise (*rechute êclatante*), and the servant of God, breaking off with this slave of the spirits, had him told never again to appear in his presence."

If the rest of the book be no more truthful than this statement, it is certainly not worth reading. The good Father de Ravignan well knew that I was not an American, and that this power had began with me before I ever saw America, for I had told him all my history. He also knew that I never invoked the spirits. No good name is, or ever will be, required to introduce or accredit a God-given truth, and I knew far too well the power of facts to think that they required the passport of even Father Ravignan's name. His biographer must have had a limited education too, both religious and historical, to write of these things being the "fine discoveries" of the New World, for they are to be readily traced in every age and country of the world of which we have any record or history pre served to us. It is perfectly untrue that I ever abjured any magical or other processes, for I never knew anything of such, and therefore I could not abjure them. The Father de Ravignan used to say to me, when I told him that the spirits had said they would return to me on the 10th of Eebruary, 1857, "There is no fear of that, my child, so long as you go on as you are now doing, observing carefully all the sacraments of our holy church; they will not be allowed to return." I fol'owed out his injunctions most conscientiously; but on the very day promised, they came as I have described, and told me they were glad to find me in so pure a state of mind, as it greatly facilitated their approach. I never yet violated any promise, to my knowledge: and as to the biographer coming in and finding me rolling on the ground, and crawling like a worm, it is an entire falsehood. But had it even been true, it would not have been the place of a priest to make such a thing public. If I took an oath, and wrote it down as alleged, that writing will have been kept. Let it be forthcoming, to save the character of this Father A. de Ponlevoy, that he may prove the truth of the statement he makes. In the meantime, I say that it is without even any foundation of truth. The last time I saw the good Father de Ravignan, I would only reason with him, for as I then said to him, no man had a right to forbid that which God gave. I left him without confessing, even—so I had not been on my knees at all, much less crawling like a worm.

As I have said, when the Abbé C—— came to see me, the conversation I had with him only tended to strengthen me in my opinion of what was right, for when priests are not agreed as touching such a matter, whom or what are we to rely on, if not on the reason

God has given us. The Father de Ravignan never had me informed that he would not see me again. On the contrary, it was I who said I would not go to him till he would reason with me. I have letters of his to me in my possession, which will show the kind feeling he ever had for me previous to this period, and I am well assured in my own mind, that he never said aught against me, even when I no longer saw him. He was so good, so pure, and so high minded, that I would that he had had a more truthful and honest chronicler to write his life.

The Countess L—— was herself a firm believer in the manifestations which she had frequently witnessed in my presence, and she was also present when I had a vision which is described in one of the Paris papers in the following words:

"The recent failure of Mr. Thurneyssen recalls to us a strange fact that signalized the sojourn of Mr. Home in Paris during the last winter. The Countess —— had a dozen years ago a strange hallucination. One evening being busy with some embroidery, alone with her brother, he was reading to her one of the most irreligious books of the eighteenth century. As she listened mechanically to his reading, she raised her head, and looking at her brother she was struck with terror at the sight of the strange expression of his face. He was ordinarily a most gentle, benevolent, and sympathetic young man, with calm, quiet features, but at that moment they were frightfully contracted, the eyebrows singularly convulsed, the eyes wide open, the corners of the mouth distorted by a bitter and despairing smile, and altogether he had the peculiar expression which painters would give to a fallen angel. The frightened Countess had immediately, as it were a thought revealed to her, (for she never previously dreamed of the possibility of such a thing), she was convinced that her brother was possessed by a demon. Frequently afterwards she saw the same infernal expression on the face of her brother, even when he was most calm and happy ; but the idea was so horrible to her that she never mentioned the circumstance. Last winter Mr. Home was introduced to the Countess. Being at her house one evening, and in his usual quiet frame of mind, his attention was drawn to a beautiful marble bust. He was not aware of its being that of the brother of the Countess, but immediately his whole visage changed, and he became in a state of most violent agitation. The Countess much alarmed, inquired why he was so affected, when Mr. Home replied, 'Madame, the man whose bust this is, is possessed with a demon.' One may judge of the astonishment of the Couuntess on hearing Mr. Home say what she had thought twelve years before. She pressed him with questions, and he, recovering from his emotion, rose and went to examine the bust more closely, then turning to the Countess he said, 'In a short time your brother will have a great misfortune, and this misfortune will deliver him from his enemies.'

" And so it has occurred, the Count de P—— has lost in the bankruptcy of M. Thurneyssen a considerable part of his fortune. The prophecy came four months previous to the failure. Could it have been that the spirits saw the dishonesty of Thurneyssen ; if so this might account why certain persons are so ready to oppose all communication with the other world, preferring the darkness to the light."

The day previous to my leaving Paris, a wonderful case of healing occurred through me in the manner which I will now relate.

On the 19th of March, 1857, when I was residing at 13, Rue des Champs Elysées, I received a letter from a stranger to me, Madame A. Mavoisin de Cardonne, of 233, Rue St. Dominique, St. Germain, stating that she had had a dream, in which she had seen her own mother and mine, and that the latter had told her to seek me at once, in order that her son, who had been deaf for four years from the effects of typhoid fever. might be cured. This was so strongly impressed upon her mind, that she wrote to me to say that she would call upon me with her son, the following morning at ten.

Accordingly the next morning she presented herself with her son at my rooms, there being present the Princess de B—— and Miss E——, who were with me, previous to my leaving Paris that very day, to proceed on my voyage to America. I had been so overwhelmed by persons wishing to see me that I had uniformly refused such visits; but on this occasion I had been so much pre-occupied by my engagements in preparing for my voyage, that I had not been able to acknowledge her letter, or to write to her either in the affirmative or negative. I therefore received her with considerable embarrassment, which was fully reciprocated on her part. It was indeed an embarrassing meeting for both of us, the mother yearning for her son's recovery, and I, not knowing how I was expected to be instrumental in healing this long total deafness; the more so that operations had been performed on the boy, as I afterwards found, by eminent surgeons of Paris, who had said that it was impossible he should ever be restored to hearing.

She sat down on a chair near a sofa, I taking a seat on the sofa, and beckoning the son to be seated on my left. The son was in his fifteenth year, tall for his age, of a delicate complexion, with large dreamy blue eyes that looked as if they would supply the place of hearing, with their deep, thoughtful, enquiring gaze. The mother began her description of the boy's illness, commencing with the attack of the fever, and ending with the entire loss of hearing. During the recital, told with all the warmth and tenderness of a mother's heart, and describing the various surgical operations to which he had been subjected, my sympathies were deeply moved, and I had unwittingly thrown my left arm about the boy and drawn him towards me, so that the boy's head rested on my shoulder. Whilst in this position, and Madame de Cardonne was telling some of the most painful particulars, I passed my hand caressingly over the boy's head, upon which he, partly lifting his head, suddenly exclaimed in a voice trembling with emotion, "*Maman, je t'entends!*" (Mamma, I hear you!) The mother fixed on him a look of astonishment, and said "Emile," the boy's name, and he at once replied, "*Quoi?*" (What?) She then, seeing that the child had heard her question, fainted with emotion, and on her recovery the scene was a most thrilling one—the poor mother asking continually questions for the mere pleasure of hearing her child reply. The boy was able to resume his studies, and has continued to hear perfectly up to the present time.

CHAPTER VI.

IN AMERICA. THE PRESSGANG.

On reaching America, I found the American press ,ad been publishing some ridiculous paragraphs about me, one of which was of a practical joke said to have been perpetrated by General Baraguay d'Hilliers and others in the presence of the Emperor, and that I myself had become greatly alarmed, and finally very angry on discovering the trick. The whole was a fabrication, as will be seen, for at that time I had never even seen either of the three gentlemen who were said to be actors in it. The following paragraph was, also, of the same character, as I had not then met M. Dumas.

"Home, the table-turner and magnetiser, who has of late caused such attention in Paris, has predicted to M. Alexandre Dumas that he would live to the age of 113 years, and be killed in a duel."

The following is another specimen ef a similar kind.

"Mr. Home, the medium who has made such a sensation in Paris, is on his way to this country, to visit his sister. He has been offered marriage by a lady of immense wealth, but has refused her."

The "New York Herald," a paper better known for its untruthfulness than otherwise, published letters from its special correspondents at Paris, stating "from the most reliable sources," that I had stolen £30,000, and was now for ever banished from France. I had at that very moment my return ticket in my pocket, and knew that an Imperial Prince, then on a visit to the Emperor, was awaiting my return. Indeed, if the public judged of my life from what the newspapers said of me, they must have been greatly puzzled by the statements and contradictions which successively appeared. I was quite content to leave both without notice, and I have never been at the pains to set them right. The following notice is of the same class as the preceding.

"The 'Indépendance Belge' states that Napoleon sent away Mr. Home, the American spirit-rapper, because the Empress was so much affected that the Emperor dreaded the continuance of the diabolical scenes. The ladies of honor were equally excited and could talk of nothing else. It is said that Home was quartered in the royal household, and was paid at the rate of £40,000 per year."

The "Hartford Courant" states:

"The 'Times' says that Daniel Dunglas Home, the famous medium, whose performances are so peculiar as to utterly baffle the most acute and sagacious minds, and who is a gentleman of education and character quite out of the range of the common mediums, was in this city last Saturday. We regard him as the most remarkable man living; and no man who has not witnessed what is done in Mr. Home's presence, can claim a right to give an opinion on Spiritualism. Mr. Home says the jokes of the newspaper correspondents about him are entirely untrue. He had some *sittings* at the Tuileries, but declined conversation on that subject."

Another paper, "The Springfield Republican," noticed my presence in America as follows:

"Home, the distinguished spiritual medium, who has recently been raising spirits in the presence of the Emperor Napoleon, is in Springfield on a brief visit. He will return to France shortly, where his services are in great request among the savans."

A New York paper gave the following account, correcting some of the misstatements about me:

"What terrible gossipers some of our letter writers are. The New York Editor of the 'London Letter,' in the last 'Sunday Times,' has the following paragraph: 'It is whispered, in Paris, that Home, the American spirit-rapper, was producing so much mischief in the Court that he was ordered off by the alarmed Emperor; and the fellow who, though playing the part of a personage with £40,000 a year, was really penniless, has left for the country of the rappers.'

"Possibly it may interest some of our readers to know something of Mr. Home, who has lately afforded a prolific subject to paragraph makers. We have nothing to say as to his 'spiritual' belongings here, but simply speak of the lad—for he is scarcely more, being but twenty-two years old now—in reference to such reports as the above. Home, the 'American,' is of an old Scottish family of standing, and was born in Scotland, but brought very young to this county. Quiet and unobtrusive in his manners, he never has thrust himself forward, nor specially sought nor avoided the notoriety which attends him; *never has exhibited himself as a public medium*, as many suppose, but has simply suffered events to take their course with him.

"As to the above story of his quitting Paris, which has gone the rounds, in various shapes, we have only to say, that some two Sundays since, while reading from the English papers an account of his doings in Paris, and supposing him snugly ensconced in the Tuileries, the door opened, and to our astonishment, in walked Mr. Home, to take dinner 'at home'—it being under our own roof that, some time since, at the age of sixteen, he found his first shelter in New York (Brooklyn,) a temporary refuge from horror-stricken relatives, who had turned the 'rapper' adrift as being 'possessed of a devil;' thus starting him as a young martyr at least, whether deservedly so or not.

"He told us of his arriving a day or two before, at Philadelphia, and stated what he had come for, and when he was going back. He has accomplished his errand—part of which was to obtain his sister, with whom he had sailed from Boston, a few days since, on his return to Paris.

"So much for the 'mischief' and the 'alarmed Emperor' who 'ordered him off,' a story made of the same bit of cloth as the Socrates joke by Baraguay d'Hilliers and others."

Whilst on the subject of these newspaper inventions, I may as well allude to a curious series of them which occurred in 1858. I had then left Paris for Rome, on account of my health, and on the 13th of March, the following telegraphic dispatch reached me there from a friend in Paris, "Tell me immediately if you are still at Rome. I have a request to make." I replied that I was still at Rome, and in course of post I received a letter of the 14th March, as follows:

"Dear Friend.—I sent you yesterday a telegraphic dispatch that you might write to me at once if you were at Rome. I made pretext of having a commission to ask you to do; but it was in reality only to have a letter from you as soon as possible. Scandal says you have been arrested, and the Hague papers say that you are in prison at Mazas. Monsieur B——, whose son is a medium, has sent to know the truth, and I have authorized him to publish that I have a letter from you, bearing date of Rome the 7th of March. I have also sent to inform 'La Patrie,' that a stop may be put to there base calumnies. I trust you will approve of what I have done."

The Parisian papers took up the report, and it was confirmed by them that I was truly in prison at Mazas. Persons even in official positions told my friends *that they had seen and spoken to me in that prison*, and one, an officer, went so far as to state that he had accompanied me there in the carriage.

Being at Rome, and altogether unaware of all this scandal which was passing about me, I had felt forcibly impressed, I knew not why, to write to M. Henri Delage, the well known mystic writer of Paris. I did so, and it will be observed by the following paragraph introducing my letter, how very opportunely my impression had been given, and how well I had acted in following it out.

Paris correspondent of "Le Nord."

"PARIS, 17th March.

"Allow me to begin by a good action; it is to free an honorable man from calumnies, arising from what source I know not, but which for the past few days have been rapidly spreading. I speak of Mr. Home, who is, for the moment, in Italy, whereas it is whispered both secretly and openly that he is in the prison at Mazas, for we know not what crimes. The letter here given, dated Rome, 7th of March, was received yesterday by M. Henri Delage, an intimate friend of Mr. Home. The letter is there before me with the postal mark, and I will give you his literal words:

"ROME, March 7th, 1858.

"'Dear M. Delage,—You were without doubt much surprised to hear of my departure for Italy; but the truth is I was very ill. I had an impoverishment of the blood, so what could I do. My power had quite left me. The dear spirits thought me too ill to see strangers. Here in Rome I go but little into society, a complete rest being necessary. Write to me soon, and will you kindly remember me to M. H———; you know I like him very much.

"Yours faithfully,

"'D. D. HOME.'

"I beg of you to give the publicity of your well-known journal to this letter of Mr. Home. It being the best reply which can be given to those base calumnies which attack his honor."

I well know the origin and cause of this intrigue, and I have in my possession a friendly letter, bearing date the 18th July, 1858, from the Bureau du Ministre de l'Intérieur, which is a sufficient refutation of the wicked calumny. His Highness the Prince Murat also made it the occasion of proving to me not only the Christian principles which actuated him, but also the true nobleness of his heart, in doing for a comparative stranger, that which a father alone could be expected to do for a son. He, at his own expense, sent persons to Germany, to Italy, and to England, to ascertain the foundation of such a libel, and generously gave me his public and private testimony to its entire untruth.

I have now to present the following letter, and the enclosed programme, which I also received while at Rome, and which disclose a case of personation, which is by no means either the first or the last of that kind which I could give. It is, however, an amusing specimen of them.

"Paris, April 7th.

"Dear friend,—I send you a programme taken from one of the Lyons papers, that was sent to M. Allen Kardee. What a shame to think such an imposition should be allowed in your name. I would advise you to write at once to the Prefect of Lyons, or to the police, that the villain should be unmasked as soon as possible, not only for the wrong he does to your name, but also to the cause of spiritualism. Do not allow a moment to pass, and we on our side will do all we can. Only think of the audacity in daring to say that he had been received by the Emperor.

"I am, &c., &c.

"P.S.—I have this moment heard that the imposture was at once discovered, and he has fled from Lyons."

I give the original programme, with an English translation.

"*Salle du Grand Théatre. Jeudi, Avril* 1, 1858, *à huit heures. Soirée Américaine ou Séance de Spiritualism de M. Home.*

"Je ne me guide jamais d'après la science, mais d'après ma conscience; je crois donc fortement aux faits magnétiques, je crois que la force magnétique augmente prodigieusement la force de vision de l'homme; je crois que ces faits sont constatés par un certain nombre d'hommes très-sincères et très chrétiens.'—L'ABBE LACORDAIRE.

"Programme: Expérience de vision par M. Home et l'Ange miraculeux.—Obéissance à l'ordre du public. —Séance de spiritualisme par la sensitive Mme. de Cabanyes.

"Production des visions demandées par les spectateurs: Frémissement, Joie, Colère, Idiotisme, Piété, Multiplication des sens, Augmentation et diminution des forces.

"Reproduction de plusieurs de ces phénomènes sur des jeunes gens que le public est prié de présenter.

"M. Home, qui a eu l'honneur de faire ses expériences devant Sa Majesté l'empereur, invite MM. les médecins, docteurs, chirurgiens, etc., etc., à monter près de lui sur la scène, afin de contrôler, la véracité des phénomènes curieux qu'il a l'honneur d'offrir au Public. Des siéges seront disposés à cet effet.

"Prix des places: Premières loges, fauteuils et stalles, 6 fr. (sans augmeutation pour la location à l'avance);—premières galeries, 5 fr.;—secondes, 3 fr.; —parterre, 2 fr. 50 c.;—troisièmes, 1 fr. 50 c.;—quatrièmes, 1 fr."

"*At the Great Theatre, Thursday*, 1*st of April*, 1858, *commencing at* 8 *o'clock, American Soirée or Séance of Spiritualism, by Mr. Home.*

"'I never allow myself to be guided by science, but by my conscience. I therefore believe firmly in the facts of magnetism. I believe that the magnetic force augments prodigiously the power of man's vision. I believe that these facts are certified by a certain number of men very sincere and very christian.'—THE ABBE LACORDAIRE.

"Programme: The vision experience of Mr. Home, and the miraculous angel.—Obedience to the order of the public.—Spiritual séance by the sensitive Mme. de Cabanyes.

"Production of visions asked for by the spectators: Tremblings, Joy, Anger, Idiotcy, Religion, Piety, Multiplication of the senses, Augmentation and diminution of strength.

"Reproduction of several of those phenomena on young persons, whom the public are requested to introduce.

"Mr. Home, who has had the honor to go through his experiences before his Majesty the Emperor, invites the Doctors of Philosophy and others, also Surgeons, &c., &c., to sit near him on the stage to satisfy themselves as to the truth of the curious phenomena which he has the honor to present to the public. Chairs will be arranged for that purpose.

"Price of places: First boxes, fauteuils and stalls, 6 frs. (no extra charge for booking); first gallery, 5 frs.; second, 3 frs.; pit, 2 frs. 50 c.; third places, 1 fr. 59 c.; fourth, 1 fr."

This was contradicted by the Paris papers, which gave only as a reason that I was in Turin, whilst at the time it happened that I was really at Naples.

But it would be wrong to confine these falsehoods to the press of America or France, when the English press vied with them in fabricating and dispensing equally false statements about me. The Socrates story was from the forge of the "Court Journal," and was disseminated through a great part of the English press. No wonder that with such teaching there should be misconception about me, and about the phenomena. I can only say that the whole of the following statements, names, dates, circumstances and persons are false from beginning te end.

Extraordinary Spirit Affair in Paris. Singular and Successful Hoax on the Spiritualists.

"Mr. Home, the all-hearing, all-seeing spirit-rapper, is gone suddenly, without warning. Many stories are afloat respecting the cause of this abrupt departure.

amid such striking success, when Paris was just filled with his renown, and even from the pulpit had threats and warnings been launched forth against those who dared to frequent his company, or believe in his incantations. Some newspapers have declared that he is gone to America in search of his sister, whom he pronounces a more powerful medium than himself; others that, in consequence of some of his tricks having assumed the character of *tours de passe-passe*, he had been forbidden to practice his deceptive arts upon the high personages whom he had chosen, on pain of *procès-verbal;* and that the metamorphosis of the Princess Mathilde's pocket-handkerchief into a living scarabeus—after which exploit the practitioner had fallen into catalepsy, and remained senseless for five hours—had awakened certain scruples and suspicions in the minds of those who had witnessed the feat, which had caused his exclusion from that circle of society. Nothing of all this is the case, and your readers may be assured of the truth of what we are about to relate, and of the adventure being the whole and sole cause of the abrupt departure of the discomfited wizard.

"A few nights ago a grand séance had been prepared for him at the house of one of the principal officials about the Court, who had witnessed the divers experiments made at the Tuileries, and which, although failing to convince him entirely, had yet not left him wholly incredulous. The company was limited, and of the first water. The names had all been submitted to the practitioner—those of Eugène Guinot, the *feuil letoniste:* General Baraguay d'Hilliers; and Nadaud the composer; all of them atrocious unbelievers, wretched infidels, and scoffers, wholly devoid of all sensibility r imagination. Numerous were the experiments tried, and all, as usual, eminently successful. The accordeon glided, as usual, from knee to knee, all round the circle, and played the tunes most loved by the inquirers; the bell wandered round the ceiling, and rang its merry peal or tolled its doleful note, according to the will of any member of the company who chose to command it. But the wizard had promised that night to evoke the spirits and render them visible to the sight, and every preliminary experiment was attended to with impatience, so great was the hurry to witness the crowning masterpiece of the performance. At length the lights were all extinguished but one, a solitary wax taper on the mantel-piece, behind the figure of the practitioner, which cast its long, gigantic shadow on the walls and ceiling of the room. The silence was complete; some of the ladies crouched behind their neighbors, and resisted the temptation to faint only by reason of their curiosity; others stared around, hoping, yet dreading, to see something awful and terrific, that they would be driven to hysterics. The voice of the wizard was heard, amid the silence, demanding whose spirit should be summoned to appear. A faint whisper, from a distant corner, thrilled through the room —"Let it be Socrates, the greatest of philosophers!" A pause ensued—no objection or opposition being manifested, the wizard raised his arm, and waving it towards the door, solemnly bade the spirit of Socrates appear and stand before him. Again the silence was resumed, and the wizard remained, with extended arm and muttering lips, gazing towards the door. It slowly opened; and, amid the utmost terror, the company beheld the entrance of a figure, enveloped in a kind of floating drapery, something like a winding-sheet, which advanced with noiseless tread over the carpet, and stood before the conjuror. The white and flowing beard, the bald head and crushed nose were unmistakable—Socrates stood, as in life, in the very midst of that gay and frivolous circle, evoked from his slumber of centuries to furnish sport for a Parisian *salon!* The awe and terror of the company was at its highest, and the figure glided back in silence while yet the effect produced was at its culminating point. When it had disappeared, compliments, of course, poured in upon the operator, who, shaken to the very fingers' ends, could not help expressing his surprise at the unusual promptitude with which the summons had been answered, and, full of the excitement of unlooked for success, yielded to the entreaties of the same voice which had spoken before, and which now implored the evocation of Frederick the Great. The wizard again stretched forth his hand towards the door, although doubtful if his electric current would be strong enough to accomplish two evocations so rapidly one after the other. He was observed, however, even in the dim light of the apartment, to turn deadly pale as the door again opened at his summons, when he called aloud for Frederick the Great, King of Prussia, to appear before him. The moment's pause was truly awful. By degrees, amid the shadows of the room could be seen gliding through the door-way, a short figure, wrapped, like the one which had preceded it, in a kind of winding-sheet clinging to its limbs, and held around the waist by the grasp of the hands. The face, however, was undeniably that of the great hero, and the head surmounted by the little traditional cocked hat which makes every Prussian heart beat with gratitude and loyalty even to this day. The figure advanced as that of Socrates had done before, close up to the magician, and there stood still and motionless within a few paces of the chimney. Presently, the excitement of the magician became intense, the perspiration rolled in huge drops from his forehead, and the teeth chattered. "Enough, enough—begone, depart!" said he, in a hoarse whisper, as the eyes of the figure glared upon him with a fierce and menacing expression. "Begone, I say!" repeated he, in a hollow tone, as the figure still stood motionless in spite of the command. In another moment, however, the spell was broken. Rousing himself by an effort which, considering the circumstances in which he was placed, may be regarded as sublime, he suddenly exclaimed, "I have been made the dupe of some mystification," and stepped close to the figure, which had still retained its menacing attitude until that moment, when a loud and uncontrollable laugh burst from its lips, and it exclaimed: "What! don't you know me? I am Nadaud, and here is my friend Socrates, otherwise Marshal Baraguay d'Hilliers, ready to appear again whenever you choose, and close at hand is my comrade, Eugène Guinot in life, and Alcibiades in death, waiting to be summoned after me, as he would most assuredly have been, had I been able to follow up the joke." You can just imagine the effect produced by the discovery of the mystification. Mr.

Home was struck powerless and dumb; when he re covered, he begged it to be remembered that he had been the first to find out the deception, and asserted that the spirit summoned would have appeared, for that he does possess the facility of raising them. In a few moments, however, he disappeared, and the next day we heard, without astonishment, of his sudden departure from Paris. It seems that the three *mauvais plaisans* who had been excluded from the company had been determined to revenge themselves; and, with the assistance of a *confrère*, aided likewise by the false white beard of Socrates and the cocked hat of Frederick the Great, had almost succeeded in duping the operator, had it not been for the uncontrollable laughter of Nadaud which betrayed the whole conspiracy.

"This is the story told of the sudden desertion of the camp by Mr. Home. Time will show us if it be truth, for he has promised to return; and should we not behold him according to his promise in the space of three months, we shall know what to believe and what to doubt of his mysterious power."

I could tell much more of a similar kind, but what I have already given is sufficient to show the reckless invention of those who assume to enlighten the public through the press. I found it the easiest to let them have their own way, for if I had begun to contradict all the falsehoods told about me, my time would have been fully occupied in vain attempts to stop a torrent, which seems as if it would never cease to flow.

CHAPTER VII.

1857–8.—FRANCE, ITALY, AND RUSSIA.—MARRIAGE.

I RETURNED from America to Paris in May, 1857, and I remained there till July, having séances every day. The power was very great at that time, and the phenomena were witnessed and investigated by many hundreds of all classes. The spirit hands were frequently visible, and were seen by many to take pen or pencil and write in the autograph of the person whose spirit was represented to be present.

One morning the *concierge* came to me saying, "Please, Sir, there is an old gentleman here, and I think you must see him, he seems so anxious and careworn." I must mention that I had been so overrun by visitors, that I had been obliged to refuse to see any strangers, as all my time was taken up by engagements with my friends. I acceded to his request, and he announced the Count de X——. At the first moment of looking at him, I saw none of the signs of anxiety and care which had struck the *concierge*, nor did he seem to me so very old. He advanced to where I stood, and taking me kindly by the hand, he said to me, "I have been sent to you, and you will yet know the reason why, though you do not even know who I am. I live at No. 4, Rue ——, and you will be obliged to come to me." I shook my head at this incredulously, and told him that my time was so taken up, that I had scarcely time even to call on my friends. He smiled, and said: "You will see, you will see." The conversation then changed, and he left me after having written his address. I was to dine that evening with the Baroness de M——, and previous to leaving the house to go to her, I heard a spirit voice saying distinctly to me, "You will go to see my father, won't you?" The voice did not seem as if it required an answer, for it was said so affirmatively, and I made no reply. On reaching the Hotel de M——, and entering the drawing-room I saw a young man standing there. I was surprised at this, expecting to have met no stranger. With his eyes fixed upon me, he said, "I am glad you have come, for we will go together to see my father," and he then suddenly disappeared. I had thought till then that he was a guest, so real was the vision. The Baroness was in the room, and saw that I was agitated, and asked me what had occurred, but I did not enter into any explanation. When about to take my seat at the dinner table, again I heard the same voice, saying, "You will go to my father, won't you?" This so unnerved me that I told the Baroness the circumstance, and she kindly advised my going. The evening passed on, and after two hours I had nearly forgotten the occurrence, and had returned to the drawing-room, when suddenly I saw by my side the same young man. His face now wore a pained expression, and I was horrified to see blood on his breast.

He said to me, "My father is waiting for you; he has had much sorrow; it is your mission to console—go to him." I told him I would on the following day, but he replied that I must go then, that very night. He disappeared, and I told the Baroness of what he said, and she allowed me to leave. On reaching No. 4, Rue ——, I was directed to the rooms of the Count, and his valet told me that his master was preparing to retire, and in all probability could not see me. Again the voice told me to announce myself, and at that very moment a door was opened, and the Count came towards me, and said, "I have been waiting for you, I knew you would come." I described to him the young man I had seen, and all that had happened, and he at once recognized him as his son who had been murdered. He showed me a portrait of him, which exactly corresponded with my visions of him, and I have since seen him often. He has told me, that on his appearance that first day, he showed the blood upon his breast, merely to impress me the more deeply with the necessity of going to his father. His father told me that he had been himself for a long time a partial medium, and that he had been told to seek me for the purpose of having his mediumship increased, in order that his son might be able the more easily to impress him with his presence. It has since been a great comfort and relief to his mind to have the certainty of his son being with him to console him in his affliction.

About this time my guardian spirits told me that it seemed necessary that I should go to Turkey, as a way was opening by which I might be the means of bringing light there. I accordingly made all preparations for my journey, and my power left me. I had received letters of introduction to persons holding high positions at Constantinople. My trunks were packed, my passport sent for *visé*. I was making a farewell call on the Duchess de A——, and while in conversation with her, the drawing-room seemed filled with rappings, the alphabet was called for, and I was told that my journey must be postponed, as some political troubles were just about to occur. Instead, therefore, of going to Turkey, I went to Baden-Baden. My power while there was not great, as my health was again failing, but I met the King of Wurtemburg, and the then Prince, now King of Prussia, both of whom investigated the phenomena.

My guardian spirits continually told me at this time that there was trouble in store for me, but that from the darkness light would come, and that whatever might seem to be a loss, would in the end prove to be a gain, and in all this they were correct.

I left Baden-Baden sooner than I had expected, and went to Biarritz. Here I was told that the first darkening of the cloud would come, and that those who might have understood me better, would be led to think ill of me by those about them, who, to serve a purpose, would farbicate a statement, the very absurdity of which ought to have been its refutation. The pre-knowledge of what was to occur to me, combined with nervous debility, made me more than usually agitated, and whilst at a séance, where almost the only manifestation was the taking of a bracelet from the lady sitting on my left, and the carrying of it to a lady opposite me, the gentleman on my right hand declared it to have been transported by my feet. If my legs were eight feet long it would have still been a miracle, but in such wonderful occurrences as these we must not be surprised at any absurdity that may be invented, however painful it may be to be charged with dishonesty and imposture.

Some instances of the manner in which it is said the phenomena are produced are sufficiently amusing to be repeated. A very popular idea in Paris was that I carried in my pocket a tame monkey trained to assist me. Another is that my legs are so formed as to be capable of elongation, and that my feet are like those of a baboon. Many people suppose that when I go to a strange house, my tables have to be sent first, and that, like Sir David Brewster's "conjectural" table, they are always copiously draped, and that I take with me wax hands and arms to show at the proper moment. Some suppose that I magnetize or biologize my audience, and that they only imagine they see what they see. Some that I carry with me lazy tongs and a magic lantern, and others have stated that when I am said to rise in the air, it is only a balloon filled with gas in the shape of a man. Others again will have it that it is done by a magic lantern, whilst some doctors declare that I administer "a thimblefull of chloroform to each of the sitters." Sir David Brewster must have had his thimblefull when he could only say that the table "appeared to rise," and that "spirits were the last things he would give into." Some have enough spiritual belief to say that I have the devil at command. Others that I raise spirits by forms and incantations. Then we have involuntary muscular motion to account for the phenomena by the learned Professor Farraday. Dr. Carpenter speaks of their being produced by unconscious cerebation, and Mr. Morell, the philosopher, tells us that they are caused by "the reflex action of the mind." A common explanation is ventriloquism. Electricity is another, and it is said that I have an electric battery concealed about my person. Then there are the od force and fluid action, and the nervous principle, and collusion, illusion and delusion. Mechanical contrivances attached to the lower extremities are also suggested by Sir David Brewster, but without specifying their nature. But the most scientific and learned explanation, leaving no room for conjectures, was given by an old woman in America, who when asked if she could account for what she had seen, replied, "Lor, Sirs, it's easy enough, he only rubs himself all over with a gold pencil." The rappings are produced in many ways, each philosopher having his own theory, beginning low down with the snapping of the toe-joints, others getting up to the ancle, whilst some maintain it to be in the knees, or thigh bones. Professor Huxley has his own "spirit-rapping toe" with which he amuses his friends. It has even been attributed to a strong beating of my pulse. Some say I rub my boots together, others my thumb nails, and that springs are concealed in the table and about the room. It has been said that I have an electrical quality which I can throw off at the command of my will. A general belief is that I bribe the servants at whatever house I visit, that they may aid me in concealing my machinery. The intelligence displayed in obtaining names, dates, and other circumstances, is previously communicated to me either by my own inquiry, from servants or by visiting the tombstones of the relatives, or even by a body of secret police who are in my pay. Others know that I am clairvoyant, and that I read the thoughts of those present. I am an accomplished juggler according to others, and have always refused to be seen by any others of the craft, although the fact is quite the contrary, and the greatest juggler of France has stated that he could not at all account for what he witnessed by any of the principles of his art.

However flattering this might be to my vanity, in conferring upon me such astounding qualities and scientific acquirements which I do not possess, it has been to me a source chiefly of amusement and wonder, to see how learned persons could so widely and absurdly disagree among themselves, and strain at gnats, though swallowing camels with such surprising greediness. I have wandered from my narrative to give my readers these attempted explanations of mediumship, hoping, however, that they will never try any of the experiments suggested by the learned in the presence of persons of average understanding. The excellent establishment at Earlswood, at the head of which is the good Dr. Conolly, would be more likely to furnish the sort of audience suited to these explanations of the men of science.

My good friends, the Count and Countess de B——, left Biarritz with me on a visit to the château of a mutual friend, near Bordeaux; and here there were several instances of direct spirit-writing on paper placed before us on the table in full view. Whilst we were sitting one evening, hands appeared distinctly above the table, and we saw them successively take up a pencil and write. One of these hands was a small one, apparently of a child, another appeared to be that of a full grown man. The hand of the child wrote a little message to her mother who was present, and signed it with her christian name. There was a striking peculiarity in this, as the child had always left out the last letter of her name, which then, instead of being a female name, became a male one. Her name was Denise, but she wrote it "Denis." Her mother had often spoken to her of this, and yet the child had not corrected herself of the habit during her life, and now to prove her identity, the final letter was again left out. This was of course unknown to me, and to all except her father and mother, both of whom were there. The larger hand wrote several communications in our presence, some for his wife, who was at the table, and others to persons who were not there present. This handwriting was in his peculiar autograph.

The lady of the house turned to me and said abruptly, "Why you are sitting in the air;" and on looking we found that the chair remained in its place, but that I was elevated two or three inches above it, and my feet not touching the floor. This may show how utterly unconscious I am at times to the sensation of levitation. As is usual when I have not got above the level of the heads of those about me, and when they change their positions much, which they frequently do in looking wistfully at such a phenomenon, I came down again, but not till I had remained so raised about half a minute from the time of its being first seen. I was now impressed to leave the table and was soon carried to the lofty ceiling. The Count de B——— left his place at the table, and coming under where I was, said, "Now, young Home, come and let me touch your feet." I told him I had no volition in the matter, but perhaps the spirits would kindly allow me to come down to him. They did so, by floating me down to him, and my feet were soon in his outstretched hands. He seized my boots, and now I was again elevated, he holding tightly, and pulling at my feet till the boots I wore, which had elastic sides, came off, and remained in his hands. The Count has all his life been well known, holding an important public position, and as truthful as his heart is good. To him and his dear wife, who has recently passed from earth, I owe a deep debt of gratitude, they having been my firm and fast friends ever since I made their acquaintance, six years ago. This was, I believe, the first time of my being raised in the air in France, and it has been of very seldom occurrence there, though it happened so frequently afterwards in England, as will be seen in future pages. Since I wrote the narrative of this séance, I have applied to the Count for his verification of it, and I have his letter stating its correctness.

Another incident occurred in the presence of the Count de B———. The Countess X——— was present for the first time at a séance, when a spirit manifested himself, purporting to be that of her son. The accordeon was being played, and she asked if he could remember a piece of music which had particularly struck them both whilst they were travelling together for his health in Germany. It had escaped her mind, she said, but it could be easily recalled to her if he would play it. Upon this the accordeon played some intricate passages from the opera of Norma, which she at once recognized.

I now returned to Paris, and went to reside with my friend the Count de K——, and whilst there I had sittings almost every day. I also went on a visit to the Chateau de R——, to the family of the Marquis de ——. The second evening of my stay, as we were about to take tea, a table standing at the further end of the large saloon where we were, came up to us with extreme violence. We were all rather startled, as we were not expecting any manifestations, and for the next two hours they were unceasing. The elder son of the family, the Count L——, came to my room when I had wished the family good night, and these proofs of a spirit presence were again made most evident Amongst others there were the sound of heavy footsteps which shook the room. I also saw the distinct form of a boy, and described his appearance to L——, adding that I could recognize him if I could see his portrait. On meeting the family at breakfast the following morning the Marquis said—"What time did L—— leave you last night, and what were you both doing jumping about the room?" We told him that we had both of us our slippers on, and that he must have heard the noises made by the spirits. The chateau, being one of the very oldest in France, has the walls in some places nearly twenty feet thick—indeed dressing-rooms have been made in them, and they are quite spacious. There is a solidity to every floor. In order, therefore, to have been heard in the room beneath, the manifestations must have been of very great force. After breakfast the Marchioness asked me if I would not like to go over the chateau, and on my assenting, she said we will begin with my boudoir. We went there, and on reaching the centre of the room I looked round, and there I saw the very face I had seen the night previous. For a moment I could not bring myself to believe it to be other than the spirit himself, but it was only a portrait. My emotion was such that I caught hold of L——, who stood near me, and said, "There, that is the boy I saw last night." I was so overcome that I had to leave the room, and they then told me that L—— having related what had occurred to his mother, they had arranged to put me to the test, and not having even told me of the existence of the portrait, they wished to see if I could recognize it.

In an hotel situate on the Boulevard des Italiens in Paris, I was introduced to a family, consisting of Mr. H——, his wife, and their two sons, both of whom were at that time in the English army, and had just returned from the Crimean campaign. The father, a cool-headed, truthful minded man, was a countryman of mine, and our conversation soon turned upon the wonders of second sight and ghost-seeing. Presently, whilst we were talking together, we were startled at hearing loud sounds coming from a distant part of the room, and slowly approaching us. I at once suggested to them that some spirit desired to communicate with us. The unseen one assented to this by making the sounds for the alphabet, and the name of "Gregoire" was spelt out, with the additional information that he had passed from earth, giving the time of his departure. This the two young officers at once and strongly contradicted, for they recognized in the name a very intimate friend, an officer in the French army in the Crimea, whom they had only just left there suffering under a slight wound, but so slight that it gave no apprehensions of an unfavorable kind. He, however, now gave them other proofs of his identity, and during the whole of the remaining hours of the afternoon and evening he continued to make his presence manifest. Several times things were brought from parts of the room distant from us, and there were frequent raps, and his friends felt touches. Sounds resembling the firing of musketry were heard, and indeed so indisputable were some of the signs given, that no one could fail to have been convinced of spirit power and presence, though having seen him so lately, and having since heard nothing to make them think his death probable, they could hardly realize the likelihood of it.

I left the family late in the evening, bidding them good-bye, as they were to leave for England the following day. From a member of the family who resides in Paris, I ascertained shortly afterwards that they had written to ascertain the truth as to what had been communicated to them by the spirit calling himself Gregoire, and that in every detail, they were informed, the spirit had been correct. I ought here to state, however, that the eldest son, previous to this corroborative testimony reaching his family, had been sent with his regiment to Canada, and he was sitting in his tent when a letter reached him from his father, relating the results of their inquiries from the Crimea. While he was reading his father's letter, informing him the details of his friend Gregoire's departure from earth, he was startled by hearing a rustling sound amongst some loose papers and pens, which were carelessly strewn on his table. Fearing lest his imagination might be taking advantage of his reason, he called for his servant to come in and look at the table—and, to their mutual astonishment, they saw a pen move itself into an erect position, and deliberately write the name of Gregoire on some blank paper. This fact was told me by the father of the young man, and I see no reason to disbelieve it. What object could tempt the young man to tell so deliberate and wilful an untruth, if it were one, on such a subject? Other strange occurrences continued with other members of this family after their return to England, for many months, and then left them in as sudden and unexpected a manner as they had made their appearance.

In January, 1858, I went to Holland, accompanied by Mr. T——, and was presented to the Queen. The manifestations at the Hague were in some instances very strong, and again sometimes I had séances at which nothing would occur, and this although in the presence of persons who were most desirous of witnessing them.

I went to Amsterdam for the purpose of meeting the proprietors and writers for a magazine of infidel tendencies. I well remember it. We were staying at a large old-fashioned hotel; the cheerless cold of the rooms with their bleak walls and their beam-bare ceilings, as I sat before the fire, which was but the ghost of such as we are accustomed to in England, when these eight or ten gentlemen were announced. None of them were known to me or to my friend, and I desired them at once to sit down, and see if any manifestations would occur. They appeared clever, shrewd persons, deeply read and thinking men. Cold reason had wrapped her chill mantle about their minds, and all that was not tangible could have no truth in it for them. The first tremulous sensation in the table and floor, which often precedes other manifestations, was felt. They delegated two of their number to sit under the table to watch me and my movements. Faint rappings were heard, and the table legs were examined to see that I had no springs concealed there.—These manifestations increased in force, and they, after the most close and strict scrutiny, were obliged to acknowledge that they had witnessed that which they could in no wise account for. The alphabet was called for, and intelligent communications were received.—This was a step in advance of their philosophy, and to them most singular, and soon the manifestations ceased—but not until they had each expressed their conviction that there was no imposture. I have since been informed, by letters from Amsterdam, that one of them became a medium, and that their general disbelief in spiritual causation was greatly modified. I remember as my friend and I sat together after the party had left, we expressed a wish that they had seen more, and we spoke of ourselves as being sorry prophets for such a mission. This idea pursued me after I had gone to bed, and the spirit of my mother came and comforted me by saying that sufficient had been given, and that "the wind must be tempered to the shorn lamb."

We returned to the Hague, and a deputation of young gentlemen from the University of Leyden called to ask me to visit Leyden. My engagements, however, were such as to necessitate my departure, and we left the following day for Brussels. There the power left me, and I was told by the spirits that it would be some time before it would return, and that many things of the utmost importance to me would occur in the meantime. I had taken a severe cold while in Holland, but had intended to have remained some time in Brussels to have séances with my young friends there, and when I found that my power had gone, I considered it better to return to Paris to consult my medical adviser there. I accordingly went there, and he pronounced my disease to be impoverishment of the blood and great nervous depression, and advised my going to Italy. I strongly objected to this, inasmuch as every time I leave Paris some silly stories are put in circulation, such as my being ordered away by the Emperor, or that I go to fly from the law. I remained, therefore, growing daily worse for two or three weeks, when I left, intending to stay at Turin with my friends there. On reaching Turin in February, I found the snow covering the ground to a considerable depth, and the cold more intense than it had been in Paris, and so I left the same evening for Pisa, to join some friends there. I found Pisa very cold, and was advised to proceed to Rome.

I reached Rome in March, and refused nearly all invitations out, wishing to be quiet to regain my health. A friend mentioned one afternoon, whilst we were walking together to the Pynchon, the name of a

Russian family of distinction then in Rome, and added that they were anxious to make my acquaintance. I excused myself on the ground of my health. At this moment a carriage was passing us and stopped—and my friend, before I was aware of what he was doing, introduced me to the Countess de Koucheleff, who asked me to come and sup with them that evening, adding that they kept very late hours.

I went about ten in the evening, and found a large party assembled. At twelve as we entered the supper-room she introduced to me a young lady, whom I then observed for the first time, as her sister. A strange impression came over me at once, and I knew she was to be my wife. When we were seated at table the young lady turned to me and laughingly said, "Mr. Home, you will be married before the year is ended." I asked why she said so, and she replied, that there was such a superstition in Russia when a person was at table between two sisters. I made no reply. It was true. In twelve days we were partially engaged, and waiting only the consent of her mother. The evening of the day of our engagement a small party had assembled, and were dancing. I was seated on a sofa by my *fiancée*, when she turned to me and abruptly said, "Do tell me all about spirit-rapping, for you know I don't believe in it." I said to her, "Mademoiselle, I trust you will ever bear in mind that I have a mission entrusted to me. It is a great and a holy one. I cannot speak with you about a thing which you have not seen, and therefore cannot understand. I can only say that it is a great truth." The tears came welling into her eyes, and laying her hand in mine she said, "If your mission can bring comfort to those less happy than ourselves, or be in any way a consolation to mankind, you will ever find me ready and willing to do all I can to aid you in it." She was true to this noble sentiment to the last moment of her short life, and she is still my great comfort and sustainer since we have separated in this earthly sphere. She was my own true, loving wife for, oh! too short a period for my happiness here, but for hers I was content to lose her for a time, till it shall please God that I too pass away to join her!

Shortly after our engagement the family went to Naples, and I with them, and we remained there six weeks. Then the family left for Florence, and my *fiancée* was entrusted to the care of a Russian family about to return by Paris to Russia, that she might join her mother, and get ready the necessary papers, that the marriage might take place as soon as the family returned to St. Petersburgh. I accompanied them to Paris, and after they had left I went to Scotland for my certificate of birth, the parish clerk having sent me one with my name written Hume instead of Home. Knowing this to be incorrect I was obliged to make a journey to have it rectified, and then I returned to Paris, and joined the family who had arrived there from Italy.

We left for St. Petersburgh in June, accompanied by M. Alexandre Dumas, who was to officiate as godfather at my marriage. An amusing account of our journey may be read in Dumas' book entitled "De Paris à Astrachan." On reaching St. Petersburgh I was honored by a most kind invitation to be received by the Emperor, but which I was obliged to decline not being in power at the time, and his Majesty most graciously sent to me to say that under any circumstances he would be pleased to see me. I excused myself on the ground of having so much to attend to previous to my marriage. A month after this, certain difficulties having arisen, and the papers which were necessary not being forthcoming, the marriage seemed on the point of being postponed. I had no manifestations for several months, but on this evening I was told by the spirit of my mother to inform the Emperor the next day that my power had returned. I did so, and was received by his Majesty at the Palace of Peterhoff, where I spent a week, and all the obstacles in the way of my marriage were removed by his most gracious Majesty, who upon this, as upon every occasion, has shown to me the greatest kindness. I have the highest veneration for him, not only as a monarch, but as a man of the most kind and generous feelings.

We were married on Sunday the 1st of August, 1858, or according to the old style, on the 20th of July, first in the private chapel at the country house of my brother-in-law, according to the rites of the Greek Church, and afterwards at the Church of St. Catherine, according to the rites of the Romish church. A short time after our marriage, my wife being in a sound quiet sleep, I saw the spirit of my mother come into the room, followed by one, who though I had never known him on earth, I knew to be my wife's father. My impression was one of relief that my wife was asleep, and thus that she would not see what I feared would frighten her. My surprise was therefore very great on hearing her say, "Daniel, there is some one in the room with us. It is your mother, and near her stands my father. She is very beautiful, and I am not afraid." Her actions, however, betrayed a certain shrinking, for she turned to the side of the bed where I lay, trembling violently. The spirits now disappeared, but loud rappings were heard in and about the room, and our questions were answered. This was my wife's first introduction to anything of the kind.

CHAPTER VIII.

RUSSIA, PARIS AND ENGLAND.

In two weeks after our marriage we left to visit some of my brother-in-law's estates, some of which were situate on the Crimean coast, and others in the interior of Russia. The journey lasted about six weeks, and we then returned to a country house of his in the neighborhood of Moscow. At the end of November, 1858, we were at St. Petersburgh, in the house of my brother-in-law, the Count Gregoire Koucheleff Besbo-rodko, from whom and the Countess I have ever met with the readiest sympathy and brotherly welcome, and to whom I owe, and ever shall owe, a debt of the deepest gratitude. Here from time to time my power returned, but generally only faintly. Still a great deal of good was done. As an instance, I may mention that a young officer, who having been convinced of the truths of immortality by what he saw in my presence, gave a supper to his friends, at which he publicly announced that in place of laughing at religion as he had done, he had seen in these phenomena what convinced him of the reality of a future life, and that thenceforward he should lead a different life.

In the middle of January, 1859, I fell ill with severe internal inflammation. This lasted some time, and was increasing to an alarming extent, and beyond the power of the physician who attended me, and the dangerous symptoms were greatly increased by my usual nervous debility. Friction was recommended, but the extreme pain which it caused precluded its use. I was in this state when one evening my wife and a friend, the Baron de M——, were present, and my hands were suddenly seized by spirit influence, and I was made to beat them with extreme violence upon the part which was so extremely sensitive and tender. My wife was frightened, and would have endeavored to hold my hands, but my friend who had had sufficient kmowledge of spirit manifestations prevented her. I felt no pain, though the violence of the blows which I continued giving to myself made the bed and the whole room shake. In five minutes' time the swelling had visibly decreased, and the movements of the hand began to be more gentle. In an hour I was in a quiet sleep, and on awaking the next morning I found the disease had left me, and only a weakness remained. The expression of the doctor's face baffles my description when he visited me early that morning, expecting to have found me worse, and felt my pulse and saw that a great change must have occurred beyond his skill to account for.

On the 26th April, old style, or 8th May, according to our style, at seven in the evening, and as the snow was fast falling, our little boy was born at the town house, situate on the Gagarines Quay, in St. Petersburgh, where we were still staying. A few hours after his birth, his mother, the nurse and I heard for several hours the warbling of a bird as if singing over him. Also that night, and for two or three nights afterwards, a bright star like light, which was clearly visible from the partial darkness of the room, in which there was only a night lamp burning, appeared several times directly over its head, where it remained for some moments, and then slowly moved in the direction of the door, where it disappeared. Tnis was also seen by each of us at the same time. The light was more condensed than those which have been so often seen in my presence upon previous and subsequent occasions. It was brighter and more distinctly globular. I do not believe that it came through my mediumship, but rather through that of the child, who has manifested on several occasions the presence of the gift. I do not like to allude to such a matter, but as there are more strange things in Heaven and earth than are dreamt of, even in my philosophy, I do not feel myself at liberty to omit stating, that during the latter part of my wife's pregnancy, we thought it better that she should not join in séances, because it was found that whenever the rappings occurred in the room, a simultaneous movement of the child was distinctly felt, perfectly in unison with the sounds. When there were three sounds, three movements were felt, and so on, and when five sounds were heard, which is generally the call for the alphabet, she felt the five internal movements, and she would frequently, when we were mistaken in the letter, correct us from what the child in dicated.

Our child was christened a fortnight after his birth,

his godfather being the Marquis de Châteaureynard, at present Minister of France at Hesse Cassel, and his godmother his aunt, the Countess Luba. His second godfather was his uncle, the Count Gregoire, and his second godmother was his relative Sophie.

A week after the christening, we went to the residence of the Count in the immediate environs of St. Petersburgh. Whilst here, there were many striking manifestations which were witnessed by many, who investigated as others had done before, and with the same results. One evening I remember, one of my friends was converted from his previous unbelief by seeing a female hand, which was visible to all of us in the room, slowly forming in the air a few inches above the table, until it assumed all the apparent materiality of a real hand. The hand took up a pencil which was on the table, and wrote with it a communication which deeply affected my friend, who recognised it as being from his mother. The general belief is, that the spirit hands always appear from beneath the table, and already formed, but this is incorrect, for on many occasions in the presence of several persons at a time, they are seen to be formed in full sight of all, in the manner I have just described, and to melt away, as it were, in the same way. Often, too, they have been seen to form themselves high above our heads, and from thence to descend upon the table, and then disappear.

The anniversary of our wedding-day found us on the steamer 'Baltic,' bound for Dunkerque, from whence we went to Ostend on a visit to my mother-in-law, who was there for her health. On seeing her, at the moment of our embracing one another, I had another of those singular impressions which so often come to me at the moment of external contact. It has seemed to me as if they were caused by the disturbing element of a physical substance which causes some secret chord of the soul to vibrate and awaken what I may call a memory of the Future, or that a flower of the spring-time has been shadowed forth among the chill blasts of autumn, as a token of the never ceasing care of God, our loving father, for His children whether in the Past, Present, or Future, all being alike known to Him. My sensations are so peculiar at the time when such foreshadowings are granted me, that words can but feebly express them. I distinctly saw at the first moment of touching my mother-in-law, that after I should leave Ostend, we should meet no more on earth. This impressional prediction did, as has ever been the case with those which have come to me in this way, prove correct.

We arrived in Paris in August 1859, and whilst there, I paid a short visit to a friend then in Switzerland, and there we had one or two sittings. On returning to Paris, a friend had kindly offered us the Château de C—, where we remained about two months, at the expiration of which time we came to England. This was in October. My power had left me for some weeks. One evening in November while I was absent, my wife being in the room with the child and his nurse, loud raps were heard upon the ceiling. They both supposed that the sound proceeded from some one walking overhead, when they changed their position, and were heard upon the wall of the room, and in a few moments they came on the table. My wife asked who was the medium upon the occasion, and the reply was given that it was the sleeping child. It was further said, that they had power to manifest through him, but that they would not, "as the atmosphere which they made use of was necessary for his physical development in the natural world." From this time we have but once had any external evidence of any spirit presence through him, though he has given us many indications of his being a seer.

In the latter part of November we were in England, and the power returned, and I began to hold séances as usual, and continued to do so until the 24th of July in the following year. During this time, the manifestations were seen and investigated by persons of all ranks and classes, from statesmen down to those in humble life, and to them again I would rather refer for the accounts of what they witnessed, than to give my own descriptions. I select, therefore, portions of their writings, a few of which have already been published in "The Spiritual Magazine" and other Journals, and the others now appear for the first time. These will give the reader an idea of the nature and extent of my mediumship during this period.

The subjoined is a portion of a letter from Mr. Pears, who was accompanied by my friends Mr. and Mrs. Cox. He now saw the manifestations for the first time. "Almost immediately the table tilted towards Mr. Home, who, raising his hands from the table, which still retained its inclined position, invited me to look under it, to see that no material means were used to produce this result. I did look, and saw none. On resuming my seat, the table returned to its position, and then it passed into an undulatory movement, as if it were in motion on waves; it seemed, indeed, almost as if the top of the table were flexible: then from this movement it passed into a directly horizontal state, so that a vessel filled to the brim, would not, I think, have spilled a drop, and it rose from eighteen to twenty-four inches clear from the floor, all hands at the same time continuing on the top of the table; and finally with perfect evenness it gradually descending to its place.

"Raps were then heard on the table, in the vicinity of Mrs. Cox, which, by reference to the alphabet, purported to be produced by a deceased child of hers. Then faint deliberate raps came near to Mrs. P., purporting—by the same mode—to come from Phœbe, our deceased little daughter to whom I referred before.

"Raps were then heard under my own hands, and at the same time the depending cloth covering the table seemed to be moved up by something under it, and was made thus to strike against my wrist. I called my wife's attention to this, and she confirmed the fact that it really did seem as if some one's hand was under the cloth trying to touch my wrist. I said, half laughing, which you might expect from my scepticism, that I should not wonder if there were not some one for me also. Immediately there were raps under the same hand, strong enough to shake the table.

"Perhaps I looked dubiously at a phenomenon so unexpected, for Mr. Home said, 'I should like Mr. Pears to be convinced that we do not make these sounds; perhaps he would get under the table and observe.' I did so; and while I saw that they were not produced by any visible agency beneath, they were sounding as vigorously as ever; Mrs. P. being witness to their not being produced by the hands, or any other visible means above board.

"When I found that the raps under my hand purported to come from my grandfather's 'spirits,' I asked if he could take the large bell from me if I held it. It had already been taken out of Mr. Home's hand and rung under the table. The response to my question was given by strong knocks. I held it under the table, being careful to hold it in the direction of my wife, whose hands were on the table, and I felt it tugged with strength out of my hand; it was rung, and then deposited on the floor.

"Many little things which struck me at the time, occurred during our séance, which lasted between two and three hours. But there was one part of the séance which forcibly struck me, and which I must relate. Mr. Home, soon after I had assumed the presence of my grandfather's spirit, passed into a singular state—half unconscious as it were—and said, 'Here's a tall, old, upright, Quaker like man, yet not a Quaker;' then he seemed to take on the manner and gesture, as closely as a young man can, of those of an old one—held out his hand to me, and grasped it in a way that further reminded me of my grandfather, and addressed me in words somewhat characteristic of him, and went on to speak of one whom he had held very dear, but from whom he had been long separated to his great grief, but that they had happily met in the other world and were reconciled. All upon this point was said in a broken way, but with gestures and allusions which were intelligible solely to myself, as the person and events so alluded to touched closely upon my grandfather's history in conjunction with my own. My astonishment was increased when, from Mr. H.'s lips, fell the name of her to whom the allusion had been made—my grandfather's daughter! both dead when Mr. Home must have been a boy in America! Long as I have known you, friend Dixon, I think I never told you that my grandfather was of a Quaker family, which was the case.

"I was by this incident astonished beyond expression, and acknowledged to Mr. Cox that the history which had been sketched, and the reflections upon it, were just what I should have expected might have been made by my grandfather.

"I have not yet found a place in my system for these phenomena, but that they are genuine phenomena is settled in my mind."

Another account is given by Mr. J. G. Crawford, a gentleman who had for years resisted all belief in such phenomena as being impossible and absurd. It happened that a friend of his from Liverpool was coming to meet me at the house of Mr. Coleman, in Bayswater, and he induced him to accompany him. He shall tell the story in his own frank and truthful words:

"Mr. Home laid his left hand on the table and with his right lifted an accordeon, which he held under the table. My friend and I were asked to look below, when we distinctly saw it move up and down, apparently held and touched by one hand only.

"We continued to sit round the table. The room was made so dark that we could not see each other. The table gave a violent stamp upon the floor; still we kept our hands upon it. Then it rose in a mass twelve or fifteen inches quite off the floor, so far as I could judge.

"Mr. Home now said that he held the accordeon under the table by one hand only, when it played our beautiful English tune, 'Home, sweet Home!' in a most finished style.

"Shortly after this occurred, a very curious affair took place, in explanation of which I cannot hazard a conjecture. Mr. Home remarked, 'I feel as if I am going to rise.' The room was quite dark. He said, 'I am getting up,' and as I was only a few feet from him, I put out my hand to him; I indubitably felt the soles of both his boots, some three feet above the level of the floor. On my doing so, he said, 'Don't touch me, or I shall come down;' of course I instantly desisted, but down he came. In less than five minutes after this, he remarked, 'I am again ascending,' and from the sound of his voice, we could not but infer that he was actually rising towards the ceiling of the anteroom.

"He then appeared to float under the archway, then to rise to the cornice of the room we were sitting in, and we heard him quite distinctly make three cross marks on the ceiling, besides doing some other writing. Then he came softly down, and lay stretched out with his back upon the table, in which position we found him when the gas was lighted, and when we distinctly saw the marks on the ceiling, which we had heard him make.

"I am well aware there is a ready answer by many well-disposed persons to what I have written—that it is all done by collusion and trick. In many countries at the present time, and in our own not a century back, all phenomena of a then *extra*-ordinary kind, were quickly put down to the account of the devil. He prompted Galileo to the adopted system of astronomy; Harvey to the circulation of the blood; he was the cause of witchcraft in Scotland, and had much to do with the wonders of chemistry, before it attained its present scientific certainty and value to the arts and agriculture. But the testimony of thousands of excellent witnesses cannot be set aside by any such plea. Not many years ago it was fashionable to deny the facts and uses of chloroform, homœopathy, hydropathy, magnetism, mesmerism, &c.; now the curative powers of these agents are commonly received amongst us as 'household words.' There appears to be a law of progressive development in the universe. Should the supposed facts of Spiritualism be found to be real, after oft-repeated experiments, we cannot doubt but they also will have a permanent place with recent discoveries. No one, now-a-days, who thinks at all, can be so bold and unwise as to deny that 'there are more things in heaven and earth than are dreamt of in our philosophy.'

"In the simple statement I have given of what my friend and I were satisfied occurred on the evening of our visit to —— Villas, I have avoided coloring the events, and for the sake of greater definiteness, have given figures of sizes, which, however, must be taken merely as a near approximation to the actual measurements.

"J. G. CRAWFORD."

Mr. Crawford mentions the circumstance of my immediately coming to the ground again on his touching my feet. I have observed that this is invariably the case when I am touched, or even anxiously gazed at, until I have risen above the heads of those who are in the room; but after I have attained that height, their looking at me, or touching me, has no effect upon me. What the cause may be I cannot explain, but it may perhaps be some break in the magnetism which is caused in the former case, and which does not occur in the latter.

On the 3d of April, 1860, I had been with some friends to a lecture given in St. John's Wood, by M. Louis Blanc, "On the Mysterious Persons and Agencies in France towards the end of the eighteenth century." His lecture was a good deal occupied with Cagliostro, and during the time he was speaking, I had the strongest impression of the presence of Cagliostro, and the lady who was sitting next me, was also aware of some strong spirit presence by having her dress pulled, and by other manifestations.

On returning home, I found that my wife had retired earlier than usual in consequence of a severe headache. In the course of conversation together, she having asked how I had liked the lecture, I said, "I have been haunted all the evening by Cagliostro," on which she exclaimed, "Pray do not use that word haunted, it sounds so weird-like, and quite frightens me." I had by this time extinguished the light, and was now in bed, when to my amazement the room became as light as if the sun had for an instant shone fully in at the window. Thinking that this effect might have been only on my spiritual perception, I said, "Sacha, did you see anything?" Her reply was, "No, nor could I, for my face was quite buried in my pillow, the pain is so intense." I asked her to observe, and I then mentally asked that if the light had been external, it might be reproduced. Almost simultaneously with the thought, came the light again, so distinct, and with such brilliancy, that no noon-day was ever brighter. My wife asked if this was the spirit of Cagliostro, and the affirmative reply was instantly given by three flashes of light, so vivid as almost to be blinding and painful to the sight. Answers were given to various questions in the same wonderful manner, and then in answer to a question asked, came a musical tinkle, as if a silver bell had been touched directly over our heads. In this way our farther answers were now given, and we then heard a footstep on the floor, falling so gently as if it feared to disturb us by its approach. My wife asked that it should come nearer, and it approached us till we felt a form leaning over the bed. In doing this, it pressed upon the bed-clothes just as an actual material presence would have done. We asked him if he had been a medium when on earth, and a distinct voice, audible to both of us, said in answer, "My power was that of a mesmerist, but all-misunderstood by those about me, my biographers have done me injustice, but I care not for the untruths of the earth." Both my wife and myself were by this time so impressed by such startling and almost terribly real evidence of the presence of one who was in no way related to us, that for a few moments all power of utterance seemed to have left us. We were, however, soon recalled to ourselves by a hand being placed on our heads, and she, seizing my hands in hers, held them up, saying, "Dear spirit, will you be one of my guardian angels—watch over me with my father, teach me what you would have me do, and make me thankful to God for all his mercies?" Our hands were clasped by a hand, and her left hand was gently separated from mine, and a ring, which was the signet-ring of my father-in-law, was placed on her third finger. This ring was previously in the room, but at a distance of at least twelve feet from where the bed stood. "Good night, dear ones, and God bless you," was then audibly spoken, and simultaneously with the sound came three wafts of perfume, so delicious that we both exclaimed, "How truly wonderful!"

Her headache was perfectly cured, and although our nerves had been greatly agitated, we slept soundly. The following day, and indeed for several days afterwards, my wife had occasional proofs of the presence of this spirit, and he remained with her up to the time of her passing from earth, and during the last months of our stay in England she frequently saw him.

About the middle of May, 1860, my mother-in-law wrote to us from St. Petersburgh, as follows:—

"Dear children,—You may not be aware that to-morrow I am to undergo a surgical operation. I have seen my confessor; I have taken the sacrament, and I now feel quite happy. Do not be alarmed, but do as I do—trust in God."

On the morning of Monday, the 29th May, my wife being then engaged at a bazaar held at the Crystal Palace, Sydenham, I proposed to visit with a friend the establishment of Messrs. Barclay and Perkins. We drove there, and had gone over nearly all the establishment, when in the barrelling-room one of the workmen proposed our tasting the porter. My friend was tasting it, and the attendant brought me a pot. I put out my hand to take it, and as my fingers came in contact with the metal, a deep shudder convulsed my frame, and I suddenly knew that my dear mother-in-law, who had been for many years a patient sufferer, had been released from her earthly troubles. I refused the porter, and requested my friend to accompany me home. In an hour's time I was calm, and I reasoned with myself how I could best conceal the painful intelligence from my wife That evening at a séance she asked how her mother was. The reply given was, "It is well with her now." All present but herself understood well to what this alluded, and a friend on my left did all she could to conceal her tears.

On the Thursday afterwards I heard my wife running up to my room. As she opened the door, and before she had time to speak, and indeed before I had seen her, I said, "Why, Sacha, I knew it last Monday." She came to my bedside, and gave me a letter addressed to me from my sister-in-law, containing a telegraphic dispatch, announcing that my mother-in-law had passed from earth on the Monday, and this letter my wife had opened. Two nights after this, at a séance where the Count T—— and an atheist friend of his were present, her dear spirit came, and her hands were made visible, resting on her daughter's head, and afterwards on mine. She wrote in her own peculiar handwriting, "You will love her always, won't you?" and she signed it "Nathalie." He who came an atheist, was one no longer.

I take the following account of some new manifestations from the "Spiritual Magazine." It is called "Two Evenings with Mr. Home," and is introduced by the editor who says:

"We have received from two correspondents, well known to us, the following account of manifestations on the evening of the 1st and 9th of May last, each evening in the presence of nine persons whose names have been furnished to us, and which we are permitted to supply privately to any inquirer who feels that the knowledge of the names is necessary for his belief. In the meantime we can vouch publicly for the perfect confidence which the narrative inspires us with, having heard the whole account from the lips of the narrators, previous to receiving the MS. from them.

"May 1st, 1860.

"The party was composed of Mr. and Mrs. Home and seven other ladies and gentlemen. We sat at the round table in the large drawing-room. Mr. Home's hand was moved to write—'The spirit of John is one who was kind to your father during the voyage to America.' No one understood this; but Mr. —— entering the room a minute afterwards, expressed his conviction that it was intended for him, as his father had been to America. Three loud raps gave assent to what he said. The table then moved away from us, and we inquired if they wished us to draw it to the window. It was answered 'Yes.' We accordingly did so, leaving a vacant space against the window, unclosing the shutters, and by their directions extinguishing the candles. The fire burned brightly. It was spelled out, 'There is a little too much light.' Mr. —— and —— screened the fire as much as possible, and the moon and gaslight from the street then alone lighted up the table; but did so completely, as the moon was very bright. The spirit of Albert then took the accordeon, and played a beautiful air of unearthly harmony. Mr. Home and I held the accordeon together under the table, for the power was very strong, and the music loud—and the instrument at times was nearly carried away from us.

"After a short time there rose slowly in the space made by the window a most lovely hand of a female—we saw also part of the beautiful arm as it held it up aloft for some time—we were all greatly amazed.—This hand was so transparent and luminous, and so unearthly and angelic, that our hearts were filled with gratitude towards the Creator for permitting so wonderful a manifestation. The hand was visible to us more from the internal light which seemed to stream as it were out of it, than from the external light of the moon. As soon as it slowly vanished, Mdlle. ——, who sat next to the open space, saw another hand forming itself close to her; and a man's hand was raised and placed on the table, far more earthly and life-like in appearance, and one that I thought I recognized—(we were subsequently told that I was right in conjecture.) Then came a dear baby hand; then the baby (Mrs. L——'s adopted child) showed its head; and finally, spirit-hands held up the little child, so that all nine of us saw her shoulders and waist. After this, a hand and arm rose luminous and beautiful, covered with a white transparent drapery; and this hand remained visible to us all for at least five minutes, and made us courteous and graceful gestures.

"Then spirit-hands held up to us an exquisite wreath of white flowers. I never saw any wreath made by human hands so perfect in form and design; and calling for the alphabet said, 'The spirit emblem of William's mother.' Then we were told they would show us 'The emblem of superstition;' and a black, shrivelled hand arose. On some of us remarking that we could not see it well, the curtains were at once moved aside, and the blind drawn away from the top of the window. It was beyond the reach of any of us, and they then showed us the hand again, so that we all could see it. The 'emblem of truth' was then shown. This was more beautiful than all the rest—a fairy-like fountain of apparently clear sparkling water, which threw up showers of silvery rays, vanishing from our sight like mist, and dwelling on the memory as perfection. After this it was rapped out, 'We can do no more.'

"Mr. Home was put into a trance, and as he fell back in his chair a gleam of the most vivid light fell upon me. This light fell over my shoulders, and gleamed on my right hand, and came from a direction whence no earthly light could have come. It came from a part of the room where the spirit of one who was a friend of mine when on earth has often stood before, and from whence he has communicated to us. This light was seen by no one but myself; but as I turned round in hope of seeing the spirit, Mr. Home said to me, 'Yes, he is there;' and added a communication from him. He then told us that the first hand that we saw had been that of his own mother; the second was my father's, as I had silently expected; and the hand and arm in drapery that remained so long, came for Prudence, and was the same that she had seen one night when alone, several years ago, at Paris, before she had ever heard of spirit manifestations. He also gave us the full name of the 'spirit John,' who had gone to America with Mr. A——'s father; and added some private information which Mr. A—— confirmed as true.

"The events of this evening having been so wonderful, I have begged my friends present on the occasion to read over this account, and to sign it as witnesses to the truth of what I have stated."

"May 9th, 1860.

"Mingling with those interested in witnessing evidences of spirit power, I gladly accepted an invitation to meet a few friends on Monday the 9th of May, 1860, at a house at the West end. At a quarter after eight o'clock, we went into the adjoining back drawing-room, and sat down to a loo table. There were nine of us, Mr. Home being one of the number. Immediately the table commenced vibrating and gently lifting itself off the floor. I say lifting *itself*, because no human beings in human clay were the actors. Nothing occurred for a few minutes, during which conversation was kept up, and then the table gradually rose up off the floor about four feet, or rather more than a foot beyond our outstretched arms, the hands of which had rested gently on the table before its ascent. It then descended. Mr. Home took the accordeon in his right hand, by the rim at the bottom of the instrument, leaving his left hand on the table, and then were played some beautiful voluntaries, exquisitely attenuated, yet clear and melodious. They then came out gradually fuller, and yet more full, till the room seemed filled with the volume of sound like a pealing organ, and still no false note. A friend, sitting next to me, forgetting himself, exclaimed, 'My God, how wonderful!' and after a breath, asked 'if they would give us some air we knew?' and having asked for 'God save the Queen,' it was played at once.

"A lady present, whose little boy had recently died, had indications of her son being in the room; and the accordeon suddenly commenced playing a well known air, which on earth the little boy was very fond of, as tallying with his mamma's name. Reader, was not there a truth of *life* and of *love* in the incident? The mother thought so, and her tears betrayed her thoughts.

"The detonations on the table, and sometimes under

my hands, were as sharp, and as clear, and as loud, as if struck vigorously with the edge of a penny-piece.

"It was then rapped out by the sounds—'Go to the window.' We rose, and moved the loo table to about eighteen inches from the window. We sat down again, but more closely, so as to allow a vacant space at the side of the table, opposite the window. The sounds then gave out, 'Put out the lights,' which was done. We found that though the room was dark, yet the light from the window was sufficient for us to faintly see each other. The window-blind then commenced moving up and down—no one near it—evidently to tone the light; and while we were remarking the singularity of the phenomenon, and how high it went, all looking at it—suddenly it sprung up to the top, and then came gently down to its original position. Mr. Home felt something on his head, and found it was a leaf. Suddenly the leaf of a geranium was taken and dropped into the lap of a lady sitting at the table. We heard the snap as if breaking off the stem of a flower, and immediately came down past the ear of my friend, and on his knee, a sprig of geranium; while he held it up for us to see, I expressed a wish to have one, when a sprig came past my right ear on to my knee. I picked it up, and while showing it, another came past my face as if from the ceiling. The geranium plant was in the room several feet from any of us, and the sprigs came down both on the right and left of me.

"After a pause, Mr. Home said he felt as if he were about to be lifted up; he moved from the table, and shortly he said, 'I am rising'—but we could not see him—'they have put me on my back.' I asked, will you kindly bring him, as much as possible, towards the window, so that we may see him; and at once he was floated with his feet horizontally into the light of the window, so that we all saw his feet and a part of his legs resting or floating on the air like a feather, about six feet from the ground, and three feet above the height of the table. He was then floated into the dark; and he exclaimed: 'They have turned me round, and I am coming towards you.' I saw his head and face, the same height as before, and as if floating on air instead of water. He then floated back, and came down and walked up to, and sat on the edge of the table we were at, when the table began to rise with him on it. Mr. Home was then taken behind to the settee next to me, and while there, we heard sounds several times as of some one giving utterance to a monosyllable in the middle of the room. Feeling a pressure against my chair, I looked, and saw that the ottoman had been brought along the floor about six feet, no one touching it, and close to Mr. Home. He said, 'I suppose it is for me to rest on,'—he lay down, and the ottoman went back to its original position—'Oh! I am getting excited, let some one come and sit with me.' I went, and sat beside him; he took my hand; and in about a minute, and without any muscular action, he gently floated away from me, and was lost in the darkness. He kept talking to let us know where he was. We heard his voice in various parts of the further end of the room, as if near the ceiling. He then cried out, 'Oh! they have brought me a cushion to sit upon—I am sitting on it—they are taking it away.' Just then the tassel of the cushion of another ottoman in the room struck me on my hair and forehead as if coming from the ceiling, and the cushion was deposited at my feet on the floor, falling as if a snow flake. I next saw the shadow of his body on the mirror as he floated along near the ceiling. He said, 'I wish I had a pencil to make a mark on the ceiling. I have made a cross with my nail.' He came down near the door, and after a pause, he was again taken up; but I did not see him, but heard his voice as if near the ceiling. Again he came down, and shortly returned to the table we were at; and the sounds on the table bid us 'Good night.'"

This is an account of "Another evening with Mr. Home." It it given us in the words of the lady at whose house the manifestations occurred. I have not, for good reasons, the liberty to give her name, but I can answer for her position and character, and for the truthfulness of the narrative. I have, in addition, the names of the nine persons who were present.

"*May the 3rd*, 1860.—The table was moved away from the remaining seven of us, and we followed it; suddenly it rose in the air, and without any help from us was placed on a large sofa that stood before the window. The spirits told us to move this sofa away which we immediately did, and the table then moved of its own accord up to the window where the hands had appeared to us on former occasions. The shutters were opened and the candles extinguished by their desire. Mr. Home sat next to the window, and I sat next to him with Mrs. H. on my other side. After sitting a few minutes quietly I felt a form glide behind me: it touched my chair, placed two hands on my shoulders, and then drew the heavy silk curtain from a window behind me (we sat in a bow formed by three windows) and folded the drapery round me like a cloak. The hands and arms which enfolded me felt as palpable as human arms would feel. On one of the party guessing the name of the spirit, it was answered by three startling raps, which shook the table, and felt as if produced by a bar of iron—no human hand could have knocked with such force. As I was intently listening to catch any sound, and straining my eyes to see any form that could make itself visible, my comb was taken out of my hair by a spirit hand, and laid on a table at a distance from me. By tiny gentle raps my darling spirit child told me that he had taken it. Then a hand rose under the window, and pulled down the blind. We distinctly saw the fingers clutch the string — this is a green transparent blind, through which the light can fall softly. The hand then made graceful gestures and pointed upwards, and when it disappeared, it was followed by another, and then by a child's hand. Suddenly I was touched on the shoulder, as if by some one standing behind me and wishing to draw my attention. I thought it was my daughter, and turned to speak to her, but I found no one. I had hardly turned round, when my left shoulder was more strongly touched, and on turning my head a spirit hand held out to me a box taken from a table at the other end of the room. I received it with emotion, and as a precious gift; and the sweet hand that gave it was placed on my shoulder with a loving pressure. The spirit of A— G— then showed his hand, touched his sister with it, and played on the accordeon, which by degrees was moved up in Mr. Home's hand over his head, the knocks at the same time beating measure, like a drum, very loudly on the table. The accordeon was finally taken entirely away by the spirits, who played on it at a distance from us, the drumming continuing all the time on the table, whilst another drum accompanied it from the other side of the room. As soon as this ceased the table rose up in the air, and floated away from us high above our heads, passing over sofas and chairs in its way. We were naturally greatly interested at this wonderful manifestation, and followed it into the darker part of the room, and here arose a scene of indescribable confusion, but still producing feelings in no way unpleasant, though we knew not when we touched each other, who were spirits, and who were fleshy human beings. The four cushions of the ottoman were virtually hurled in the air at once, and flew to the other side of the room. In answer to a remark made, a hand came down on my head, as from a spirit floating above me, and pressed my forehead and stroked my hair. As we gathered round the table nine or ten chairs flew up like lightning, one behind each of us; the chair next to me was empty (to the sight,) but when I tried to move it I could not do so, it appeared as if nailed to the ground, and by raps we were told that L— sat there. The united strength of several could not move this chair. The heavy sofa on which G— sat was moved suddenly to the other end of the room, and the spirit of her brother placed his hand in her's, and held it for several minutes. Before leaving her he gave a most touching manifestation He blessed her by making the sign of the cross on her forehead. During these manifestations almost every article of furniture in the room was moved out of its place."

My dearly valued friend, Mr. Wason, who, after twenty-nine years of outer scepticism, takes pride in dating his new birth to the belief of a spiritual life and a spiritual philosophy, from his observations of the phenomena which he witnessed in my presence, wrote at this time the interesting letter which I now give.

"In July, 1860, I was at a séance at the mansion of a person of distinction, in Hyde Park Terrace, London.

"Two baronets—one an M.P., and the other the heir and representative of a deceased M.P. of eminent ability; the wife of a distinguished living M.P.; and others, including Mr. Home, making eight in number present. The hour was a little after nine, P.M. Neither of the three first-named parties had ever seen any spirit manifestations, and were evidently sceptics: the rest of the party were mediums of greater or lesser power, and seemed as much interested in watching the effects of the spirit manifestations on the three new comers, as in the manifestations themselves. We all made a circle round a heavy loo table, capable of seating nine persons comfortably (crinoline included). It was covered with an ordinary damask cloth, (a powerful non-conductor of electricity, completely negativing the theory that spirit manifestations were brought about by electricity); and we were desired by Mr

Home to chat and talk as naturally and cheerfully as we could, and not to be too eager or expectant of spirit manifestation, which he stated had a strong tendency to defeat the object. There were six lights burning in the room. The floor (a first floor) shook and trembled in a manner that all thought resembled the vibrations and movement on a small steamer's deck when the paddles are in full work: some said it nearly resembled the tremulous motion on a *screw* steamer's deck, in which I concurred. This tremulous motion ceased at intervals and was renewed, and this seemed to strike the new comers very forcibly; it was amusing to notice their startled looks, though they said little beyond concurring in the observations as to the tremulous movements. The walls also shook at times with a tremulous motion. The table, which was a very large and heavy one, was frequently lifted a few inches from the ground, and at last it rose from the ground at least three feet, and remained thus suspended 'twixt heaven and earth, like Mahomet's coffin, for a minute or thereabouts, probably more than less. The gentlemen were invited by Mr. Home to ascertain if any machinery was underneath, and the two gentlemen who were new comers swept with their legs under the suspended table, to catch any prop or other machinery that might be applied to raise the table, and they confessed that no such machinery or prop was present.

"This séance, wonderful as it will appear—'stranger than fiction'—was not considered to be an entirely successful one; and the lady of the house, with characteristic kindness, after speaking of the meagreness of the manifestations, invited me to another séance on the following evening, an invitation I most gladly accepted, although it kept me in London an extra day, and overthrew my previously arranged movements. At this second séance we met rather earlier, a little after eight o'clock p.m., in the same first-floor room. The séance consisted of a barrister of eminence and standing at the bar, and well known to the public, a literary man—an author of established reputation, and others to the number of eight—all on this occasion being believers, except the author.

"The same tremulous motion of the floor and walls as on the preceding evening, took place; and the table was tilted and turned with even greater power than before, and rose perpendicularly from the floor, from three to four feet, and remained in this position suspended (Mahomet's coffin fashion) for about a minute, and then descended to its original place as softly and gently as the fall of a snow-flake. An accordeon was played by an unseen hand, whilst it was held by one of the party present, and afterwards by myself. I held it over the back of the chair on which I was sitting, using the back of the chair as a rest to my arm, the accordeon hanging over the back of the chair. I sat on the opposite side of the table to Mr. Home and the lady of the house. The accordeon was also played whilst lying on the floor, and also on the table, and was lifted without visible means from the floor on to the table. The music was of a solemn and impressive character.

"A small spirit-hand, warm and soft like that of a child, touched my hand, and placed in it a small hand-bell, and, at my request, took the bell from my hand underneath the table to its mother, who was the lady of the house. She seemed perfectly satisfied that it was the spirit-hand of her little boy, who died three or four years since, aged about eight years, and she received repeated responses, spelt out through the alphabet, such as might be expected from the spirit of a deceased child to its mother.

"The bell was carried to several of the parties present and placed in their hands; and lastly, was elevated above our heads, and rung in mid-air, revolving round and touching our heads (my own included). I could see the bell when it passed round my head opposite the window. I could see the bell occasionally as it passed between me and the window, the blinds of which had been drawn down by invisible agency. Pieces of mignionette and geranium flowers were placed in my hands by spirit hands, and inside my waistcoat. I saw one of the hands distinctly, which, as it came between me and the window, was distinctly visible, as the blinds did not altogether exclude the light of a summer evening and of the gas lights in the street.

"The curtains at last were drawn by invisible means, and then Mr. Home stated he was being lifted up in the air, and he crossed the table over the heads of the parties sitting around it. I asked him to make a mark with his pencil on the ceiling. He said he had no pencil. I rose up and said I would lend him mine, and by standing and stretching upwards I was enabled to reach his hand, about seven feet distant from the floor, and I placed therein a pencil, and laying hold and keeping hold of his hand, I moved along with him five or six paces as he floated above me in the air, and I only let go his hand when I stumbled against a stool. Mr. Home, as he floated along, kept ringing the small hand-bell to indicate his locality in the room, which was probably forty by thirty feet, and I saw his body eclipse two lines of light issuing from between the top of a door and its architrave—such door leading into an adjoining room that was brilliantly lighted. Mr. Home was replaced, as he stated, with the greatest care and gentleness in the chair from which he rose, but this I could not see.

"Previously to Mr. Home's being raised up, the spirit-hands of two of the barrister's deceased children touched him. He did not doubt that the hands were the spirit-hands of his children.

"Questions were asked, and rational answers given by means of the alphabet, in one of the ordinary ways of communicating with spirits. It is right that I should say, that this séance (as in the preceding evening) was commenced with prayer, which I understood was the usual course.

"I make no comments on the above, and advance no theory or hypothesis. I have confined myself simply to facts, which I can substantiate by legal evidence in a court of justice; and I add my name, address, and profession, and have only one desire, and that is—that truth may prevail.

"I am, sir, your obedient servant,

"James Wason, Solicitor.

"Wason Buildings, Liverpool."

CHAPTER IX.

THE "CORNHILL" AND OTHER NARRATIVES.

IT was at this time that the manifestations occurred which are described with such accuracy and intelligence by the eminent literary friend who wrote his account of what he saw in the "Cornhill Magazine," under the title of "Stranger than Fiction." This paper travels over nearly the whole ground of the physical manifestations, and is written with such masterly observation, and ability of description, that I feel it will be a boon to the reader to have some few extracts from it. He commences by quoting:

"The reply of Dr. Treviranus to inquiries put to him by Coleridge as to the reality of certain magnetic phenomena which that distinguished savant was reported to have witnessed. 'I have seen what I would not have believed on your testimony, and what I cannot, therefore, expect you to believe upon mine.'"

For the information of Professor Faraday and other such persons who believe in his foolish theory of involuntary muscular motion as being the cause of the phenomena, he says: "While we were seated at the table, we barely touched it with the tips of our fingers. I was anxious to satisfy myself with respect to the involuntary pressure which has been attributed to the imposition of hands. In this case there was none. My friends kindly gratified my request to avoid resting the slightest weight on the table; and we held our hands pointing downwards, with merely the nails touching the wood. Not only was this light contact inadequate to produce the violent evolutions that took place, but the evolutions were so irregular and perplexing, that we could not have produced them by premeditation. Presently, however, we had conclusive proofs that the vivacity of the table did not require any help from us.

"Turning suddenly over on one side, it sunk to the floor. In this horizontal position it glided slowly towards a table which stood close to a large ottoman in the centre of the room. We had much trouble in following it, the apartment being crowded with furniture, and our difficulty was considerably increased by being obliged to keep up with it in a stooping attitude. Part of the journey it performed alone, and we were never able to reach it at any time together. Using the leg of the large table as a fulcrum, it directed its claws towards the ottoman, which it attempted to ascend, by inserting one claw in the side, then turning half way round to make good another step, and so on. It slipped down at the first attempt, but again quietly resumed its task. It was exactly like a child trying to climb up a height. All this time we hardly touched it, being afraid of interfering with its movements, and, above all things, determined not to assist them. At last, by careful and persevering efforts, it accom plished the top of the ottoman, and stood on the summit of the column in the centre, from whence in a few minutes it descended to the floor by a similar process."

The writer makes the following pertinent reflection on what he has just described. "It is not to be expected that any person who is a stranger to these phenomena, should read such a story as this with complacency. Yet here is a fact which undoubtedly took place, and which cannot be referred to any known physical or mechanical forces. It is not a satisfactory answer to those who have seen such things, to say that they are impossible: *since, in such cases, it is evident that the impossibility of a thing does not prevent it happening.*

Upon many subsequent occasions the writer says that he has witnessed phenomena of a similar nature, and others of a much more startling character. He tells us, for instance, "When I saw a table, at which two ladies were seated, moving towards me without any adequate impulse being imparted to it by visible means, I thought the fact sufficiently extraordinary; but my wonder abated when, on subsequent occasions, I saw tables move apparently of their own volition, there being no persons near them; large sofas advance from the walls against which they stood; and chairs, sometimes occupied, and sometimes empty, shift their places for the distance of a foot or a yard, in some cases easily, and in others with a slow, laborious movement."

As to the peculiar trembling of the table and room, he says, "On the first occasion when I experienced the effect I am about to describe, there were five persons in the room. In other places, where it occurred subsequently, there were seven or more. The architecture of the houses in each case was wholly dissimilar, both as to the area and height of the apartments, and the age, size, and strength of the buildings. We were seated at a table at which some singular phenomena, accompanied by loud knocks on the walls and floor, had just occurred, when we became conscious of a strange vibration that palpitated through the room. We listened and watched attentively. The vibration grew stronger and stronger. It was palpably under our feet. Our chairs shook, and the floor trembled violently. The effect was exactly like the throbbing and heaving which might be supposed to take place in a house in the tropics during the moment immediately preceding an earthquake. This violent motion continued for two or three minutes, then gradually subsided and ceased. Every person present was equally affected by it on each occasion when it occurred. To produce such a result by machinery might be possible if the introduction of the machinery itself were possible. But the supposition involves a difficulty somewhat similar to that of Mr. Knickerbocker's theory of the earth standing on the back of a tortoise, which might be an excellent theory if we could only ascertain what the tortoise stood upon."

He now speaks of the raising of the table altogether from the floor, which he repeatedly witnessed. "Presently the table rises with a slight jerk, and steadily mounts till it attains such a height as to render it necessary for the company to stand up, in order still to be able to keep their hands with ease in contact with the surface, although that is not absolutely necessary. As there are some present who have not witnessed this movement before, a desire is expressed to examine the floor, and a gentleman goes under the table for the purpose. The whole space, open to the view of the entire party, is clear. From the carpet to the foot of the table there is a blank interval of perhaps two feet, perhaps three,—for nobody has thought of providing a means of measuring it, and we must take it by guess. The carpet is examined, and the legs and under surface of the table are explored, but without result. There is no trace of any connection between the floor and the table; nor can it be conceived how there could be any, as the table had shifted to this spot from the place where it originally stood a few minutes before. The inspection is hurried and brief, but comprehensive enough to satisfy us that the table has not been raised by mechanical means from below; and such means could not be applied from above without the means of immediate detection. In its ascent, the table has swung out of its orbit, but it readjusts itself before it begins to descend, and, resuming its vertical position, it comes down on the spot from whence it rose. The downward motion is slow, and, if I may use the expression, graceful; and the table reaches the ground with a dreamy softness that renders its touch almost imperceptible.

"Of a somewhat similar character is another movement, in some respects more curious, and certainly opening a stranger field for speculation. The table rears itself up on one side, until the surface forms an inclined plane, at an angle of about 45°. In this attitude it stops. According to ordinary experience everything on the table must slide off, or topple over; but nothing stirs. The vase of flowers, the books, the little ornaments are as motionless as if they were fixed in their places. We agree to take away our hands, to throw up the ends of the cover, so as to leave the entire round pillar and claws exposed, and to remove our chairs to a little distance, that we may have a more complete command of a phenomenon, which, in its marvellous development at least, is, I believe, new to us all. Our withdrawal makes no difference whatever; and now we see distinctly on all sides the precise pose of the table, which looks, like the Tower of Pisa, as if it must inevitably tumble over. With a view to urge the investigation as far as it can be carried, a wish is whispered for a still more conclusive display of the power by which this extraordinary result has been accomplished. The desire is at one complied with. The table leans more and more out of the perpendicular; two of the three claws are high above the ground; and finally, the whole structure stands on the extreme tip of a single claw, fearfully overbalanced, but maintaining itself as steadily as if it were all one solid mass, instead of being freighted with a number of loose articles, and as if the position had been planned in strict accordance with the laws of equilibrium and attraction, instead of involving an inexplicable violation of both."

Of the music from an accordeon playing by itself on the floor, he says :—"Apart from the wonderful consideration of its being played without hands—no less wonderful was the fact of its being played in a narrow space which would not admit of its being drawn out with the requisite freedom to its full extent. We listened with suspended breath. The air was wild, and full of strange transitions; with a wail of the most pathetic sweetness running through it. The execution was no less remarkable for its delicacy than its power. When the notes swelled in some of the bold passages, the sound rolled through the room with an astounding reverberation; then, gently subsiding, sank into a strain of divine tenderness. But it was the close that touched the hearts, and drew the tears of the listeners. Milton dreamt of this wondrous termination when he wrote of 'linkèd sweetness long drawn out.' By what art the accordeon was made to yield that dying note, let practical musicians determine. Our ears, that heard it, had never before been visited by a 'sound so fine.' It continued diminishing and diminishing, and stretching far away into distance and darkness, until the attenuated thread of sound became so exquisite that it was impossible at last to fix the moment when it ceased."

The writer disposes of all questions of fraud or mechanical contrivance, by telling us:—"We need not speculate on what might be done by skilful contrivances, since the question is removed out of the region of conjecture by the fact that, upon holding up the instrument myself in one hand, in the open room, with the full light upon it, similar strains were emitted, the regular action of the accordeon going on without any visible agency. And I should add that, during the loud and vehement passages, it became so difficult to hold, in consequence of the extraordinary power with which it was played from below, that I was obliged to grasp the top with both hands. This experience was not a solitary one. I witnessed the same result on different occasions, when the instrument was held by others."

He also several times was present when I was raised from the ground; and he gives the following description of what he observed:—"Mr. Home was seated next to the window. Through the semi-darkness his head was dimly visible against the curtains, and his hands might be seen in a faint white heap before him. Presently, he said, in a quiet voice, 'My chair is moving—I am off the ground—don't notice me—talk of something else,' or words to that effect. It was very difficult to restrain the curiosity, not unmixed with a more serious feeling, which these few words awakened; but we talked, incoherently enough, upon some indifferent topic. I was sitting nearly opposite to Mr. Home, and I saw his hands disappear from the table, and his head vanish into the deep shadow beyond. In a moment or two more he spoke again. This time his voice was in the air above our heads. He had risen from his chair to a height of four or five feet from the ground. As he ascended higher he described his position, as at first perpendicular, and afterwards horizontal. He said he felt as if he had been turned in the gentlest manner, as a child is turned in the arms of a nurse. In a moment or two more, he told us that he was going to pass across the window, against the gray, silvery light of which he would be visible. We watched in profound stillness, and saw his figure pass from one side of the window to the other, feet foremost, lying horizontally in the air. He spoke to us as he passed, and told us that he would turn the reverse way, and recross the window; which he did.. His own tranquil confidence in the safety of what seemed from below a situation of the most novel peril, gave confidence to everybody else; but, with the strongest nerves, it was impossible not to be conscious of a certain sensation of fear or awe. He hovered round the circle for several minutes, and passed, this time, perpendicularly, over our heads. I heard his voice behind me in the air, and felt something lightly brush my chair. It was his foot, which he gave me leave to touch. Turning to the spot where it was on the top of the chair, I placed my hand gently upon it, when he uttered a cry of pain, and the foot was withdrawn quickly, with a palpable shudder. It was evidently not resting on the chair, but floating; and it sprang from the touch as a bird would. He now passed over to the farthest extremity of the room, and we could judge by his voice of the altitude and distance he had attained. He had reached the ceiling, upon which he made a slight mark, and soon afterwards descended and resumed his place at the table. An incident which occurred during this aërial passage, and imparted a strange solemnity to it, was that the accordeon, which we supposed to be on the ground under the window close to us, played a strain of wild pathos in the air from the most distant corner in the room."

A most able, quiet, and philosophical description of these and others of the phenomena which he witnessed, is closed by some remarks which it is too much to hope that many will profit from. There is so much unreasoning opposition to the facts, that an appeal to reason in favor of them is almost out of place. He says:—"To say that certain phenomena are incredible, is merely to say that they are inconsistent with the present state of our knowledge; but knowing how imperfect our knowledge is, we are not, therefore, justified in asserting that that they are impossible. The 'failures' which have occurred at *séances* are urged as proofs that the whole thing is a cheat. If such an argument be worth noticing, it is sufficient to say that ten thousand failures do not disprove a single fact. But it must be evident that as we do not know the conditions of 'success,' we cannot draw any argument from 'failures.' We often hear people say that they might believe such a thing, if such another thing were to happen; making assent to a particular fact, by an odd sort of logic, depend upon the occurrence of something else. 'I will believe,' for example, says a philosopher, of this stamp, 'that a table has risen from the ground, when I see the lamp-posts dancing quadrilles. Then, tables? Why do these things happen to tables?' Why, that is one of the very matters which is desirable to investigate, but which we shall never know anything about so long as we ignore inquiry. And, above all, of what use are these wonderful manifestations? What do they prove? What benefit have they conferred on the world? Sir John Herschel has answered these questions with a weight of authority which is final. 'The question, *Cui bono?* to what practical end and advantages do your researches tend?—is one which the speculative philosopher, who loves knowledge for its own sake, and enjoys, as a rational being should enjoy, the mere contemplation of harmonious and mutually dependent truths, can seldom hear without a sense of humiliation. He feels that there is a lofty and disinterested pleasure in his speculations, which ought to exempt them from such questioning. 'But,' adds Sir John, 'if he can bring himself to descend from this high but fair ground, and justify himself, his pursuits, and his pleasures in the eyes of those around him, he has only to point to the history of all science, where speculations, apparently the most unprofitable, have almost invariably been those from which the greatest practical applications have emanated.'*

"The first thing to be done is to collect and verify facts. But this can never be done if we insist upon refusing to receive any facts, except such as shall appear to us likely to be true, according to the measure of our intelligence and knowledge."

This article was received by the public in the only way which was likely, from the novelty to so many of the subject of the phenomena; and those who were acquainted personally with the marvellous occurrences so well described in the Magazine, well knew their truth, yet the writer and the Editor of the "Cornhill" were severely blamed by many for allowing the appearance of what they designated as absurdity. As the article was anonymous, the facts stated in it were deliberately denied by the press, and to stem the torrent of abuse and unbelief, a gentleman, who has since become my very esteemed friend, wrote, giving his

* Preliminary Discourse on the Study of Natural Philosophy, p. 10.

name, the following letter, which is introduced by some prefatory remarks, in the "Spiritual Magazine." The letter of Dr. Gully, of Malvern, first appeared in the "Morning Star," which of all the London papers has been the most fair and candid in dealing with the facts of Spiritualism :—

"Sir,—In Mr. Coleman's letter of the 11th inst., he gives his opinion that the gentlemen who were present at the meetings recorded in the 'Cornhill Magazine,' under the head of 'Stranger than Fiction,' should confirm or confute the statements made in that article. I was one of the persons present at the evening meeting. The other gentlemen were a solicitor in extensive practice, and two well-known writers of solid instructive works—not writers of fiction—who, by-the-by, appear to be so used to inventing that they cannot believe that any one else can possibly be employed in stating facts. It will be seen that the joke about 'fools of fashion' does not apply to the gentlemen alluded to, but that we were all workers in callings in which matters of fact, and not of fancy, especially come under observation. Further, it may be useful to some persons to know that we were neither asleep, nor intoxicated, nor even excited. We were complete masters of our senses ; and I submit that their evidence is worth a thousand conjectures and explanations made by those who were not present. Scores of times I have been much more agitated and excited in investigating a patient's case, than I was in observing what occurred at the evening meeting in question.

With this state of senses at the time, and revolving the occurrences in my mind again and again, since that time, I can state with the greatest positiveness that the record made in the article, 'Stranger than Fiction,' is, in every particular, correct; that the phenomena therein related actually took place in the evening meeting; and, moreover, that no trick, machinery, sleight-of-hand, or other artistic contrivance produced what we heard and beheld. I am quite as convinced of this last as I am of the facts themselves.

"Only consider that here is a man, between ten and eleven stone in weight, floating about the room for many minutes—in the tomb-like silence which prevailed, broken only by his voice coming from different quarters of the room, according to his then position—is it probable, is it possible, that any machinery could be devised—not to speak of its being set up and previously made ready in a room, which was fixed upon as the place of meeting only five minutes before we entered it—capable of carrying such a weight about without the slightest sound of any description? Or suppose, as has been suggested, that he bestrode an inflated balloon, could a balloon have been introduced inflated large enough to hold in mid-air such a weight? Or could it have been inflated with hydrogen gas without being detected by ears, eyes, or nose?

"It seems to me a much stronger sign of credulity to believe either of these suggestions, with our present knowledge, than to adopt the wildest statements or dreams of what is called Spiritualism. Let it be remembered, moreover, that the room was, for a good part of the evening, in a blaze of light, in which no balloon or other machine sufficient for the supposed purpose could be introduced; or, if already introduced, could remain unobserved; and that, even when the room was comparatively darkened, light streamed through the window from a distant gas-lamp outside, between which gas-lamp and our eyes Mr. Home's form passed, so that we distinctly perceived its trunk and limbs; and most assuredly there was no balloon near him, nor any machinery attached to him. His foot once touched my head when he was floating above.

"Then the accordeon music. I distinctly saw the instrument moving, and heard it playing when held only at one end, again and again. I held it myself for a short time, and had good reason to know that it was vehemently pulled at the other end, and not by Mr. Home's toes, as has been wisely surmised, unless that gentleman has legs three yards long, with toes at the end of them quite as marvellous as any legion of spirits. For, be it stated, that such music as we heard was no ordinary strain; it was grand at times, at others pathetic, at others distant and long-drawn, to a degree which no one can imagine who has not heard it. I have heard Blagrove repeatedly, but it is no libel on that master of the instrument to say that he never did produce such exquisite distant and echo notes as those which delighted our ears. The instrument played, too, at distant parts of the room, many yards away from Mr. Home, and from all of us. I believe I am stating a fact when I say that not one person in that room could play the accordeon at all. Mr. Home cannot play a note upon it.

"To one whose external senses have witnessed these things, it is hard to increase the insufficiency of those attempted explanations which assert the use of tricks and machinery. As I said before, it requires much more credulity to believe such explanations than to swallow all the ghost stories that ever were related. I may add that the writer in the 'Cornhill Magazine' omits to mention several curious phenomena which were witnessed that evening. Here is one of them. A distinguished *littérateur*, who was present, asked the supposed spirit of his father, whether he would play his favorite ballad for us, and, addressing us, he added, 'The accordeon was not invented at the time of my father's death, so I cannot conceive how it will be effected; but if his favorite air is not played, I pledge myself to tell you so.' Almost immediately the flute notes of the accordeon (which was upon the floor) played through 'Ye banks and braes of Bonnie Doon,' which the gentleman alluded to assured us was his father's favorite air, whilst the flute was his father's favorite instrument. He then asked for another favorite air of his father's, 'which was not Scotch,' and 'The Last Rose of Summer' was played in the same note. This, the gentleman told us, was the air to which he had alluded.

"I have thus borne testimony to the truthfulness of the facts related by the writer in the 'Cornhill Magazine,' whom I recognise as having been my neighbor during the meeting. And I have endeavored to show that, as regards the principal and most wonderful phenomena, there could have been no contrivance by trick or machinery adequate to produce or account for their existence. How, then, were they produced? I know not; and I believe that we are very—very far from having accumulated facts enough upon which to frame any laws or build any theory regarding the agent at work in their production. Intelligent phenomena, such as the music played at request, point to intelligent agents; and spiritual bodies that have quitted fleshly bodies may be at work. I, for one, wish that it were proved to be so; for a more solemn discovery than that of a means of communication between embodied and disembodied sentient beings cannot be imagined. It giddies the brain to think of the possible result of such a discovery. But, whilst I obstinately stand up for the integrity of my senses during my observation of the wonders above related, my inner senses cannot but observe many gaps that must be filled up before the bridge between the spiritual body's life here in the flesh, and its life elsewhere out of the flesh, can be finished. Meantime the facts must be patiently and honestly accumulated, and enthusiasm must be banished from the minds of the enquirers. And as regards the denials, and abuses, and jests of the non-enquirers, let it be remembered that scurillity and laughter never discovered or disprove anything in the world's history.

"Respecting the purely physical phenomena, such as the raising of weights whether of human bodies or tables, it *may be* that we are on the verge of discovering some physical force hitherto undreamed of; who shall say that we know all the powers of nature? Here, too, dispassionate inquiry must go on, regardless of the noise outside; regardless, too, of the ignorant and malicious prejudice which would blast the reputation of those who enquire in a direction opposite to that prejudice.

"Enquirers, unlike routine people, must be prepared to rough it among their fellow-creatures. And I suppose that I, for having asserted that I have five senses as yet unimpaired, and for having testified to what the majority disbelieve, shall come in for my share or abuse. Let it be so, if it helps on a truthful search.

"I am, Sir,
"Yours faithfully,
"J. M. Gully, M.D.

"Malvern, Oct. 14."

CHAPTER X.

MIRACULOUS PRESERVATION. FRANCE AND ENGLAND.

We left London the 24th of July, 1860, for the Château de C——, near Paris. One of the most remarkable interpositions of Providence which have ever happened to me occurred at this place. Many doubt the possibility of such interpositions, but I have not been allowed to doubt them, and I have to thank our Heavenly Father that I have so often been made aware of His ministering care and kind Providence. I do not suppose for a moment because of this, that His Providence is more over me than over all His children, and I believe that in looking back over our past lives, there are none of us who can fail to recognise the finger of God directing and protecting them, often in some remarkable and even almost physical way, though generally, perhaps, through means apparently more remote than those which saved my life on the 16th September, 1860.

I had just returned from Naples, whither I had been to visit a friend—but who had passed from earth before I had arrived—and I found my health affected by fatigue of travelling and mental depression. Being recommended to take much out-door exercise, during my stay at the Château de C——, I used to take with me my gun—more that it might be said I was out shooting than for any great attraction the sport has for me. The Château de C——, distant half-an-hour by railway from Paris, stands in a beautiful old park. Some of the trees are of very great height; one of the largest, a northern poplar, stands a quarter of a mile from the château at an angle of the park, where it is separated from the outer grounds by a hedge. To this spot, when there is much shooting going on in the neighborhood, the game used to come for shelter; and I, who am but an indifferent marksman, could get easy shots by planting myself by the hedge.

On the day mentioned, I had been walking with my friend, Mons. T——, and on his leaving me, I bent my steps to this favorite corner, wishing to take home a partridge. As I neared the hedge, I stooped and advanced cautiously. When close up to it, I was raising my head to look for my game, when on my right I heard some one call out, "Here, here!" My only feeling was surprise at being thus suddenly addressed in English. The desire to have a good look out for my game, overruled my curiosity as to whom the exclamation had come from, and I was continuing to raise my head to the level of the hedge, when suddenly I was seized by the collar of my coat and vest, and lifted off the ground. At the same instant I heard a crashing ing sound, and then all was quiet. I felt neither fear nor wonder. My first thought was that by some accident my gun had exploded, and I was in the spirit-land; but, looking about, I saw that I was still in the material world, and there was the gun still in my hands. My attention was then drawn to what appeared to be a tree immediately before me, where no tree had been. On examination, this proved to be the fallen limb of the high tree under which I was standing. I then saw that I had been drawn aside from the fallen limb a distance of six or seven feet. I ran, in my excitement, as fast as I could to the château. My friends, seeing me running, hastened to the window to learn the cause of my disturbance. As soon as I recovered my power of speech, I told them how God, by his good angels, had saved my life, and they returned with me to the scene of what I must call my miraculous escape.

I will not attempt to portray the feelings of those present, but if ever heartfelt prayer of thankfulness ascended to God's holy throne, it was then and there, from us all, even to the servants, who broke off twigs to keep as mementos of the mercy shown me.

The limb which had thus fallen measured sixteen yards and a half in length, and where it had broken from the trunk, it was one yard in circumference. It fell from a height of forty-five feet. The part of the limb, which struck the very spot where I had been standing, measured twenty-four inches in circumference, and penetrated the earth at least a foot. The next day a friend made a sketch of the tree and branch. We now speculated as to how it could have happened. The tree is not a dead one, nor was the branch at all decayed, and there was scarcely wind enough to stir the leaves. The branch was so cleanly reft from the trunk that one might at first think it had been sawn off, and the bark was not in the least torn about it. I have been informed since that such accidents are not uncommon with trees of this species of poplar, and that there are trees of a similar quality in Australia, under which settlers will not remain for fear of such sudden breakages.

A day or two after, Dr. Hoefer, one of the most learned men in France, and for whom I have the highest esteem and regard, as a sincere truth-seeker, and a friend deserving every confidence, came at about noon and requested a séance. We had one, and a very good one it was. Answers were given to questions of the utmost importance. All at once it was spelled out, "Go, see the branch." Dr. Hoefer, impressed as it were, withdrew from the table, saying, "Perhaps they are going there." I went to the drawing-room, and asked the ladies if they would join us—but the day being damp and the walking bad, they declined.

I ought to have said, that the thick end of the branch rested, at a height of eight feet from the ground, firmly against the trunk of a tree, so much so that the possibility of its coming down had never for an instant occurred to us, but rather that the strength of several horses should be required to move it. Our surprise, then, may be imagined when we now found that it had been moved three or four inches laterally from its original point of support. Dr. Hoefer said—"I firmly believe that the branch will be pushed down before us." I replied, "That seems almost an impossibility." At the same time I took in my hand one of the smaller twigs and mentally said, "Dear spirits, will you push this branch down?" I then distinctly felt as if some one gently touched the twig which I held; tnis was repeated, and at the third touch, as it felt to me, the branch fell to the ground.

Four persons witnessed this, and are ready to testify to what I here relate.

I had afterwards a piece of the thickest part of the fallen tree sawn off, and sent to me in London, where it still is—and with it on many occasions, some of which will be afterwards mentioned, some very marvellous manifestations took place.

One evening, at the chateau, as we were seated at the table, the spirits having requested that the candles should be extinguished, the table drawn to the window, and the curtains opened to admit the moonlight, there had been some striking manifestations, and the time had been passing almost imperceptibly to us all, when a gentleman who was present, said that he felt very much exhausted, and he asked for a glass of brandy and water. It was brought, and he took it in his hand, and was about raising it to his mouth—when a spirit hand suddenly appeared, took hold of the lower part of the glass, and disappeared with it under the table. We laughingly said that our unseen friends surely did not believe in the use of stimulants. To this they assented by emphatic raps, and at the same moment the glass slowly rose again before him empty. The windows being closed, we supposed the water had been thrown upon the floor, and we arose to see where it was. We could discover no trace of it. About two minutes hac elapsed, when the same glass which was standing empty before him, was seen without any visible cause, gradually to approach the edge of the table, and to disappear beneath it. I do not believe that above two seconds could have elapsed before it again appeared with the brandy and water in it, apparently not less in quantity than when first brought in, though the quality had certainly undergone some chemical change, as it had now lost much of its brown color. By the raps, a warning was given to all of us against such indulgence.

In September we left the chateau to spend a month in Paris, and we paid a short visit to our relatives at Biarritz, returning to England at the end of November, 1861. My wife's health being delicate, the medical men having discovered an internal disease, which, though of a serious nature, might yet last for many years, we did not during this winter see so many friends, but I had séances as often as I could.

From an esteemed friend, who had been rescued from scepticism by the manifestations of spirit power which he had so often witnessed, I find a letter describing what he saw in London at this time.

"Seven of us were present in a large drawing-room, lighted by a good fire and three gas-burners. The accordeon was taken by one of our friends who had never been present at any manifestations, and in his hands it was forcibly pulled and several chords played —in my hand also the same was done, but the weight of the instrument made the holding of it painful to me. We then began to be touched—and I felt a soft body passing across my knees. A gentleman and I wishing our hands to be grasped by a spirit, placed our handkerchiefs over our hands, in a single fold.—Shortly, the handkerchief was taken off by what seemed to me like air fingers—so gentle, so soft. It was carried to the gentleman opposite, and by him received and handed to me; the other was restored to the owner, *tied* into a curious knot. All other hands were on the table during the whole of the time. Two of the three gas-lights were now put out—and the fire burning brightly, gave a subdued light in the room. Mr. Home then became cataleptic in his hands and arms: he was raised from his seat till he stood upright, and then he rose vertically till he was a foot above the floor—his head level with the chandelier—this was repeated twice, but he did not rise higher. On sitting down again, the table-cloth was several times raised up in different parts of the table, and I, with others, placed my hand on the substance which so raised it—and to my sense of feeling, it was as if a plastic hand and fingers touched mine, yielding to my pressure. During our conversations, approval or disapproval of some things said were given by energetic concussions. The loudest affirmatives were when it was said these manifestations were by God's permission, to prove to us the continued existence of our relatives, and of our immortality; also that we could not be alone, as there were ever about us unseen active intelligences, who saw our actions, heard our words, and discerned our thoughts.

"The lady who was with me had laughed and wondered at my foolishness for these several years past for believing in spirit-power manifestations; but now wonder, joyousness, and belief took possession of her, and the candid avowal of her conviction, and the consequences to certain materialistic members of her family seemed to be producing a powerful effect upon her mind.

"What is the use of spirits descending to the level of our educational obtuseness, and producing the class of phenomena detailed in this rough sketch? The question is answered by my giving a portion of a letter received on the 6th of this month from one of our literary celebrities, whose name has not yet been prominently before the public in connection with spirit manifestations. Having sent to the editors of the daily and weekly newspapers and magazines a printed letter on spirit manifestations, I had a reply from one of the editors, who says—

"'I *know* all you have stated, and more—I have seen and felt all you have stated, and more. I believe I am no 'fool'—I am sure I am no 'rogue.' To me the belief has been an unspeakable comfort, thoroughly taking me away from that materialism into which I had crept—and I believe *that* to be the main purpose of spiritual teaching, and the reason why the great principle is developed in our time.'

"I have had the same testimony given to me by many others.

"JOHN JONES.

"*Basinghall Street*, 14th January, 1861."

The important testimony of my friend Mr. James Hutchinson, for many years the chairman of the Stock Exchange, is one to which I would draw attention, as it appears from his well-known character and sagacity, to be just such as ought to be received as conclusive evidence of what he relates. Mr. Hutchinson says:—

"I have for some time past felt an interest in the subject of Spiritual Manifestations. Like most persons I had great difficulty in realizing the statements made to me of the wonders which were daily witnessed by others, but the evidence of friends satisfied me that there must be something worthy of investigation, and I therefore determined to take every opportunity of looking into it for myself. I have now done so, and I feel it a duty to openly bear my testimony to the *facts*, leaving others to *theorise* on the causes and tendency of these remarkable phenomena.

"Recently introduced by a friend to Mr. D. D. Home, a séance was arranged for the 23rd instant, and together with Mr. and Mrs. Coleman, Mr. G. S. Clarke, Mr. T. Clarke, Mr. Gilbert Davidson, and another lady and gentleman unknown to me, we formed a party of nine. Shortly after sitting down we all felt a tremulous motion in our chairs, and in the table, which was a very heavy circular drawing-room table. This movement of the table increased in power, and at the suggestion of Mr. Coleman, it imitated the exact action and sound of a stroke of a powerful marine engine acting on and vibrating the timbers of a weak-framed vessel.

"The rapping sounds on the table and floor were constant; the heavy table was raised up repeatedly—and these manifestations were continued whilst my friend, Mr. Clarke, and another were seated, at the request of Mr. Home, *under* the table.

"Two hand-bells, one weighing at least a pound and a half, were passed from one to another of the party by the unseen agencies. All of us in turn felt the touch and pressure of a soft and fleshy like-hand. I saw the full formed hand as it rested on my knee. The accordeon, whilst held by Mr. Home in one hand, discoursed most eloquent music, and then to our great astonishment it was taken from him, and whilst both his hands and those of all of the party were visibly imposed on the surface of the table—the accordeon, suspended from the centre of the table, gave out an exquisite air, no human hand touching it!

"These and many other incidents of a seriously impressive but private character, of which I do not hesitate to speak among my friends, occupied about four hours of what I must admit to be one of the most interesting I have ever spent. I place the facts as we witnessed them at your disposal for publicity, if you please, merely adding, that contrary to the assertions so constantly made that the manifestations are always in the dark, the whole of the phenomena of which I have spoken were manifested in a room lighted with gas, and a bright fire burning.

"Yours, &c.,

"JAMES HUTCHINSON.

"January 26th, 1861."

The following editorial remarks, introducing the letter of "A Plain Man," appeared in the 'Sunday Times,' of the 17th February. The "Plain Man" is well known to me, and I can personally vouch for his high character and intelligence, but he is in a position, which makes it a matter of prudence that it should not be known publicly that he has seen what he has seen. If science and religion are satisfied with this uncharitable state of things, I confess that I am not, and that I sigh for the days when every man and woman will be able to tell the truth without being robbed of their bread by the calumnies of those who are simply uninformed as to the facts which are observed. The editor of the 'Sunday Times,' says:—

"In accordance with the pledge we made at the time when we inserted a notice of Mr. Novra's lecture, we hasten to give publicity to a letter which we have received, accompanied by the name and address of the writer. From the high position which that gentleman holds, and the widely-admitted truthfulness of his assertions, we cannot do otherwise than believe that he personally saw all that he relates, and thus we are again thrown back on the sea of doubt—anxious to arrive at the truth, yet unable to do so. Fortunately, it is not our duty to decide, or even to give our opinion on such matters; we, therefore, publish the letter hoping that if a certain enlightening spirit is granted, which may clear up the truth, that it may be shed upon us, or that if the whole thing is fictitious and imaginary, the delusion may soon be dissipated. Too much credulity on the one hand is contemptible. A blind obstinacy has often nearly marred the best revelations which Providence has vouchsafed to science.

" *To the Editor of the 'Sunday Times.'*

"Sir,—For some time I have been waiting for a favorable opportunity to address you, and to state certain facts connected with Spiritualism, which clearly demonstrate the existence of what many persons seem determined to deny. Such sceptics, by their arguments, so far from doing any injury to the cause, have been the means of inducing many to enquire into the phenomena, who otherwise, in all probability, would never have thought of doing so, and as a consequence, have converted them into thorough believers. Nine such cases have occurred at my own house. Again, throughout all the books and articles I have read, I never have found advanced one single article against the *possibility* of a communication with the spiritual world, but merely expositions of the tricks practised by some interested persons, thus confirming those who were only half convinced, and enabling all who are fortunate enough to be present at a *bona fide* séance, more easily to distinguish between reality and deceit. Clearly, such persons deserve the thanks of us all. The columns of a newspaper could not admit, nor have I the time to write, the many reasons to be adduced in favor of the probability of spiritual manifestations; all I ask of you is to insert a plain statement, from a plain man, of certain facts so striking, extraordinary, and convincing, that those who have seen them cannot fail to believe, and by which not only are the ideas of a man's lifetime upset, but the very laws of nature and gravitation as hitherto understood, appear to be scattered to the winds.

"A few nights since, a party of seven, including Mr. Home and two ladies, assembled, *en séance* round a heavy large circular table. For a short time nothing extraordinary took place, but at length a convulsive throbbing was felt in the table, which shortly began to move, undulating with an easy, graceful movement, and raising itself at times about a foot off the ground. At the same time there were knocks in quick succession under the table, on the floor, ceiling, and round the room, a gentleman being under the table at the time, at Mr. Home's request, to guard against the possibility of collusion. After some trivial communications, a small hand-bell was held by me under the table, and in a few minutes I perceived, on looking down, a small white hand (every other hand belonging to the party assembled, being on the table), which commenced caressing and playing with mine. After ringing the bell once or twice (in my hand), I asked that it should be conveyed to a gentleman opposite, and no sooner was my wish expressed than I felt it pulled from my hand, and deposited in that of the gentleman I had indicated. This was done several times. The hand was smooth and white as a child's, and was quite visible, there being two gas jets burning in the room. An accordeon was held at the side of the table by Mr. Home, when the most lovely, plaintive, and melodious music was played, and no sooner had I expressed a wish to hear the 'Last Rose of Summer,' than that tune was played, at which moment the accordeon was resting on my feet, without a hand of earthly description near it, it having been taken out of Mr. Home's hand and deposited there. Several hands now appeared in quick succession moving different articles of furniture; and one, a particularly powerful one, having touched Mr. Home, he exclaimed that enormous strength had been given him. It certainly had, and he proceeded at once to exercise it. A block of wood, from the large arm of the tree of great weight, from the falling of which he was so wonderfully preserved, was taken up by Mr. Home as if it were a straw, carried round the room under his arm, and finally deposited near the table. It seemed of no weight to him, and yet, when two gentlemen, each of them apparently much more powerful than Mr. Home, essayed, they could hardly move it. A singular circumstance connected with Mr. Home's receiving such extraordinary strength it is necessary to mention. One of the gentlemen present had lost a very dear friend in the late war in the Crimea, and who, prior to leaving this country, gave him his photograph. It was the only one he ever sat for, and after the decease the family asked for it to get it copied, but they had not returned it. On several occasions the spirit has manifested himself, and has constantly reproached this gentleman for having parted with it. On this evening a similar message was received, when he mentally asked for such a manifestation as would fully identify him with the departed friend. When in the world, he was a most powerful muscular man; and to convince this gentleman it was he, who enabled Mr. Home, through himself, to lift this mass of timber, which at another time he could not have moved. The last words spelt out were, 'Get back a copy at least.'

"Another hand now appeared: and on Mr. Home being touched by it, he exclaimed, 'They are raising me; do not look at me till I am above the level of the table, as it might have the effect of bringing me down.' Almost at the same moment Mr. Home was raised up and floated in the air at the height of about five feet, touching one gentleman on the head slightly as he passed, but on approaching the window he came again gently to the ground. He remarked, 'Their strength is hardly great enough yet, but I feel that it will be soon.' The table which for some time had remained passive, now began to heave and throb most violently, and finished by moving towards a sofa at the end of the room, obliging all sitting round to follow it. We had scarcely resumed our seats, when our attention was attracted by seeing a small table move across the room; and finally, after much difficulty, raise itself, and stand in the centre of the large table round which we were sitting. 'Less earthly light' was now spelt out, and the two gas-lights were turned down, leaving merely a bright blazing fire, which clearly illuminated the whole room. This was scarcely done, when a small baby's hand was seen creeping up a gentleman's arm, and almost at the same time he perceived between Mr. Home and himself the form of an infant in white. Being naturally very fond of children, he thought nothing of it, merely imagining that his inclinations were known; but on his wife's asking if it was not the spirit of her little child now passed away, a timid answer in the affirmative was given—a bright light appearing close to the sofa at the same moment, which, by degrees, faded, and at last disappeared. The small table which, it must be remembered was still upon the large one, now began to move, and at the same moment the same hand that before imparted such supernatural strength to Mr. Home was again seen grasping him. His arms were raised above his head, he was again lifted about two feet off the ground and carried towards the window, and when there, he was raised to within about eighteen inches of the ceiling. After remaining floating for about two minutes he descended; but on coming near his chair, he was again elevated, and placed in a standing position in the centre of the table, together with the small one. His weight not resting on it, it had no effect, nor was there even a creak heard. In about a minute both Mr. Home and the small table were elevated for a fourth time in the air, about a foot off the surface of the large table, and, after remaining in that position for about a minute, he descended and resumed his seat.

"Such is a short account of this most remarkable and satisfactory séance. I need scarcely add that of necessity I have been compelled to omit many small details which, although interesting in themselves, sink into insignificance by the side of the wonderful manifestations above described.

"I remain, Sir,
"Your obedient servant,
"A PLAIN MAN."

By this time the health of my wife was failing, and she was sometimes confined to bed. One night the spirit of her mother came to us, and after making three crosses upon Sacha's brow, the hand being invisible but still perfectly tangible, my wife said to me, "Oh, mama is blessing me, and I feel such a strange thrill of joy." I now felt the hand laid upon my brow, and again the present was obliterated from my mind, and I saw the being so dear to me as passing from earth. It was so terrible a reality that I would have given worlds to have felt that there could be even the slightest possibility of my having been deceived. Her mother told me that the disease which would cause her to pass from earth was not the one we had so dreaded, but would be, in fact, consumption. From that moment, every time our kind-hearted and experienced doctor came, I urged him to see whether or no he could detect the slightest change, as indicating disease of the lungs; but he said, though great weakness existed, still active disease was not going on, and he thought it might be avoided. As soon as the dear one could undertake the journey, we went to Bournemouth, where our friend, Mrs. P——, joined us, and we there found the symptoms of lung-disease to have increased. Accordingly, a medical man was called in, who, with one of his colleagues, pronounced the left lung to be unsound. I was alone when they told me this; and when I entered my wife's room, she wished to know what the result of their diagnosis had been. We had, when first married, promised to each other that if ever one knew the other to be seriously ill, we would not attempt to conceal it. Still I had never had the courage to tell her what her mother had revealed to me; for to one so young, and whose life had everything to make it desirable, it seemed hard to think that a new existence so soon awaited her. I felt, however, that I must be true to my promise, and I told her what the doctors had said. She smiled, and said, "Do you think I can remain on earth ten days?" I told her that not only ten days, but that in reality she might live ten years, but that still all was uncertain. She took my hand in hers, and said, "Do you remember, Daniel, when my mother blessed me a month ago, and I told you what a thrill of joy I felt? Well, I feel that she is here now, and I feel a continuation of the self-same thrill. I am going to her, but God will not separate us. I will ever watch over Gricha and you." She asked me for her writing desk, and then wrote letters, which she sealed and addressed, adding the words, "To be opened after I am gone." Just as she was about to finish the last letter, our child ran into the room, and sitting on her knee, he caressingly stroked her cheek, saying, "Mama is too good to be ill." This so affected her that she burst into tears, and these were the only tears she ever shed at the thought of leaving the body. Distinct musical sounds were now heard every night in our room, and on more than one occasion the singing of a bird was heard for more than an hour over her bed.

We remained at Bournemouth about three weeks, and finding the climate very unsuitable, went to the country-house of our kind friend, Mr. Cox, in Hampshire, where we remained a month. My wife now frequently saw both her father and mother, and also a little boy whom she did not recognize, and her mother told her that he was her brother who had passed from earth when only a few hours old. Here occurred some curious phenomena which are described in the letter of my friend, Mr. Cox, of Jermyn Street:

"The late Robert Owen, a short time previous to his passing from earth, had given me a writing desk which had belonged to his wife, and which contained amongst other things a box of paints. As I had other things of his as remembrances, I felt it more just after his departure, that some member of his family should possess the desk, which had belonged to their mother; and I therefore gave it to his son, Mr. Robert Dale Owen, in order that he might take it with him to America. I felt, however, at the time an almost irresistible impulse to retain the desk, but the feeling of right overcame it. The fact had almost escaped my memory, when at nearly the first séance I had with Mr. Home after his return from Russia, the spirit of my old and valued friend, Mr. Owen, came and said, 'You must tell Robert to return you that writing desk; and why did you give it to him, for I did all I could to impress you not to part with it.' I wrote this to Mr. Robert Dale Owen, and in due time the desk was returned to me. We were then at my house in the country, and Mr. and Mrs. Home came to spend a short time with us. My little boy was then, and had been for some time previously, indisposed, and medical advice had been called in, but to little purpose. The spirits had previously prescribed for him, and now they said they would magnetize some pure spring water, which would benefit him. For this purpose a decanter was procured, and placed on the middle of the table at which we were sitting. I placed it there myself, and had taken every precaution that no one should touch it. The water in the decanter became agitated after a few moments without any visible cause, and a powerful aroma came from the bottle. We tasted the water, and found it was strongly impregnated with something which gave it a decided flavor, but what it was we knew not: it was not like anything we had tasted before. Mr. Home was then thrown into the trance state, and taking the decanter in his right hand, he walked a few feet from the table, holding it in full view all the time, when, to my astonishment, I saw another decanter, apparently precisely similar to the other, in his left hand. Thus, in each of his hands I saw a decanter; and so real was the second that I could not have told which of them was the material one. Even if a trick had been intended, here was no opportunity for it, and as the decanter was a large one, another one could not have been concealed up Mr. Home's coat-sleeve, or about his person. A little later, Mr. Owen's spirit came and desired his wife's writing desk to be placed on the table; and now the room was darkened to see if we could distinguish spirit lights, which were then seen by three of us. Presently we heard the writing desk opened, and a hand was placed in mine, another in my wife's, and a third in Mr. Home's, each hand differing in size from the others. The alphabet was called for, and 'I fear I may have spoilt your Claude,' was spelt out. We could not understand this; but when the lamp was relighted, we found that some paint had been taken from the box from inside the desk, and had been freely used on one of my paintings which hung several feet from where we were sitting.

"WM. COX."

We now returned to London; and the first day of our arrival our valued friend, Dr. H——, called on us, still hoping that the medical men had made a mistake in pronouncing the lung to be diseased; and as he was sounding the chest, my dear wife looked up at him laughingly, and said, "You see how very different it is now to what it used to be. I myself can distinguish the difference in the sound." He sorrowfully shook his head, and said, "It is but too true, and with your belief I would not attempt to conceal it from you." Many times did he reiterate these words during her illness, adding, "With my other patients I have to give them hopes that they are going to stay, and you are ever asking me for hopes that you are to go."

During our stay in London I had a séance almost every night, my wife feeling that they did her good both physically and spiritually. The character of the manifestations occurring at this time will be seen in the accounts which are given by my two friends. That of Mr. W. M. Wilkinson is as follows:—

My First Séance with Mr. Home.

"Though I have been on terms of intimacy with Mr. Home for some years, and have heard and read of all the wonderful things which occur in his presence, yet this 19th June, 1861, is the first time I have come to see them for myself. It has not been because I disbelieved them, or thought them of no importance; for I quite believed them, and thought them of very great importance. Having been, however, in the habit of hearing from friends of all that was occurring, I was fully satisfied with their accounts, and did not think that they were so much beneath me in observation, that it was necessary for my own eyes to convince me. I take no credit to myself for this, for it is mainly a consequence of my own experience. I remember about twenty-five years ago, when I first heard of mesmerism, and of its psychological wonders, I committed the folly of saying that I did not believe a word of it—and since I had on that occasion to surrender at discretion, on seeing for myself, I have made much fewer similar mistakes. Since that time, I have pursued this and kindred subjects, and I may fairly say that I can now readily believe in much more than I once thought possible. I have found this, at all events, convenient,—for I have not had so often to find myself at variance with facts, which is always a painful position to be in; and, besides, it has opened up to me a new world of spiritual forces, which, though generally ignored, I have found to account for many of the strangest, and otherwise incomprehensible chapters of human history.

"I had on two or three occasions, through Mr. Squire and other mediums, seen phenomena as wonderful as those which I now witnessed in the presence of Mr. Home. I had seen nearly all the wonderful things so admirably described in the 'Cornhill Magazine,' and in the letter of Dr. Gully; I had also been present when others of even a more powerful kind were done, and which were ably described by Dr. Blank, at page 161 of the first volume of the 'Spiritual Magazine.' I had several times seen, both in London and Paris, direct writing by invisible power, on paper placed beyond mortal contact, and I was well convinced also of the alleged power of mediums to float in the air, by having had one come down on my chest, as well as having on other occasions had hold of his hand, whilst he was floating about the room. I did not, therefore, on this evening care to disturb myself and others by taking those precautions which would have been necessary if I were the President of the Royal Society, and were about to make a conclusive report to that illustrious body of inquirers into physics. I did not doubt, but I sat, and saw, and heard, and felt, and made notes. There were eight of us, all well known to me, and some of them known wherever the English language is spoken. We were in the drawing-room of a house in Cornwall Terrace, Regent's Park, and we sat round a large loo table, and commenced talking. Curiously enough, one having said that Professor Faraday was coming on the following Monday to a séance, and speculating as to his guardian spirit not allowing him to be easily convinced, there were at once very loud knocks on the table in affirmation of that proposition. I was sitting next to my wife on her right hand, and immediately afterwards I felt my leg gently touched, in a position where it was impossible for Mr. Home to have reached it. Then there began a gentle but deep vibration of the table, chairs, and floor, till all the room was shaking violently, during which the table rose about ten inches, the trembling continuing all the time. The table began to rise on the opposite side to where Mr. Home was sitting, and it was clearly out of his power to have raised it. Mr Home's chair was quietly moved back, away from the table, about three feet, and whilst there the dresses of my wife and of the lady next to her were both pulled, and so strongly that I could see them dragging down. I also felt my wife's dress whilst being so pulled, and there was a powerful force expended in the act resisting my hand. At this time Mr. Home was fully six feet off, and both from distance, and from his being in full view, I could see that it was done by no force of his. Hr. Home now held the accordeon in his right hand beside his chair, and it at once began to play. He held it by the bottom, the keys being on the top, and they were therefore out of his reach. It was impossible that he could touch them. I carefully examined the instrument, opening the slide beneath the keys, and I found it to be a common instrument, with only the usual mechanism of the keys. There was nothing inside of it. I looked steadily at it, and at the hand and fingers with which he held it. There it was, being pulled up and down, and discoursing sweet sounds, whilst his hand was stationary, and his fingers motionless. I could see above and beneath the instrument, but there was no visible cause for its motion, nor for the opening and shutting of the keys which caused the music. When it ceased, my wife asked if it could not be played in her hand, and immediately the instrument emitted three sounds, which we took to mean that it would have much pleasure in trying. It was accordingly given to her, and whilst she was holding it, she said she felt one of her fingers being touched. Immediately afterwards the table was raised about a foot steadily from the floor. As there was no sound from the accordeon in her hands, she returned it to Mr. Home, but it was taken from his hand immediately, and given back to her, and whilst in her right hand it began to play. She felt it distinctly lifted up and drawn forcibly down, and she did not and could not touch the keys, which, however, must necessarily have been touched and opened to make the sounds. In Mr. Home's hands a beautiful tune was now played, during which we heard what has been so often des cribed, the full notes gradually decreasing until they died away into the thinnest streaks of sound. By three quickly repeated notes it was promised that the instrument should play the tune of the other evening, representing 'The Two Lives,' the one in this world, the other in that which follows. The first, or this world's life, was represented by discords grating painfully on the ear, and which I thought did but scant justice to a world which, though capable of improvement, still has some rich harmonies within its depths. In mercy to our ears, the first life did not last long, and was then succeeded by the second, which was made up of beautiful soft angel music, such as I had never heard. It played for several minutes, swelling into rich sounds of which the sweetness was enchanting to the ear, and gradually changed into the dear old tune of 'Home sweet Home.'

What more appropriate and happy view of the second life could be given in musical sounds than this of its being home; and what a sweet sermon on the relative values of the two lives! I believe it was received more solemnly, and yet more thankfully by all who were present, from knowing the sickness 'even unto death' of one of the party, the youngest and the happiest in her bright longings for this second life. It would be almost blasphemy to ask in her presence what is the good of Spiritualism. Such a question would not occur to a good man, and could not be asked by a wise one. The mere man of science who measures human souls by mathematics, would be out of place in such a scene, and had I not been too happily engaged with my own thoughts, I should have felt glad that we were troubled with none such. I did not during this last performance scrutinize the instrument further than to see that it was held, bottom upwards, in Mr. Home's right hand, his other hand being upon the table, as were the hands of all the other persons present, and I am not aware of any natural means by which an accordeon can be played under such conditions. I do not doubt for another reason, however, having once had an accordeon play in my own hands, when I know that I do it. I also know that Lord Lyndhurst, and many other public men whom I could name, have had a similar experience.

"But now the table rises again a clear foot from the floor, and there stands, not quietly, but strongly undulating, still so that I was able to make the following note on my paper resting on the table, whilst it was at its full height above the ground:—'Table rose a foot. Count 10. I wrote this whilst up and undulating.' It then gently descended to the floor again. We now changed places according to directions, and a gentleman became my right hand neighbor, who, in a minute after, said that he saw a hand which he believed to be his son's. I did not see it, nor did I see three fingers which my wife shortly after saw; but in answer to a question, I had three taps on my knee as from a hand, still with no such distinctness as to make me sure what it was. At this time, several at once said they saw a light cloudy appearance dart across the room, but, being behind me, I saw nothing of it.

"In one corner of the room, near where we were sitting, was a shrine with several Indian idols of bronze. Suddenly, there was a commotion amongst them, and a crash, and a large one was thrown down, and brought with some violence and noise under the table. There it appeared as if it was in the hands of some vigorous power, and presently we found a jingling of some metallic substance against it, which afterwards proved to be a metal ornamental canopy, which had been unscrewed from the back of the idol, and with which questions were now answered by knocking them together. In like manner, loud knocks were made in answer to questions, by rattling the idol against the floor. A remark was made as to the want of respect thus indicated, and at once a number of jubilant raps were produced by again knocking the two parts of the idol together. Two or three times the idol appeared, pushing up inside of the table cloth, and twice it made its appearance naked above the table, and gently reached the ground again. Some flowers were brought from the shrine, and placed in the hand of each person present. Our present consisted of a rose and several pinks. I felt the rose placed in my hand under the table, all other hands being visible and on the table.

"Several times during the evening we all perceived a cool air pervading the table, and which it was impossible not to notice. The accordeon was now placed on the floor, and all hands on the table, when it was heard to sound clearly several times, but no tune was played. It then tried to get from the floor to the table, but was not able to accomplish the whole journey, and fell gently back to the floor. The table was now again raised clear from the ground, both my feet being on its pediment, and pressing heavily downwards the whole time. The resistance and upward steady movement of the table were strangely curious, as was its careful quiet descent, my feet still pressing on it, and yet it reached the ground without noise. There was now a general rattle among the idols, and several very loud knocks, and then came an end of a very interesting evening, during which I have seen and heard what was sufficient to convince me that those are wrong who deny the possibility of the phenomena. How they are to be accounted for is another matter, which may be discussed with many honest differences of opinion; but that they exist is not a matter of doubt, but of certainty. There are some well-meaning persons who say that they are done by the devil; but I saw no signs on this evening of any wickedness, either in the work, or in the persons who looked on. For myself, I took up much the same attitude as I should do at a scientific lecture, illustrated with experiments and diagrams, and I perceived no special influence but that of a strong desire to observe the facts.

"As to the facts being impossible, because they do not square with the ideas of spirit and of matter which are current in the Royal Society, that is not my affair, for I did not make either the facts, or the opinions which make them so inconvenient. I do but state that which I have seen, and if I have done so clearly, that is my only wish. Facts will always take care of themselves, and those are the most wise to whom they administer no reproof. There is another reason why I hope to have enlarged the circle of observers, by my description of this evening's phenomena. It is impossible for many that they should see what I have seen, and so far as they can believe my testimony, the neces sity for their personal seeing is avoided. Many things must be taken on the evidence of others. 'Non cuivis contingit adire Corinthum.' It does not happen to every one to go to Corinth, and so they who can't go themselves, must take the account of those who have been there. A certain few of a peculiar turn of mind, common to all ages, cannot accept the testimony of others, and they are best left alone, till an opportunity offers of convincing them by a mode suitable to their peculiar weakness. It is not yet fashionable to believe in these impossible things, and as some one must begin and put up with the necessary ridicule, I willingly submit my name for as much as can be made to stick to it.

"W. M. Wilkinson.

"Hampstead."

Mr. William Howitt, who has made such deep researches into this subject, and has in his great work now ready for the press, brought together the testimonies, ancient and modern, to the supernatural in all ages, was present on several occasions to observe and investigate the phenomena, and in an eloquent and forcible letter which he wrote to Mr. Barkas of Newcastle, he gives an account of some part of what he witnessed.

"I wish some of your negatives could have seen what I and Mrs. Howitt, and several others saw at the house of a lady in Regent's Park, about three months ago, and the like of which some of our most distinguished nobility have seen there repeatedly of late. There were, beside us, Mr. and Mrs. Home, and a Russian Count Steinbock, aud several others. We had beautiful music played on the accordeon when held in one hand by Mr. Home, who cannot play a note, and the same when held by a lady. We had the clearest and most prompt communications on different subjects through the alphabet, and flowers were taken from a bouquet on a cheffonier at a distance, and brought and handed to each of us. Mrs. Howitt had a sprig of geranium handed to her by an invisible hand, which we have planted, and it is growing; so that it is no delusion, no fairy money turned into dross or leaves. I saw a spirit hand as distinctly as I ever saw my own. I touched one several times, once when it was handing me the flower. My wife's silk dress was pulled so strongly that she thought it would tear out the gathers, and was rustled so loudly, that it was not only heard by all of us, but might have been heard in another room. My wife's handkerchief was taken from her knee, and brought and whisked against my hand at the opposite side of the table; I thought, with the intention of my taking it, but the spirit would not allow that, but withdrew it a little, then whisked my hand with it anew, and then flung it into the middle of the room. The dress and the handkerchief were perfectly visible during these operations, but the motive power was invisible.

"Then the spirits went to a shrine of bronze idols, belonging to the lady of the house, who bought them in India. Some of these are very heavy. They pitched them down on the floor, and with such violence that the clash might have been heard all over the house. The larger of these idols—perhaps all—of that I am not certain—unscrew, and the screws work exactly the opposite way to our screws; but the spirits unscrewed them, and pummelled their heads lustily on the floor, saying, through the alphabet, 'You must all do your best to destroy idolatry, both in India and in England, where it prevails in numerous ways. Idolatry of rank, idolatry of wealth, idolatry of self, idol atry of mere intellect and learning,' &c., &c. The different parts were thrown under the table, that you might tread them under foot, and two parts of the idol Mahadeo, of heavy bronze, were placed on the table by a visible hand. The head of the idol felt to me to weigh four or five pounds.

"Mr. Home was lifted about a foot from the ground, but did not float as he frequently does, in the strongest light. The table, a very heavy loo table, was also several times lifted a foot or more from the ground, and we were invited to look under it and see that there was no visible cause. To us, who have seen so much of these things, and to whom they are as familiar as the sight of a bird flying, and far more familiar than the present comet, this was not necessary.

"A few evenings afterwards a lady desiring that the 'Last Rose of Summer' might be played by a spirit on the accordeon, the wish was complied with, but in so wretched a style that the company begged that it might be discontinued. This was done; but soon after, evidently by another spirit, the accordeon was carried and suspended over the lady's head, and there, without any visible support or action on the instrument, the air was played through most admirably, in the view and hearing of all."

CHAPTER XI.

A DIARY AND LETTER.

Nearly the whole range of the phenomena occurred during our residence with our friend Mrs. P—— in the Regent's Park, and she has been a frequent visitor at other séances, and has kept a diary of every evening, which she has kindly placed at my disposal. I propose therefore to make extracts from it of some of the more striking phenomena both of this and of subsequent dates.

Short Extracts from a Diary, 1860–61–62.

December 15, 1860.—My *mental* questions were answered by raps upon my dress. I put my right hand suddenly upon my lap, and tried to take hold of whatever it was that was touching my dress, but could seize nothing. Mr. Home desired me to put a handkerchief over my hand. I did so, and immediately on putting it down, a hand grasped mine, and I suddenly withdrew it. Determined to conquer the nervous feelings that overcame me, again I put my hand down, and it was taken by another hand, and kisses were imprinted on it from the tips of the fingers all over the palm.

An accordeon, held in Mr. Home's right hand, played tne most exquisite music, swelling forth in full harmonious tones, and dying away in notes of tenderness, and of exquisite and unearthly music. His left hand was all the time on the table.

A number of manifestations took place, and to *mental* questions I received intelligent answers, and I returned home from this my first séance with Mr. Home convinced of the truth of our being permitted to hold intercourse with those who have passed to the spirit-land.

December 24th.—The accordeon played in Mr. Home's hand, then five raps asked for the alphabet—and "Christmas Hymn" was spelled out; again five raps, and "less earthly light:" we lowered the flame of the four gas jets that were burning over the table, and "The Manger, the Life, and the passing away," was spelled out. The accordeon played a sweet air appropriate to childhood. "The Life" was represented by the most harmonious strains intermingled with discords at times, as if it were thorny and painful, and the *passing away* died on the air with exquisite tenderness.

January 29th.—A séance of eight persons. We had amused ourselves during the time with the article "Spirit-rapping made easy," in the magazine 'Once a Week,' which we left on the chiffonier. I saw something pass from the side of the room with great velocity, which vanished under the table. A curious noise was heard like the crumpling of paper, a spirit hand arose, appeared, and placed in the medium's hand a sheet of 'Once a Week,' crumpled up and torn. The spirits were at work destroying the magazine—they rubbed it strongly over Mr. Home's shoe, and then placed his foot upon it. The spirits gave each person a bit of the mangled magazine, and the remainder wa raised up by a large spirit hand, and placed on a vacant chair, which by invisible power had a short time before been moved from a distance to the table. The table was violently moved up to the centre window, before which stood a piece of the bough of the northern poplar which had been sent from the Chateau de C——, and which was a part of that, from the fall of which Mr. Home so miraculously escaped. The height of the bough was three feet eight inches, and the circumference three feet. Luminous hands were now and then visible, the table rose gently, and tipped many times against the bough; the spirits threw bits of the torn magazine about it, and placed one piece under it. I asked in Hindostanee, "Are you making Mr. Novra do *pooja* to the branch?" To which they loudly rapped "Yes." The gas lights from the street were streaming in, the spirits closed the shutters, and we heard a curious tearing noise, a spirit hand came across my hands, and placed upon them a bit of the bark torn from the poplar, the noise recommenced, and to every one of the circle a bit was given. Invisible power opened the shutters, the trunk of the tree rocked and waved backwards and forwards, and after a time it was lifted up by invisible power and laid upon the table. At this time "Oft in the stilly night" was played by the accordeon which lay on the floor, untouched by mortal hands. Mr. Home's arms were raised, and he walked to the end of the room, where he was lifted off the ground, and raised until his feet were on a level with the top of a chiffonier, between four and five feet from the ground. I distinctly saw his body carried along erect in the air, it then returned to its former place, where it remained some time—at length it floated forward in the air, passed behind the gas chandelier which was suspended in the centre of the apartment, and he descended gently upon the floor, close to the chair in which a lady was sitting.—She said that when she saw him, he was about four feet from the ground. When he had descended his arms were paralyzed, but in a short time they returned to their natural state.

March 13*th.*—The trunk of the tree that stood in the window was shaken, the roll of drums was heard on the table, and it was lifted as before. The tree shook again, and the accordeon which was on the ground, played untouched by mortal hand. Mr. Home took it afterwards in his right hand, and held it upside down—it was played upon in the most masterly style, the harmony was beautiful. A small chess table from a distance, came up of its own accord, and pushing up to the edge of the loo table, rose and stood upright upon it. Luminous hands often appeared. A beautiful little hand arose between the trunk and the curtain, the fingers distinctly plain: it rose higher, until it showed the arm up to the shoulder, and the little fingers bending over the top of the tree, played with the broken points of the wood, the upright splinters, and then after we had seen it for some time it vanished. Mr. Home was pushed back in his chair a foot or so, and a luminous head came up from his right side, stopped in front of his knees, and then coming toward me, as I sat on his left hand, it disappeared.

March 17th.—*En séance* five persons at Mr. Home's. He fell immediately into the trance, and after a time he awoke. I had in my pocket a musket ball, which in battle had broken the leg of a beloved relative. My dress was pulled, and a spirit hand rapped several times on my knee—it was his spirit. I took the bullet in my right hand, and put my handkerchief over it; spirit fingers turned the handkerchief over the bullet, and took it away. Soon after, my dress was again pulled, and the hand put the bullet which had been tied up in a handkerchief into my hand. Keeping perfectly quiet, I said, "Beloved spirit, will you kiss my hand?" and immediately my fingers were kissed four times. The spirit told me that the bullet now possessed talismanic power, not in cases of sickness, but in those of accidents. Natural flowers were taken off the table, and given to each person present. Mr. Home was now led to the end of the room, which was very dark; he was raised from the ground, a beautiful star was visible, and also one like a small comet. He said a star was on his forehead, and one on each hand; we saw the three very bright, and many others glancing about. He was fixed against the wall. The luminous appearance was so distinct as to render the papering on the wall perfectly distinct; and then he floated along the room and was placed on his knees on the sofa—again he was carried up, and the star on his forehead showed where he was—as he floated along the room, it floated above his head, and when he descended the star was quenched. Whilst he was at the table, a spirit hand raised the accordeon from the floor above the table, and when he was borne into the air, the accordeon floated above his head, playing beautifully all the time, and crossed from one end of the room to the other.

March 28th.—*En séance* nine persons at Mr. Home's house. I had a gilt whistle in my hand, Mr. Home took it in his left hand, and put it under the table cloth; in his right hand was the accordeon. "O!" he exclaimed, "it is so strange—what are they going to do with the whistle? the spirit has turned it round in my hand, and I feel a mouth against my fingers." The whistle was immediately sounded several times. This was quite a new manifestation. The spirit then took the whistle from him, the accordeon began to play, and the air was accompanied by the whistle, which I then heard drop upon the floor.

March 31st.—*En séance* seven persons. I put down my hand, and held it motionless—it was kissed by two spirits, and when the table cloth was lifted off the bracelet, I felt fingers trying to pull it off my arm, but it would not pass over my hand—then the fingers turned the bracelet round until they got hold of the clasp, which it appeared they found difficult to unfasten. At length having succeeded in so doing, they carried the bracelet away. Shortly afterwards a hand arose near a gentleman opposite, and threw the bracelet gently on the centre of the table.

June 2d.—A séance of five persons. As twilight came on, a pleasant dimness fell over the room, and a lady said, "Is the light the spirits love, like the odylic?" to which raps answered "More refined."

The spirits moved the table with violence up to the window, near the Hindoo shrine, and the accordeon, (no human hand touching it) played in the most charming manner, exquisitely and with great power—There was much noise at the Hindoo shrine, the image of Vishnu and the Holy Bull were brought and put on the top of the table, then a large hand, which appeared dark, being between us and the light, put up the accordeon entirely above the top of the table—a second hand on the other side took it down again, another hand took a bell off the table and rang it. Mr. Home was raised from his chair erect into the air, and descended on a footstool. Then he was drawn to the other end of the room, and raised in the air until his hand was on the top of the door; thence he floated horizontally forward, and descended. I saw a bright star constantly flashing forth, the raps died away in the distance, and the séance ended.

June 3rd.—A séance of nine persons. I placed a large bouquet of natural flowers on the shoulder of the great marble idol Ganesh. The accordeon in Mr. Home's right hand playing most beautifully, harmonized the circle, and the spirit hands touched almost every one present. A rustling sound was heard about the idol, and something passed under the table. The spirits rapped, "They are not so beautiful as those you will find with us," and immediately the bouquet was placed in Mrs. Home's hands. Mr. Home, untying the bouquet, returned the flowers to Mrs. Home, who asked the spirit to give them a talismanic power, and take one to each of us. The first flower, a rosebud, was carried to a lady, and the spirits rapped, "From one who is a mortal, but will ere long be with us—emblem of Sacha." This announcement drew tears from us all; we were deeply affected, and Mr. Home sank back overcome with emotion. A narcissus was given to me, and a flower to every one present—also some for those who were absent, but who were loved by Mrs. Home. She spoke for a length of time consolations for those whom she was about to quit; her voice was very weak, and I lost the greater part of what she said. She shook hands with us all, a farewell we wept, but not a word was uttered.

June 5th.—A séance of four persons. Mr. Home immediately went into the trance, and after many communications said, "If you could only see the mass of spirits near Sacha! A veiled female is near her—when Sacha goes to the spirit land, there she will be, her veil off, she will place it on Sacha's brow, heavy with its own stars, shimmering, shimmering down.—Beautiful features, long flowing hair, her hands crossed thus—looks upward—upward—no sorrow, no pain! prayer is carried up by loving hands and placed before God's holy throne—they bear His blessings down to earth. A staff is placed in their hands, a cloud to shade the heart from the sunbeams—by the side is suspended the bread of life—the Hope star high in the heavens to lead them from earth, and to trust only in God."

June 11th.—*En séance* seven persons. The spirits played beautiful music, and brought to us sprigs which they tore off a sweet-scented verbena which was in the room. They brought the *Deir*, a brass idol holding a mirror from the shrine, and put it under the table. Mr. Home saw a spirit at the shrine; then they rapped, "Faith in God, and the change of world will be most glorious, all other——" (the idols which they had placed under the table were rattled violently) "gods" were rapped out; again they rapped the idols violently, and beat them against one another with great noise and force, and spelled "must;" they raised the great idol *Mahadeo*, and put it on the table. It is the large brass idol overshadowed by the expanded hood of the *cobra di capella*. Then they rapped "be brought." They took the idol off the table and pitched it down violently with a clang and noise, then rapped "down low before him." In this manner they elucidated the words they rapped out, "Faith in God and the change of world will be most glorious; all other gods must be brought down low before Him."

June 12th.—A verbena plant in a flower pot stood by the shrine. A hand touched Mrs. Home, and the verbena plant, with the little sticks that supported it, having been broken off at the roots, was thrown by the spirits upon the table. Then they rapped, "We regret, but in taking the flower, we have also taken the earth with it." They shook Mrs. Home's dress violently, earth was thrown on Mr. Home's shoulder, and over it on the table. He saw a spirit hand which was full of earth, and then the remainder which had come out of the flower pot in a mass, was placed in his hand; not a bit of the living flower remained in it.—The spirits rapped—"Life-giving—and the casket that remains only fit to be broken." Immediately they broke the empty flower pot to pieces, as it lay on the ground by the window, emblematic of drawing the soul from its earthly tenement.

June 13th.—Mr. Home went into the trance, and said, "There are more spirits around Sacha, and the veiled spirit is coming nearer and nearer." Mysterious sounds which we had before heard in the chamber above were repeated. When asked, "How do you feel when you go into a trance?" he said, "At first a heaviness in my feet comes on, I feel as if fainting away on the brink of a precipice—there is a moment of suffering, and then all is agreeable."

June 22d.—*En séance* seven persons. A spirit hand arose and came to Mrs. Home—it moved about—she was anxious to touch it; a long finger pointed to and motioned her to be quiet. A hand and arm were distinctly seen, and a spirit hand closed the shutters.—Flowers were given to some, and were placed on the heads of other persons. My head was twice touched, and twice an arm waved over the table; three times an open hand was strongly pressed on my forehead. A spring-bell from the shutters, used as an alarum, was rung above our heads, and we saw the hand which held it. Mr. Home went into the trance, and said, "Where the eye ought to be are placed two crosses; the Christian faith will put the eye out. I do not understand what they mean—the spirit is doing it! Hark! hark! don't write!" I ceased writing—we listened, and heard a noise like scratching on the shrine. Mr. Home woke from the trance, and the séance ended. On going to the shrine, we saw on the forehead of the great white marble image of Ganesh, two crosses made in pencil by the spirits, just over the centre triple eye of the idol, which denotes its having all-seeing power. This was the noise alluded to by Mr. Home in the trance.

June 24th.—Seven persons *en séance.* A scientific gentleman who had written to disprove spiritual manifestations, was to have joined the party; however, he requested to have a programme! which he said is due to him as a scientific man, and to his position! It being impossible to give a programme, he declined joining the séance.

June 25th.—*En séance* eight persons. The accordeon playing of itself, was raised above the table—then it was shown a second time. The spirits rapped to a lady whose child had passed away—"She only went to God, she did not die." At the word God the most peculiar sounds were made, as if to impress us with solemnity.

June 27.—A séance of eight persons. Numerous manifestations took place. Flowers were given, the accordeon played, and an American cane chair which was at the other side of the room, was moved by unseen power up to the table. A hand touched our foreheads, and an arm waved in the air over the table several times. Mr. Home was drawn back in his chair, and an arm, the hand holding the alarum bell, waved over the table; it rang in the air, and by my shoulder, which it touched and then fell to the ground. The accordeon, now in the air, untouched by mortal hand, played beautifully as it floated round the table, and touched each person present.

June 28.—A séance of eight persons. Mr. Home was raised from his chair, and carried up a little in an erect posture, and then put down again. Music was heard in the air, and then strange sounds—we marvelled what it might be. "Is it a spirit?" "Yes." Then the spirit spoke many times, but the words were unintelligible. Mrs. Home was afraid, and begged them not to speak; and Mr. Home said, "It is their difficulty to make the material sounds of speech." It reminded me of Bournemouth, where in Mr. Home's room I had heard music, the chirping of a bird, and spirit voices very distinctly.

June 30.—A séance of three persons. The table trembled and tipped so much, we were surprised the decanters did not fall off. Then it was shaken so violently that froth was produced, and the wine in the decanters splashed up their long necks, whilst the water was scarcely affected. The spirits rapped out their dislike to wine. The table was made excessively heavy—four of us stood up and tried to lift it with all our power; it would not stir, neither could we turn it round. Soon after, it was lifted by the spirits a foot or more from the ground, with all the things upon it, and then it gently descended. One person could now lift it, and it was rendered heavy several times.

July 3rd.—*En séance* seven persons. The table was shaken, and rose and undulated in the air, whilst I counted sixty-two aloud. Mr. Home was lifted up a little in his chair, and went into the trance. His arms were then raised, and he ascended about a foot from the ground, descended, and rose again a couple of feet. He leaned over until he touched Mrs. Home, and then he was carried up, his body being bent forward in a circular form, until his head was above the centre pane in the large window; he ascended some feet, and came down again. It was quite light in the window, and we were close to it. He then went to the end of the room into the darkness, and we could not see him ascend, but three bright stars were shown which denoted where he was. He descended, returned to the table quite stiffened, awoke soon afterwards, and came out of the trance.

July 7th.—We, four persons, were sitting at the centre window in the front drawing-room, talking together, when the spirits began to rap on the floor. Mr. Home brought up a small table, and we had many manifestations, in the midst of which a sofa-table at the end of the room, on which was a large lamp and two flower-pots containing fine lemon-scented verbenas. One of them rolled up, untouched by any one, and placed itself between Mr. and Mrs. Home. It was a fine summer evening, and the room was perfectly light. Mr. Home fell back in his chair, and went into the deep sleep for some time; then he walked about the room, led apparently by a spirit, a very large bright star shone on his forehead, several clustered on his hair, and on the tips of his fingers. He made passes over the verbena plant, but did not touch it. Immediately the air was filled with the scent which he wafted to each of us, and it remained most powerfully on his hands. Making more passes, still in the trance, he said, "Thus we extract the essence from the flower; in the same manner the soul is taken from the body; to-morrow you will see the lower leaves are withered, and the plant will die in a few days." Which fact occurred as he had said, yet no apparent cause could be assigned why it should have died. We then went into the dining-room below; and after refreshments our guests quitted, leaving only Mr. Home, who was seated in an easy chair by the fire-side, Mrs. Home sleeping on the sofa, and I sitting by the table reading by lamp-light. Suddenly loud raps were heard on the large heavy dinner-table; it trembled, rose, and balanced in the air. Mr. Home was led about the room, the shutters were closed, I put out the gas-lights, and we were in darkness. A spirit touched my fingers as they lay on the table, voices were were heard in the air, and Mr. Home said, "The spirits are trying to talk." "Yes," then a voice said, "we are trying to come." I heard two voices of very different tone, and asked, "Who are you, dear spirit?" The name was given and repeated several times. Mr. Home was led about the room, showing stars on his forehead and fingers as he held his hands up. A cross of stars was seen by him and Mrs. Home. I only saw the cross-bar of stars, not the uprights. He was led up to the shutters, and he opened the lower part; immediately spirit power closed the lower and opened the upper part. Mr. Home was now led to the further end of the room, and passed in front of a very large mirror—a sea of glass. I saw a form leading him, over the head of which was thrown a tinted robe flowing to the ground, marking the shape of the head and shoulders. He followed close upon it; I saw them both in the mirror, his features, face and hair, perfectly distinct, but the features of the form that led him were not visible beneath the dark blue tinted robe that covered them. They passed from before the glass, and then we all saw a female figure with a white veil thrown over her head, which fell to the ground; at the same time, but rather higher, was the form of a man in oriental costume. The startling vision faded away, and the great mirror remained with only the light from the window, which streamed in upon it.

July 12th.—*En séance* six persons. Stars appeared above Mrs. Home's head, and a light was seen, with fingers passing over it as it floated above our heads. It was the VEILED SPIRIT. I saw the hand which held the veil, which was spangled with stars, and the fingers moved distinctly as it floated just in front of us. A star was seen on Mr. Home, and flowers were given. Mrs. Home's mother made the sign of the cross on her brow, and then on Mr. Home's. Two fingers touched my forehead, and one all wet made the sign of the cross. The tearing of paper was now heard, and soon after a spirit hand took hold of my left hand as it lay on the table, and put a piece of paper into it. Other pieces of paper were torn off, and then a pencil was thrown to the other end of the room. A bell was rung in the air, the accordeon floating above our heads played the most joyful and martial music, and Mrs. Home saw her spirit-father. "God bless you all, good night," was now rapped. On looking at the paper that had been put into my hand, I found the initials of a beloved spirit, beautifully written in pencil, a *fac-simile* of his writing when on earth. A paper had been given to Mrs. Home by her father, and on it was a cross surmounted by a crown, to show us that we must bear the cross to wear the crown.

February 18, 1862.—A séance of six persons. After

various manifestations, Mr. Home went into the trance, and addressing a person present said, "You ask what good are such trivial manifestations, such as rapping, table-moving, &c.? God is a better judge than we are what is fitted for humanity, immense results may spring from trivial things. The steam from a kettle is a small thing, but look at the locomotive! The electric spark from the back of a cat is a small thing, but see the wonders of electricity! The raps are small things, but their results will lead you to the Spirit World and to eternity! Why should great results spring from such causes? Christ was born in a manger, he was not born a King. When you tell me why he was born in a manger, I will tell you why these manifestations, so trivial, so undignified as they appear to you, have been appointed to convince the world of the truth of spiritualism."

The foregoing extracts will be read with interest by those persons who were present, and perhaps by a larger circle. I give no names, but merely the facts as they occurred, because it is *impossible* for any one to give credit to such marvels, until by investigation they are forced to believe the truth.

F. C. P.

In this diary there are several remarkable manifestations, and amongst them that of the presence of the veiled spirit, who thenceforth was frequently seen by my wife and by me, as will be read in the beautiful memoir of my wife, written by that most inestimable type of womanhood, Mrs. Mary Howitt. The veil of that spirit kept gradually being raised through the successive stages of my dear wife's painful illness, and became almost an index of the insidious advances of her disease.

There is one phenomenon, however, which has happened to me only on the occasion described in the diary. I allude to the wonderful case of the verbena plant, and the drawing of its scent, and of its very life out of it, by a few passes of my hand, wafting its whole perfume in the faces of the sitters, and leaving the tree to die for want of the vital principle which had been thus extricated from it. I have heard before of experiments tried in mesmerism upon plants with some apparent results, but never of any so marked as this, of the verbena. It is not wise to judge of isolated cases, but probably there may occur, or may be found, other instances of a similar kind, which may throw light upon the power of the human will, over the lower forms of life.

I am sorry that in so many instances I am obliged to conceal the names of my friends who have witnessed wonderful things; but if the reader is disposed to complain of this, let him remember the reason, and take the greater part of the blame on himself. No sooner is the name of some honest and courageous person given in obedience to the call for testimony, than it becomes a target for all the ridicule, jests, and abuse of the unscrupulous, the sceptical, the orthodox, and the scientific; in fact, of all who are not wise enough to think, and observe, and weigh, and judge, before they decide. There is small encouragement for men, and still less for ladies, to come forward, and stand in front of all this obloquy. If an example be needed of the truth of this, if it be not an obvious fact already in this uncharitable day, let my adventurous friends watch the extent to which I shall be abused, and called bad names, and given to the devil, for simply and truthfully writing in this little book a few of the incidents of my life, with the production of which I have had nothing to do. It has been my good fortune never to have cared much for bad opinions of me, which have been formed in utter and acknowledged ignorance; and my silence hitherto when the most gross and foolish statements have been made to my prejudice, and when a word from me would have corrected them, is sufficient proof of my indifference to such attacks.

I am sorry, however, for the want of kindness and the folly which so many exhibit, for their own sakes, more than for my own. I do not expect that they will behave differently now in regard to what they see in my book, for in the present state of their minds, the truth cannot be received. The facts become to them impossible, while to me, and many of my friends who have been in the habit of seeing them, and watching them, studying them and their consequences for so many years, their strangeness even has well nigh disappeared. We ought certainly to make some allowance for those ignorant persons who sit quietly at home, saying that such things are impossible, without having ever taken the trouble to try to witnesss them, or to get together even the first elements for forming a judgment upon them. These are not so unjust and dishonest as that class, of which Sir David Brewster is the type, who, in the interests of what they consider their position in the scientific world, have no scruple in telling falsehoods, and in denying what they have seen, and in deceiving still further the former class of merely ignorant persons.

I hope, therefore, that both I and my friends may be in some measure excused for giving their narratives without their names. If I were at liberty to make them public, they would add greatly to the value of the narrative, and the public would have an opportunity of being greatly surprised at finding out who are the persons who have investigated the subject and vouch for these remarkable facts. In society they are well known to many ; and, perhaps, nothing is more strange than the entire belief with which these facts are spoken of and received in large mixed companies, when compared with the expression of entire disbelief with which they are accompanied in nearly all notices of the press. Of those who will openly comdemn this narrative in their journals, hardly one does not reckon amongst his intimate and valued friends, or relatives, or co-contributors, several who are with good reason entire believers. It would be curious to contrast the language he holds to such persons with that he uses in describing my book to the ignorant masses, who, he meanly knows expect such abuse at his hands he will be pleased to hear it. If it were necessary, I could give some names which would amply justify what I have said of these poor leaders of the blind.

The testimony which I now give is that of a lady, whose word and powers of observation are entitled to the most unreserved acceptance, and I am sorry that

I can only give her initial, and call her Mrs. S——. She had become a widow not long before I had the pleasure of making her acquaintance.

"I first attended a séance at Mr. Home's in the summer of 1861, when I was put in very deep affliction. I had never seen anything of Spiritualism before, but had heard a good deal of it from a dear old friend who introduced me to Mr. Home. My own experiences that night were far more wonderful than anything I had ever heard or read of, and were to me most convincing. After many raps, movements of the table, &c., my handkerchief was drawn from my hand, the knocks given for the alphabet, and the words 'Shed no more tears' were spelt out, and my handkerchief *came up of itself* at the oposite side of the table, moved gently across, and settled itself *on* the table in front of me; this I *saw* without a possibility of mistake or doubt. After this, Mr. Home fell into a trance, and described my dear husband most accurately, said how noble he was in mind and body, and how he should have loved him had he known him in life, and then said, 'But who is that Mary standing by his side? What a noble woman, and how she loves him, and how happy they are together, and how they both love you; you were *his* star in life. But what was that misery about his watch? you forgot to wind his watch, and how miserable it made you.' Now this was a fact known to no human being but myself. I had wound the watch the night I lost my husband, and resolved never to let it go down again; but more than a month afterwards, when I returned to our old home I forgot to wind it one night, and my agony was great when I discovered it in the morning, but I never mentioned it even to my husband's sister, who was in the house with me. A great deal more took place at the séance interesting both to myself and others.

"A month later I attended a second séance. Some remarkable things were told by Mr. Home, who was in a state of trance, to a lady present of her departed friend. He then went to the opposite end of the room, and she remarked to me in a low voice. 'How very wonderful, he has been dead these thirty years,' when Mr. Home, whom I thought much too distant to hear, called out, in a loud thrilling voice, 'Do not say dead; he is not dead, but gone before; nothing kills but sin, sin kills through the devil, but those who live in Christ will never die.' Mr. Home came soon afterwards to me, and said that my dear husband and his mother (the Mary spoken of before) were behind my chair, and that both longed to comfort me. He gave me the following message:—'My own Adelaide, all your prayers are heard, your pure thoughts seen, your patience and loving hope. We are *not*, nor shall we be separated, we are one in CHRIST.'

"He then went on to say that I had had a conversation with my husband eight months before, and that he blessed me for that conversation now; that we were sitting in our drawing-room at home, he in his arm-chair and I in mine, with *the little round table between us*, that I had just been reading a chapter in the New Testament, and that on that night the angel of the Lord laid his hand upon my husband's brow, and he had faded from that time. I remember *perfectly* the con versation alluded to, and it was a very remarkable one. I had been reading prayers to the servants, and we were sitting in the manner prescribed, and talked for more than half an hour before going to bed. These are facts for which I can vouch, and though my name is not given here, Mr. Home will give it to any one wishing to be convinced. To me the comfort has been unspeakable; but did I believe Spiritualism to be sinful or forbidden by our Lord, NOTHING would induce me to have anything to say to it, but I believe the reverse in this case. I have felt more at peace, more perfect trust — utter childlike trust—in my God and Saviour, than I have ever done before. Mr. Home told me that my dear husband was always with me when I prayed, and I feel that he is, through Christ."

We spent July, August, and September, 1861, at Folkestone. My power had left me, but my wife continued to see spirits daily. We went to Brighton, where we remained till the month of December. Late in the evening of one day in November, my wife being in bed, I was in the drawing-room with a friend, when a strange chill air seemed to surround us, and creaking noises were heard. In fact, a feeling of great discomfort came upon us both, when we heard my wife knocking on the floor, this being her signal of requiring my presence. I ran up stairs, and she said, "Daniel, do not leave me; there is a spirit-presence in my room which is strange and unpleasant to me. I feel as if something had occurred, or was about to happen." I remained with her, but we no longer felt or heard anything of the kind. In the morning on the breakfast table was a letter from a much loved friend, announcing the departure of a son under most painful circumstances. It was evident that it was his spirit who had been with us the previous evening.

We came back to town in December; and in January, 1862, the power returned, in me but far from strongly. On one occasion whilst we were seated, the strange trembling so often noticed was felt in the table, and almost simultaneously with it I heard the nursery-bell ring. I heard the servant go up stairs, the nursery being on the third floor, and soon she came with a message from the nurse requesting my presence I went, and found the child sitting in his bed, and a look of alarm on his face. He said to me, "Oh, papa, I don't like to have my bed rocking." I thought that he might have a headache, or some slight indisposition, which might have caused a giddiness, but he said he was very well. I remained a short time with him, and then joined my friends in the drawing-room. In about half an hour the trembling was repeated, and again the nursery-bell rang. I had to go him, and I found that the rocking had been more violent than before, and he begged me to lay down with him till he got to sleep. I did so, and in about ten minutes he was fast asleep. The spirits then told us that they had "accidentally caused his bed to shake."

Another instance of this trembling being felt outside the room has occurred within ten days previous to my writing this. A deaf and dumb maid living in a house where I was, and knowing nothing either of my presence, or of spiritual manifestations, said to the young lady, her mistress, on her going upstairs to her,

"How you must have been dancing, all of you, for the whole house has been shaking so that I have been made quite dizzy." We were upon the ground floor, and the principal manifestation that evening was the strong vibration of the room. She was upon the third floor, and the house is a large well-built one in one of the best parts of Kensington.

CHAPTER XII.

IN MEMORIAM.

On the 20th of February, 1862, we left England for the Château Laroche, near Perigueux, the residence in the south of France of my brother-in-law. I need not to go through again the scenes of those last days on earth of the dear one whom it has pleased God to take away, in the spring time of her life, to the bright morning land. It is well with her there, and she is only more than ever my hope, and my beaming guiding star. My good guardian angel, watching over her dear child, and me, her husband—separated, but not lost—in spirit more than ever present. In God's loving mercy we shall meet again, and find our lasting habitation in the eternal inner world.

Let me have the pleasure of adding the sweet tribute to her memory of Mrs. Howitt, which gives such few facts as may be made public of one who amongst her friends required no written words to be embalmed in their hearts' best memories. To those who knew her not, these words will serve to show the effect of spiritual communion during the long stages of disease, and the placid contemplation of the passing onward, by one to whom the bright spirit-world has become a calm reality, from her frequent intercourse with the good angels who had gone before.

In Memoriam.

"Madame Alexandrina Home, the wife of Mr. Daniel Dunglas Home, passed from earth on the 3d July last, at the Château Laroche, Dordogne, France, the residence of her sister, the Countess Luboff Koucheleff Besborodka, in the twenty-second year of her age.

"Mrs. Home was the youngest daughter of the General Count de Kroll, of Russia, and she was the god-daughter of the late Emperor Nicholas. She was educated at the Institute of St. Catherine at the same time as the present Countess de Morny, of Paris. Mr. Home, who had been at several of the Courts of Europe, where he was received with much distinction, and where the marvellous phenomena which occur in his presence excite deep attention, was at Rome in the spring of 1858 for the benefit of his health, and there first saw the lady who became his wife on the 1st of August of that year. The marriage took place at St. Petersburgh, and was celebrated in the presence of M. Alexandre Dumas, who went from Paris on purpose to be present, and to officiate as god-father to Mr. Home, according to the custom of the Romish Church. The Emperor Alexander also was represented there by two of his aides de-camp, whom he sent as groomsmen, and the Emperor presented to Mr. Home on the happy occasion a magnificent diamond ring of great value. On the birth of the only child of the marriage, a son, the

Emperor evinced his continued interest in Mr. and Mrs. Home by presenting to them as a memento of his friendship a ring of emeralds and diamonds. Mr. and Mrs. Home thus commenced their married life with all the outward accessories of station and wealth, together with hosts of friends, as a matter of course, whilst the measure of their happiness was completed by that calm domestic bliss, which is the purest source of earthly enjoyment, and to which her kindly and tender nature contributed its full share. They could not but be happy, for their affection was pure as it was sincere, and when their union was blessed by the birth of their little son, there was no more to hope for, but to bring him up worthily to be a partaker in their happiness.

"In the midst, however, of these bright human hopes and anticipations, the decree went forth that her days were numbered. About eighteen months before her departure, the physician who was called in on the occasion of some trifling illness, as it was supposed, detected, to the surprise and grief of all who loved her, such undoubted signs of consumption in her constitution that in all human probability her life could not be of long duration. Such tidings to a young and happy woman, surrounded by everything that can make outward existence attractive, would, in ordinary circumstances, have come as the direst calamity; but it was not so in the case of Mrs. Home. Though at that time only in her twenty-first year, she received the announcement with entire calmness. God's will be done, was the cheerful law of her life, and He who had hitherto made that life so rich would not fail, she knew, to continue His love and mercy to her in that higher life to which He was calling her. Nothing but the deepest religious conviction of the Supreme Wisdom and Love can bring the human soul into a state of submissive obedience to His otherwise apparently severe and mysterious decrees. Let us now see how the Divine Father had led and schooled His young disciple into that highest, that profouudest of all knowledge, the firm possession of which makes obedience and submission easy, and keeps the soul calm and even joyful under the most startling and adverse circumstances. We shall then in part, if not fully understand whence came the strange, and apparently most unnatural, willingness to depart from the earthly life amidst its most attractive circumstances. *She was a deeply-believing Spiritualist.* God's love had made known to her the reality of the spiritual world; she had been permitted to solve the great, mysterious, and perplexing riddle of the Hereafter, and so loyal was she to the knowledge which had thus been given her, that she was ready to attest it in life or in death. Like all experienced Spiritualists she knew that the outward life, be its term longer or shorter, is but a school in which God wills to train the immortal being to a higher knowledge—is but a pilgrimage, or passage by which he is willing to conduct it to another and a still happier home. She knew that in that other state of existence, though unclothed by the body, and apparently separated from the beloved on earth, she might yet be permitted to watch over and love them as their guardian angel, and to be in the close companionship of those who had gone before—of those living and glorified spirits who should lead her to the throne of grace and love ineffable. If it be the highest heroism to meet death with unflinching courage, this amiable, gentle young woman, this child of affluence and fortune, displayed an almost unequalled degree of this noble quality of mind, and so doing, proved how strong and all-sustaining in life's extremity is the faith of the Christian Spiritualist.

"The first startling intelligence that her disease was mortal came to a mind so prepared with wholly abated force. The sting was already taken from death; nor through the whole after trials and sufferings of her physical frame did she lose her equanimity or firm confidence in the future. This calmness, indeed, became the most striking feature of her long and painful illness. It was so profound and marked as to be almost phenomenal, and was noticed as such by the eminent physicians who attended her in London, and subsequently in France, as well as by the Bishop of Perigueux, who frequently visited her during the latter part of her earthly life. The last sacraments were administered to her by the Bishop, who wept like a child, and who remarked that 'though he had been present at many a death-bed for Heaven, he had never seen one equal to hers.'

"Whilst residing in London the most remarkable spiritual gifts and manifestations exhibited through Mr. Home, and the many attractive qualities of his young and lovely wife had naturally gathered around them a large circle of friends to whom the singular exhibition of her calmness, her meekness, her playful, winning ways, even in the midst of suffering, and the joyfulness with which she anticipated her removal, were, if possible, a greater anomaly, and almost for the time, cast into the shade the wonderful gifts and powers of her husband. If Addison called to his death-bed his infidel son-in-law that, witnessing his composure, he might learn with how much calmness a Christian could die, so here disbelievers in Spiritualism looking on this gifted young woman, saw with wonder not only how calmly, but how joyously the Christian Spiritualist could face death. Another equally anomalous feature to the Protestant Christian was not to find in her the self-depreciation of the guilt-awakened sinner; not to hear on her lips the usual phraseology of the dying but suffering saint; no mention made of the atonement; of the works of grace on her soul, of the sufferings of a crucified Savior for her sake. Nevertheless, with the simplicity of a little child who accepted the Divine love as his natural gift, she loved the Savior and rejoiced in Him, responding to His unspeakable goodness with the whole allegiance of her soul, but Gethsemane and the bloody hill of the crucifixion were not present to her mind; the agony and woe had no place in her experience. She was, it must be remembered, the embodiment of her own Greek church; of that church in which she was educated, the most ancient faith of which has ever recognized the Savior less as the Crucified than the Arisen, the triumphant over suffering, sin, and death, as the Victor not the Victim, as the Lord who said to his chosen ones, 'Rejoice that your names are written in heaven!' Such, it appears to me, who frequently saw her during this portion of her short stay on earth, was the fact which made her relationship to the Savior so joyous, whilst her own single-heartedness left her free from all established phraseology or any wish to produce effect, and these happily combined with her actual knowledge of spiritual existence, strengthened that remarkable state of calmness and cheerfulness with which she waited the close of her outward life. Her Savior had indeed risen for her, and with the unquestioning, unreasoning faith of a loving, obedient child-like nature, she was not only willing to go when He called her, but cheerfully to give up all at His bidding, knowing that a more enlarged, a more glorious sphere of usefulness and angel ministration would be unfolded to her through His love, and that thus she should be enabled more tenderly and more effectually to watch over and become a blessing to the beloved ones whom she left behind.

"During that short but interesting time of her declining health in London, her remarkable unselfishness became another endearing characteristic to all her friends. She made, even amidst her increasing sufferings, constant exertions to see them, and séances were held frequently at the house where she and her husband were then residing, in which she took a glad part. On these occasions many wonderful and touchingly beautiful incidents occurred, and few, if any, who thus met her, but retain with tender and affectionate regard some tender flower or fragrant spray—am emblem of herself, which was presented to her by spirit-hands, as a little memento for each.

"In the earlier stages of her disease her spiritual perception began to open, and she commenced, and throughout her illness continued to see and converse with the denizens of the spiritual world. Her most frequent visitants were her mother and her father, and the mother of her husband. From them she received the most loving messages of endearment, and the most cheering words of welcome to her spirit home. She was also constantly attended by a veiled female spirit, whom she did not know, but whose very presence gave her great comfort, though she never spoke, nor raised her veil. Mr. Home was told that this kind guardian spirit would continue veiled until the last, when the veil would be thrown over her own new-born spirit, to keep her from the sight of the tears and mourning around the bed where her body would be lying. Through the six months previous to her passing away, the veil was slowly and gradually gathered from the feet of the guardian spirit towards the head, until two days before her release, when for the last time she saw the spirit with the veil gathered in the form of a crown about her head, but with one part, as a festoon, still concealing her face.

"On one occasion several persons, who were in the room with Mrs. Home, saw the hand and arm of the spirit to the shoulder, the appearance being that of a luminous body, most beautifully perfect in form, and covered as if with a veil of light.

"The eminent composer, M. Magnus, of Paris, came to the Chateau Laroche to visit Mrs. Home during the last three weeks of her earthly stay, and almost daily she asked him to play for her, and whilst lying placidly listening to his music, her face assumed an almost beautiful expression whilst she kept time to the music with her hands. On one occasion she said, when he had finished playing, 'Those strains are very beautiful, but I shall soon hear more beautiful still.'

"Frequently also, during the first three months and the last two months of her illness, not only she, but all those about her, heard delicious strains of spirit music, sounding like a perfect harmony of vocal sounds. During the last month, also, the words were most distinctly heard, and were recognized as the chants for the dying used in the Russian Church.

"She departed on Thursday, the 3rd of July, and on the Saturday morning following, her little boy, of three years old, said to his nurse on awakening, 'I have seen mamma, and she is quite well now. She is with God, and she told me that my uncle Gregoire, and my aunt Luba are my godfather and my godmother, and that they would be very good to me, and I must love them.'

"At her funeral, the service at which was performed by the vicar-general of the diocese, four of the men servants of her sister asked each to lead a horse of the hearse to the burial ground, saying that they could not allow hired persons to be near the dear body of her who had ever had a kind word and a loving look for all. The peasantry, instead of, as is customary, throwing earth upon the coffin, first covered it with flowers—fittest for her last garment, and fittest for the expression of their love.

"Such is a brief memorial of a short but lovely life on earth. But short as it was, rarely has the oldest and most experienced orthodox Christian attained to a higher degree of religious consciousness, clearness and trust in God, than did this young and attractive woman, by those very means and teachings which the religious world as yet so much ignores and questions.

"Blessed, however, be God the Saviour for every fresh revelation and manifestation of his Divine life, and for every renewed teaching of his Holy Spirit.

"MARY HOWITT."

To another esteemed friend, Mrs. S. C. Hall, also well known for her true woman's heart, and for her power of expressing the best feelings of the soul, I am indebted for her written impressions of my dear wife, and in which she embraces a most interesting account of her observations of the phenomena:

"It pleased God to remove from this life only a few months since, a much beloved lady, who during her brief residence among us, entwined herself closely round the hearts of her and her husband's many friends —I speak of one, dear to us as 'Sacha,' the wife of Mr. Daniel Home.

"Educated as befitted a Russian lady of rank, she was still more richly endowed by grace, feeling, a peculiar beauty, which I may term loveliness, and a sweet simplicity of nature, that rendered her transparent and pure as crystal; she was also gifted with a rare appreciation of the beautiful. Her interest in, and admiration of whatever was excellent in art, was the result of innate perception, not often met with where observation has not been matured by age; with a refinement on the natural quickness of her sex—she felt while others reasoned—indeed, all her perceptions were vivid, and she was entirely feminine.

"When first I knew her, she was radiant with life and joy—a playful girl numbering just twenty years, and yet in the full tide of her sweet joy—loving her husband, her child, her friends, and feeling keenly how much she was beloved. If something touched her quick sympathies, her eyes in a moment grew deep and dark, her sweet lips quivered, and the girl became at once the deep-hearted, tender, earnest woman. Wise too she was, and in her wildest moods something would come of wisdom, a sentence, or even a single word, so full and suggestive.

"Soon, however, it became certain to us that this sweet happy life was not to remain here, and to none was this so evident as to herself; not for a moment did she doubt that she had received her warning for the 'better land.' She would talk with her husband, and with all of us, her friends, of her passing away, believing—nay, knowing—that she would be permitted still to watch over her child, to companion her husband, to communicate with her friends; and this in calm, unconstrained cheerfulness, surrounded by the happy realities of a loving life, and loving, as he deserved, her devoted husband. It was almost impossible to hear the full sweet tones of her voice, to feel the affectionate pressure of her little hands, observe the life-full expression of her face, and realise her approaching change, when the mortal shall have put on immortality.

"How bitterly hard it is to *feel*, however we may repeat the words, 'Thy will be done!' As the spring advanced each time I saw her, I perceived some change, and yet the 'change' could not be defined—it was more in her spirit than her person. Suffering, wearied the young fragile form, and she longed to be away—she desired freedom from the body's pain, from the perpetual endurance of restlessness— she craved to be out of the body that she might be in the spirit.—She talked about this change as invalids talk of change of air, and with hope in her beaming face. I confess that I do not comprehend this phase of mind—I look forward with joy to meet those I have loved and lost from earth, and I look to the time when those I leave behind will, trusting in the same Mediator, bend before the dear Redeemer, and join in His presence, the 'spirits of just men made perfect,' so that we all shall be one in Christ—but this young creature's certainty that she should return and watch over her husband, child, and all she held in her expanding heart, was to me incomprehensible; it was as if she thought that after death heaven would descend with her to earth. Her faith in her future happiness was fine; but death, like life, was to her a poem, and all her thoughts and actions were poetic—with all her suffering, hers was the poetry of daily life. She enjoyed beyond description a séance with those she loved. One of her pleasures was tying up little bouquets of flowers with one of her long dark hairs, flinging a bouquet under or on the table, or into the room, and expressing a wish that a spirit would give it to one or other of her friends. This was invariably done, and I preserve these flowers as tokens of her sweet love, and shall do so while I live. These little tender acts of kindness were mingled with promises of coming to us when she should have no mortal body—suffer no pain. She never doubted that this would be permitted, and she loved to dwell upon the delight it would be to her to be with us. There was in her no taint or tone of sadness. I never saw a more joyful, a more perpetual belief in the soul's immortality. We could not avoid observing at times an occasional abstraction, her eyes—illuminated by a bright light, wandering round the room, her whole face smiling as if recognising some spirit friend. Daily—daily was the end, as regarded her earthly tenement advancing, and still nearer came the angels!

"At times, her patience under the accumulated sufferings she was doomed to endure was marvellous; and when at last she longed to anticipate our summer, so tardy that year in arriving, and when I bade her adieu, she pressed her tiny hand into mine, 'feel it—feel it well,' she said in her pretty English, no longer broken but accented—'feel it, for when I come to you, you must remember it.' Some months passed, and then at last came the news, early in last July, she was called home.

"I had several times the full conviction (as I have at this moment) that she was with me, but I have no medium power, and beyond the cool breeze that passes across my hand or brow, 'the air of the angel's wing,' I receive no sign of such presence—nor do I need it.

"Mr. Home returned to England, and after our first meeting (those who loved her could not call it sad, for he was assured of her happiness) we arranged an evening séance in the drawing-room, which was lit as usual —only five persons present, five who had known and loved Sacha!

"Before what the world calls death, she had asked

her husband to give me a little lace cap, the embroidery by her own hands, and I had asked him for a braid of her hair; he brought both, tied in one of her white handkerchiefs, and placed them on the table.—More than the usual manifestations came that night; not only the table but our chairs, and the very room shook, and the 'raps' were everywhere around us. A lady, whose consolation through spiritualism has been indeed blessed, received several messages in answer to her thoughts; and a very eminent sculptor, whose engagements on public works are unceasing, had been rising before day to finish a bust of Sacha, which he desired to present to her husband—*this fact was not even known in his own household*—he received a message thus: 'Thanks for your early morning labor—I have been often near you.' While the message was rapped out, he felt her little hand repeatedly on his, in loving confirmation of her thanks. This was the first time he had ever felt the touch of the 'spirit-hand,' and it affected him deeply. Mr. Home then placed the embroidery and the hair under the table. 'Sacha,' he said, 'wishes to give them to you herself.' Presently my dress was pulled. I put down my hand, and the cap was not only placed in it, but my fingers closed over it, *by her hand*, I could not be mistaken, I knew that hand so well! My dress was again pulled, and I laid my hand in my lap, then I felt her hand more distinctly; it was placed entirely in mine, and after a pressure, left me the lock of hair!

"Again the alphabet was demanded, and the passage spelt out. 'Give me the handkerchief, I want to give it to Mrs. S——. Oh, I thank her for her beautiful flowers,' (flowers she was in the habit of sending her during her illness.) Mr. Home threw the handkerchief that had contained the hair and embroidery down. It was rolled up and knotted, and given into Mrs. S——'s hand. There was much more that evening, the revealings were all continued evidence of spiritual power, and spirit presence, such as come to us with healing messages on their wings, making us thankful that to us Spiritualism has been the handmaid of Christianity.

"But dear Sacha is far from being the only one of my beloved friends, departed, or rather removed, from whom I have received sweet, and consoling, and comforting messages. One whom I love and reverence beyond all who are gone before, has given me by unmistakeable proof, the blessed certainty of the interest she is permitted to take in our spiritual welfare, and has, by her precepts, and apt quotations of holy writ, strengthened our armor of faith, and if it be possible, brightened the hope of the glory that shall be revealed hereafter. Is not this comforting? I do not prolong this brief record of happy memories, but I could do so. Spiritualism has been to me a blessing, for which I cannot be enough thankful, less for my own sake, than for the sake of others who are very dear to me; for though it brought me more sunshine, it has given me no new light. I testify here of spiritualism, as it is known and believed by me and mine; I say known, for nearly five years we have had abundant proofs of its reality. I will briefly say how this is. I thank God that I never had a doubt as to the divine truths of Christianity, neither did I receive them as cold facts. My dear mother was of pure Huguenot descent, and would, at any period of her life, have gone calmly to the stake sooner than have even seemed to abate one jot of her belief in the Existence, Mission, and Miracles of Christ-God. I drank at the fountain of this faith from my earliest years, and every night the accustomed 'chapter' was read, prayed over and discussed; thus religious faith grew to be my enjoyment, as well as my hope and trust. Moreover, she held the belief that the spirits of those we knew, loved, and reverenced, were permitted to watch over us, and it might be to communicate with us—but how such communication was to take place, was a mystery as much to the parent as the child. She believed that our holiest thoughts and actions were suggested to us, under Divine permission, by ministering angels; and that perseverance in prayer would protect us from the evil influences that were ever on the watch to whisper, or even to inculcate, what was contrary to God's holy law.

"This was, and is pure Spiritualism—pure Christian Spiritualism!—yet having believed this all my life long, believing also that the supernatural was often permitted as one of the missionaries of Christianity, I laughed at what was called 'Table-turning.' I had never seen spiritual manifestations, but that did not hinder my laughing at the idea of a spirit giving a message by raps on a table; all my belief in the 'Cloud of Witnesses' did not prevent my catching at what seemed the absurdity of such a means of communication, and instead of investigating, I laughed. I did worse, I became angry. I said I had all my life believed in *su-*

perna ural presences, I believed that, *if necessary*, CHRIST-GOD would give one of His 'Cloud of Witnesses' permission to communicate with me, but what had that to do with raps? I never called to mind that at this moment the world is filled with 'Thomases,' who will not (if they can avoid it) believe except on the testimony of their senses. Because I believe in Gospel truths, I thought that others ought to believe as I did, from the testimony which had sufficed me and mine. *I* did not want to see the Saviour's wounds, I believed in them, *that* was enough for me. I did not think those 'stiff-necked and stubborn,' who require, as Thomas did, a 'sign;' and we must remember (which I did not) that the MASTER *did not refuse him that sign—no, He called him to examine those marks of His suffering.* HE not only permitted the unbeliever to examine for himself, but He *called* upon him to do so.

"At length we were prevailed on to meet a young lady-medium, one in all respects above suspicion; we were a mixed party of twelve or fourteen at that dinner-table: and while questioning myself how it was possible that educated and intelligent men could receive as testimony of spiritual presence the 'raps' and 'tilts,' which though I could not account for, I did not believe in, my attention was awakened by the young lady's saying that a spirit was present, who desired to communicate with me. She described a presence which I recognized, and then gave me a message, a portion of which could only be intelligible to us two—the spirit who gave it, and I who received it. This was so positive and conclusive to *me*, that believing as I always did that such a power existed, I was *forced* to believe that there was truth in mediumship, and that *here* was the means used for communicating from the spirits of those gone before to those who still lingered in the flesh.

"This was the confirmation of a blessed reality to me, but to others, particularly to one other at the table, it was thrice blessed; his past had been clouded with doubts as to the existence of spirit-life, he had refused to believe what he could not understand; his lamp of reason, trimmed with ever so much care, only made the darkness, so as to say, more visible. Faith was to him a dead letter. His heart ached to believe, but, like Thomas, he wanted a 'sign.' The first 'sign' was given him that night, and since then directed invariably to THE BOOK which leads to life eternal he goes on his way rejoicing.

"Only those who have stumbled amid the doubts and uncertainties of a sadly unsatisfying materialism, can comprehend the inspiration which the assurance of future existence, amended, enlightened, purified, gives. I am frequently asked, what is the use of Spiritualism? My answer invariably is, that I believe it is permitted to check the growth of materialism. No one, however sceptical, can receive messages from the spirit world, *knowing their truth*, and disbelieve in spirit-life, in a immortality! This is the key-stone to a belief in the Holy Scriptures. Scores, hundreds, thousands, at this day say as I did, 'Why don't people believe? They have Moses and the prophets.' *I* believed on Bible testimony. Yes, but those thousands do *not* believe in Bible testimony; they ask for a *sign*. Will they not seek 'the sign,' and investigate its truth?

Would not they give all they possess for a 'sign' proving immortality? Do they not desire intercourse which, sanctified by prayer, will, (I have often seen it done) direct them to particular passages in Holy Writ, which for the first time they comprehended, and which became sanctified to them? And again, there are many who receive Spiritualism as a fact; well-minded, timid persons, who fear that Spiritualism is dangerous. I have seen quite enough to convince me that carnal-minded people bring their evil angels with them into many a circle; and they suggest what is evil more palpably than in those silent whispers that lead as surely astray. 'By their fruits ye shall know them.' We know that 'lying spirits' endeavor to distil their poison into the purest hearts; and be sure they are on the watch around the circle assembled for manifestations, and can only be 'sent behind' by faithful prayer; but every Christian knows that he is perpetually beset by such like.

"Spiritualism, as we know it, commences each séance with prayer; and usually (though not invariably) has reason to finish with praise. I would not join a circle where this was neglected. I could name many who have been lifted out of the slough of materialism by, in the first instance, seeing the marvelous manifestations that arise from Mr. Home's mediumship, and the mediumship of the young lady I have already mentioned. Ridicule on the one side, and asseverations on the other, cannot alter *facts.* There must be a *coin* to create a *counterfeit,* and, doubtless, charlatanism has found its way into 'circles,' whence it has been driven as soon as discovered.

"MEDIUMSHIP is a mystery we cannot fathom, nor understand why the power should be delegated to one more to another. We have the highest authority for the belief that there are 'diversities of gifts' all from 'the same spirit;' and amongst them is specified, 'To some the discerning of spirits.' Why should one have 'the gift of healing,' and *not* that of 'divers kind of tongues,' or 'the seeing of spirits.' *That* is one of those marvels we shall comprehend when we no longer see through a glass darkly. I can only add, with no large amount of humility, that 'mediumship' is not the only thing I do not understand.

"But I must cease here. I do not attempt to give any further description of the 'manifestations' I have witnessed, the wonders I have seen, and examined, and *questioned*, and after my examinations and questionings, could not doubt their being permitted for the ONE purpose, which I again repeat, is the missiom of high and holy Spiritualism.

"I do not feel called upon to write in defence of Spiritualism, nor to quote from the volume of facts by which that defence is to be sustained, and its truth proved. I have no talent for argument or controversy; there are others who have, and are willing, as well as able, to be its defenders. I believe it to be sanctioned by GOD, and that therefore it must be for a good purpose; and I content myself, as I must content those who may read what I have written, with expressing my conviction that Spiritualism is TRUTH."

CHAPTER XIII.

CONCLUSION.

I CAME to England from Perigueux, and have been since engaged, as much as my time and health would permit, in having séances, at which most of the manifestations recorded in the previous pages of my work have been repeated. I have been several times lifted a short distance from the ground, but not so high as to float above the heads of the persons in the room. Many persons have seen and been convinced of the occurrence of what they previously deemed impossible, and have had their faith in immortality renewed and strengthened when all other means had failed in making them believe. On the 20th January, 1863, I went to Paris on a short visit to my friend, Count de K——, and there also the same phenomena have occurred in the presence of great numbers of persons. I have also been frequently received by their Majesties at the Tuileries, and by the imperial Princess and the nobility of France, who have shown a great interest in investigating the manifestations; but enough has been given of the facts to enable the reader to form an opinion of them, and there is no need to go into further details. I have already told the main incidents, and must now leave them to be judged and analyzed by the various classes of persons who may devote their thoughts to the subject.

It would be hard if I were held answerable for facts which occur in connexion with my physical organization, and towards which I am, in mind and intent, wholly passive, even if there were any harm in them. As there is no harm in them beyond their disturbing certain prepossessions, on the contrary, some likelihood of good; and as they are independent of all moral action my feet; I trust that with the candid and enlightened I shall be held, as I am, innocent.

It will have been observed that they began with me when I was an infant in my cradle, and they have since with a few exceptions, formed a part of my daify life. Their range includes nearly all the phenomena which are known under the incorrect name of Modern Spiritualism. I say the name is incorrect, because there is not one of them which is new, and which may not be traced in every age of which we have any record preserved to us. The great difference, however, is, that during the last two centuries a great change has come over the world, and by a kind of re-action, men have reversed the belief which previously existed as to the supernatural. Up to two centuries ago, it was not considered a point of wisdom to disbelieve in such manifestations and actings from the inner world, but on the contrary, such disbelief was reprehended as unscriptural and wrong.

I am, however, fortunately relieved from the necessity of showing at great length the prevelance of spiritual action and phenomena in the past ages of the world, by the publication of the elaborate and almost exhaustive work of Mr. W. Howitt,* to which I refer my readers, in full confidence that in his pages they will find not only the facts but the arguments necessary to show that the spiritual has been ever present, and that nothing had occurred to me but what has been frequently observed before. I trust that this work will be extensively read, in order that much of the present ignorance on the subject may be dispelled, and that the minds of men may be led to inquire more deeply into this great subject. As a brief summary of the same subject, I may likewise point to an article in the Appendix which has been framed by a friend from a series of historical notes, gathered by a literary gentleman who has, with great kindness, placed them at my friend's disposal.

It will be readily admitted that such facts as those I have described, are calculated to throw great light upon the hitherto neglected science of pneumatology —and that it is in the direction pointed out by such facts that further search is to be made into the hidden questions of the soul, and its relations with the body and external things. For such a study, no facts, however small or apparently trivial, can be dispensed with.

Of those which are of a physical kind, such as the moving of furniture, the raps, the raising into the

* "The History of the Supernatural in all Ages and Nations, in all Churches, Christian and Pagan, demonstrating a Universal Faith." By William Howitt, Author of "Colonization and Christianity." London, Longman and Co.

air, or levitation, and similar classes of phenomena, they are to be investigated, and their uses ascertained by the man of science and the philosopher. At present such persons have fixed *à priori* that such things have never occurred, and are impossible and absurd; and for this very reason, if for no other, it will be admitted that they are of the highest use in order to correct such notions of the relations between spiritual forces and natural things. There is no study which could be of such value to philosophers as that of facts now known to thousands, but which their present philosophy deems impossible. For their philosophy must be radically defective when that which they say is impossible, is nevertheless of daily occurrence. The physical side, therefore, of these phenomena is to be studied by students of experimental science, in order to enlarge their views of material forces, and if this can be effected, as it has been in so many instances, by the movement of tables, and by the rapping sounds, and by the raising of bodies into the air without touch or contact, they will no longer complain of the triviality of such phenomena. Indeed, already so little are they trivial or unimportant, that the noted men of science, such as the Faradays and Brewsters, have gone out of their way to inveigh against their possibility, and to bestow the name of credulous dupes upon those who have publicly stated what they have seen and heard. The very denial of these things by these men, and by the mass of the public, shows that they are not trivial to them, but that they are really of the utmost importance. For why are they denied by the men of science, but that they contradict all their previous knowledge of the laws of nature, upsetting "the philosophy of a lifetime," and are therefore impossible to them, until they enlarge the present boundaries of their knowledge, and find out those higher laws under which these become not only facts, but possible facts.

There is of course no religious revelation, properly so called, in such phenomena, any more than there is in the phenomena of gravitation, electricity, or magnetism, but that has not latterly been a reason why such laws should be repudiated. At the institution of the present Royal Society, there was a great outcry on the part of the religious persons of that day, against the formation of such a society, on the ground that it was blasphemous and wicked to attempt to inquire into what were called God's mysteries; and it was said that men already had their Bibles, and knew enough, and ought not to seek to know more. Such is not the general opinion now-a-days, and the time is not far distant, I hope, when the manner in which this subject has been received, will in the same way be brought forward to prove the same great truth, that all knowledge is to be pursued, and that we need not fear that we shall ever have too much of it. God is able to preserve His own mysteries, and whatever is possible for us, it is our right and duty to search into and fathom, and to bring forward as a part of the general stock of human intelligence. I anticipate, therefore, that when the real men of science find these facts not to be impossible, they will by their aid, be led into a knowledge of higher laws, which at present they conceal from themselves; and that at greater discovery awaits their research than that which has adorned the name of Newton, who did not find it a trivial fact when an apple fell before his eyes.

As to the other great division of these phenomena, into such as are of a mental kind, and betoken intelligence, a much larger question is raised.

The former class of manifestations we could only commend to the scientific investigator; but so soon as we are assured of the fact of manifestations directed by intelligence, we are put upon an inquiry of another kind. We are not aware of any other being but man, who is endowed with the kind and amount of intelligence which is disclosed in many of the manifestations and we are at once brought to the inevitable conclusion that such intelligence is exhibited by human beings, either in body, or out of the body. Neither the od force, nor electricity, nor magnetism, nor any of the imponderable forces, has ever yet been detected in betraying intelligence, or in carrying on a conversation between themselves, or in taking part in one with others, and though they are largely engaged in their proper offices throughout nature, and in that epitome of it which is contained in a man, yet there is nothing human nor intelligent about them in the true sense of the words.

We feel instinctively, therefore, when we meet with this intelligence, that we are dealing with a man either embodied or disembodied. The wonders of clairvoyance and internal perception (if we are to consider these faculties inherent in the living, independent of spiritual aid,) may account for some of the phenomena; but there are others which my reader will not have failed to note, which infallibly point to the intelligence being that of disembodied human beings. The intelligence declares itself to be a human being, and gives information known to it alone. It says that it is a spirit, and in the spiritual world. It is seen as a spirit, and recognised as that of one loved on earth. It says that its office is to be our guardian, and helper, and comforter. It tells us of things that have passed, of things that are happening in distant parts, of things that are to come. Can this be ourselves, who unknwingly counterfeit such a presentment, and tell this false intelligence to ourselves? No such quality or power has hitherto been recognised or known to exist in the mind of man. No such quality has been recognized or known to exist in the od force, nor in electricity, nor in magnetism, as the ability to tell either truth or falsehood. Whence is it then? Is the question so entirely a new one as to the existence of spirits and their power to communicate with man, as that we can ignore it or deny its possibility? Are we inevitably thrown upon finding some natural hypothesis to account for such facts? and are we as Christians, to say like Sir David Brewster, that "Spirit is the last thing I'll give in to." I thank God that I have been taught otherwise, and I refer to the bible, and to the spiritual books, and authorities, and beliefs of all ages and of all churches, in support of my belief. Let us then say at once that there are spirits and a spirit world, and see what difficulties are thrown in their way by the men of science, who deny them all power of communicating with this world.

It would indeed be a very difficult matter to conceive by what possible means a spirit could satisfy some minds of its actual presence. "Suppose," says the Rev. Charles Beecher, "a departed spirit, the wife of Oberlin, for example, were permitted to attempt to converse with her husband; not to establish a new revelation, not to display divine power, but merely to exercise such potentiality as might pertain to a disembodied spirit, for her own and her husband's edification and satisfaction. How could she do it in the face of the apneumatic theories. She speaks to him, moves his furniture, touches his dress, his person; all automatic action of some brain *en rapport* with that locality. She sings, plays the guitar or piano, takes a pencil and writes, and he sees the pencil in free space tracing his wife's autograph—automatic still. She shows him a cloudy hand, nay, a luminous form, and smiles and speaks as when in life—that is an optical illusion, or hallucination, or a particle exhaled from her body has impinged on his sensitive brain, and created a subjective vision. She communicates facts past, present, and future, beyond the scope of his knowledge;—that might be clairvoyance or cerebral *sensing.* Alas, then, what could she do more? She must retire baffled, and complaining that he had become so scientific that all communication with him was *impossible.*"

It is, therefore, very difficult to influence some minds by any proof that could be brought forward, for want of their having any point which such proof can penetrate; but assuredly such proofs as I have given in my book, of the existence of spirits, and of their ability to communicate with us, are of the kind most likely to be useful to them.

It is to be observed also, that such persons, to be consistent, must, and too many of them do, apply the same argument to all analogous facts in the past, as well as to those occurring at this day. On this all-important point the Rev. W. Beecher says truly, "Whatever physiological law accounts for these phenomena in all ages, will in the end inevitably carry itself through the whole bible, where it deals with the phenomena of soul and body as mutually related, acting and re-acting. A large portion of the bible, its prophecies, ecstacies, visions, trances, theophanies, angelophanies, are more or less tinged with odic characteristics. The physiology, the anthropology of the bible is highly odic, and must be studied as such. As such it will be found to harmonize with the general principles of human experience in such matters in all ages. If a theory be adopted everywhere else but in the bible, excluding spiritual intervention *in toto*, and accounting for everything physically, then will the covers of the bible prove but pasteboard barriers. Such a theory will sweep its way through the bible and its authority, and its inspiration will be annihilated. On the other hand, if the theory of spiritual intervention be accepted in the bible, it cannot be shut up there, but must sweep its way through the wide domain of 'popular superstitions,' as they are called, separating the element of truth on which those superstitions are based, and asserting its own authoritative supremacy."

It is on such grounds as these amongst many others, that I have found as a fact that these manifestations have a religious tendency, and bearing on the subject of religion of the most important kind. I do not claim for them the character of a new revelation, but that they are a recurrence in our day of some of the phenomena of a very old one; and that it is not a small matter to be able to convince many who stand in need of such knowledge and conviction, of the immortality of the soul, of its immediate and continued existence in the spiritual world, and of its power of communion and communication with us who are left behind. These are not new doctrines, but old facts, and whatever spirits may tell us, we must judge of, as we judge the other affairs of life, by its own intrinsic evidence, and not rely on the infallibility of what comes from the other side merely because of its spiritual origin. For instance, suppose that if any one of the sceptics of the day should go to swell the numbers of the spiritual world, and should come to me in vision, or through any of the numerous modes which I have narrated in the previous pages, and should tell me that there are no spiritual laws, and no spiritual world, and no spiritual beings, and that the many phenomena I have experienced throughout my life did not occur to me, and that such never occurred to others, and were in fact impossible, I should not believe what he said, merely because of its spiritual origin, for the reason that it would be opposed to the experience and knowledge of myself, and of many others in the present and former ages of the world. I should, as I do, on the contrary, recognise in the very fact of his being able to come and give me this false information, matter of the utmost importance to religious truth, directed to a point which of all others in this materialistic age, the most requires assurance and comfirmation.

The fact, therefore, of any intelligence whether true or false, coming from the inner world, is one from which conclusions must be deduced, the value of which it is impossible to over estimate. The real and intimate communion of saints may be difficult to realize, on account of our own state being too low for such holy communion, but we need not abandon to scepticism the whole spiritual world, and deny the possibility of one of the most glorious tenets of Christendom.

THE END

CPSIA information can be obtained
at www.ICGtesting.com
Printed in the USA
LVHW040025180422
716440LV00005B/417

9 783752 592207